Memories and Visions

Memories and Visions

Women's Fantasy & Science Fiction

edited by Susanna J. Sturgis

❋

The Crossing Press
Freedom, California 95019

"Signs of Life," by Barbara Krasnoff, is scheduled to appear during 1990 in *Amazing Stories*; "womanmansion/to my sister/mourning her mother," by Hattie Gossett, was first published in *presenting... sister noblues* and is reprinted by permission, Firebrand Books; "The Amazing Disappearing Girl," by Judith Katz, first appeared in *Sinister Wisdom* #34 in a slightly different form; "The Chaos Diaries," by Lorraine Schein, was first published in *EOTU* (December 1988).

ISBN 0-89594-391-3 (paper)
ISBN 0-89594-392-1 (cloth)

For Maggie, who read it first —
"Live long and prosper!"

Contents

Editorial Memories & Visions, or Why Does a Bright Feminist Like You Read That Stuff Anyway?

•

Susanna J. Sturgis

Unlike most science fiction readers, who caught the speculative bug reading male writers in early adolescence, I was infected at age twenty-eight by Sally Gearhart's *The Wanderground: Stories of the Hill Women* (Persephone Press). I interviewed Sally for *off our backs* while she was on the east coast promoting the book; our hour-long conversation provided a bibliography that kept me busy for months: Joanna Russ, Marion Zimmer Bradley, Elizabeth A. Lynn, Suzy McKee Charnas, Anne McCaffrey, James Tiptree, Jr. (Alice Sheldon).

In the late 1970s — after decades in which the few women in the field were often camouflaged by initials or androgynous first names — women's sf was blooming. A neophyte reader could luxuriate in novels by all the above writers and more: Ursula K. Le Guin, Octavia E. Butler, Marge Piercy, Vonda N. McIntyre, C. J. Cherryh, Marta Randall, Tanith Lee, Chelsea Quinn Yarbro, Lynn Abbey, Lee Killough . . . There were also several excellent anthologies of short fiction, headed by Pamela Sargent's landmark "Women of Wonder" series. All featured female characters who thought for themselves and had their own adventures.

I was soon convinced that the fantasy/sf shelves harbored some of the best feminist fiction around. Here were writers who imagined women grappling with the logical conclusions of patriarchal culture: violence against women, ecological collapse, nuclear holocaust, christian fundamentalism, state repression. They envisioned societies in which gender was not an issue and worlds where men did not exist — a utopian tradition, I learned, that went back at least a hundred years.

1

As an activist, I had to share my discoveries. I wrote reviews. In 1981, as the new book buyer for Lammas, Washington, D.C.'s feminist bookstore, I immediately started an f/sf section. Since 1984 I have written an f/sf column for the bimonthly trade journal *Feminist Bookstore News.* Through the 1980s, despite the continuing proliferation of women f/sf authors and their wonderful books, my feminist eye started to notice what wasn't there.

The worlds of women only, from Monique Wittig's *Les Guerillères* to Joanna Russ's *Whileaway,* that had so inspired me in the late 1970s seemed to have vanished. Of the few exceptions, Pamela Sargent's *The Shore of Women* (1986) and Sheri S. Tepper's *The Gate to Women's Country* (1988) were differently inspired. They took the absence of men as tragic deficiency rather than great opportunity. Tepper's book, astonishingly enough, precludes lesbian relationships; homosexuality was genetically eliminated centuries before.

To be sure, Joan Slonczewski and Suzette Haden Elgin explored women's worlds as an exhilarating frontier. In Slonczewski's *A Door Into Ocean* (1986), the Sharer women of the water planet Shora struggle successfully both to maintain their cooperative, nonviolent ethic and to defend their culture against the military and economic threats of neighboring Valedon. In Elgin's exhilarating tales of women's resistance, *Native Tongue* (1984) and its sequel, *The Judas Rose* (1987), elder women of the privileged male-dominated Linguist families take advantage of their relegation to "Barren Houses" to develop a women's language, Láadan, which insinuates itself into and begins to undermine patriarchal thought and culture.

On their all-too-infrequent ventures into women's fantasy/science ficton, U.S. feminist and lesbian publishers generally chose works that focused on otherwhere/other-when women's communities: Jana Bluejay's *It's Time* and Sunlight's *Womonseed,* both from Tough Dove Books; Donna Young's *Retreat: As It Was!* and Katherine V. Forrest's *Daughters of a Coral Dawn,* from Naiad Press; and Sandi Hall's *Wingwomen of Hera* from Spinsters/Aunt Lute. But until now no independent press in this country has attempted to develop a series of feminist f/sf.

Through the 1980s, feminist publishers in Great Britain have been more active. The f/sf list of The Women's Press

2

includes original novels, reprints of works by U.S. writers, at least one anthology, and Sarah Lefanu's well-reviewed critical work, *In the Chinks of the World Machine*, which Indiana University Press reprinted for U.S. distribution in 1989. Onlywomen has contributed two originals: Caroline Forbes' collection *Needle on Full*, and Anna Livia's novel *Bulldozer Rising*.

In the 1980s, mainstream media discovered "post-feminism." Separatism was not popular in feminist or even lesbian-feminist circles, and most women-only spaces happened by accident. In women's fantasy and science fiction, the woman hero took center stage, solitary, unsupported by female friends, lovers, kinfolk, mentors, protegees, or peers. In fantasy, Jungian-style dichotomies prevailed — good/evil; dark/light; male/female — with similar result: women were paired with men but strangers, if not rivals, to each other.

I found refuge in Marion Zimmer Bradley's Darkover novels. Like our own, Darkovan culture is patriarchal, and also like our own its women have created an alternative: the Guild of Renunciates, informally known as the Free Amazons. Renunciates make their home in the Guildhouses in various towns and cities; they support themselves at trades from mercenary to midwife. Whether they choose for their lovers men, women, or both, they all take oath not to become dependent on any man.

Renunciates make cameo appearances in many Darkover stories, but Bradley has explored their lives most fully in three novels: *The Shattered Chain* (1976), *Thendara House* (1983), and *City of Sorcery* (1984). Darkover has so captured visitors' imaginations that it has its own network of conferences, and Bradley has edited several collections of Darkover stories, some by her, most by other writers. Most of these writers are women and, Bradley frequently notes, by far the favorite topic is the Free Amazons. The anthology *Free Amazons of Darkover* appeared in 1986.

Since women were writing so prolifically about the Free Amazons, and contributing to Bradley's multi-volume "Sword and Sorceress" series, I assumed that writers were still envisioning women's communities and collaborations. What was happening to the stories that weren't about either Darkover or sword and sorcery? I fantasized collecting them

3

myself. In 1987 Sharon Yntema took on the task of editing women's f/sf for Crossing Press. I was glad — and a little envious.

The following March Elaine Gill of Crossing Press contacted me: Sharon hadn't the time to continue the project; was I interested? I sent out my call in June: "WANTED: FANTASY/SCIENCE FICTION BY AND ABOUT WOMEN." It solicited the works I was missing, specifically female protagonists over the age of 35; women with female friends, lovers, colleagues, and kinfolk; fantasy that does not simplistically equate dark with evil and light with salvation; and future and never-were worlds where the social structure is not neo-, pseudo-, or crypto-feudal.

What did I expect? Well, I was most afraid that no one would send me anything and I'd have to spend weeks in Boston (90 miles from home by road and water), scavenging through yellowing magazines and mimeographed newsletters in libraries public and private. In July, when the announcement had appeared only in *Feminist Bookstore News*, a large envelope arrived from London. It contained four stories by Caro Clarke, any of which would have done an anthology proud. (You'll find Caro's "The Rational Ship" included here.) It was a good and accurate omen.

A surprise as the manuscripts rolled in was the number of horror stories. In recent years horror, or dark fantasy, has been rapidly increasing in both readership and the number of titles available. I knew that women wrote horror novels. But I didn't anticipate that women would submit horror stories to a women's (read: feminist) anthology.

Suspicious, I read often grisly tales — of insects that persecuted humans; of shapechanging dogs with no eyes; of a killer crossbred kudzu vine that devoured some nasty neighbors and their unpleasant poodles; of beautiful people who serve grilled human flesh at their soirees; of street toughs hideously disposed of by an old movie studio.

Plainly, horror stories could differ as much from one another as science fiction or fantasy stories. I was least enthusiastic about those that mainly gave women yet another reason to be terrified. Others piqued my interest, or grabbed me by the gut, plumbing the psychological or emotional

4

depths of horrifying situations all too recognizable. Still others dealt with natural and/or supernatural retribution for genocide and ecological violence. Not a few I found immensely satisfying emotionally.

I came to realize how often my favorite f/sf writers had juxtaposed horror with hope. Suzy McKee Charnas's *Motherlines*, with its clans of spirited Riding Women, followed the grimly dystopian *Walk to the End of the World*. In *The Female Man*, Joanna Russ offered not only the all-women's society of Whileaway but also the horrific detente of Manland and Womanland. Even the women of the idyllic Wanderground must remain personally engaged with the cruelly patriarchal city.

I jettisoned my original blanket injunction against horror and tried to read each story without prejudice. Several stories in this volume incorporate what I would now call horror elements: Shirley Hartwell's "Third Wave of Armored Daughters," Rosaria Champagne's "Womankind," Charlotte Watson Sherman's "Killing Color," L. Timmel Duchamp's "O's Story," Laurell K. Hamilton's "A Token for Celandine," and Mary Ellen Mathews' "Children of Divers Kind."

Fear is part of our lives as women, and a fiction that flinches from it will be not only escapist but flat. But how about fiction that wallows in horror, that uses language to terrify, and then washes its hands of the aftereffects? Like pornography, it can provide writer and user with a short-term control, but the question remains: Do the images leave us when we want them to, or do they subtly work to alter our view of the world and each other?

Despite the profusion of women writers, among women readers science fiction seems to retain its historical reputation as a man's genre. As a bookseller, I had the opportunity to observe close up the book-buying habits of feminist women, to recommend titles from the store's respectable f/sf collection — subtly and not-so-subtly expounding my theories about women and science fiction — and to talk with customers about what they read and didn't read.

Some were already converted, others were willing to try, but many more were not even tempted by the well-drawn women characters and feminist themes, even lesbian love stories, of Lynn, Bradley, Le Guin, Charnas, and Russ, among others, at cover prices roughly a third of the trade paperback alternatives. "I don't read science fiction" was the explanation. "It's too unbelievable. I can't deal with space-ships and elves." They bought lesbian romances instead.

I could recommend plenty of titles with neither space-ships nor elves, and as to "unbelievable" . . . Well, did you hear the one about the beautiful, brilliant woman with no apparent income who runs off to a secluded resort with an equally beautiful but shy, recently divorced woman, has perfect sex on the first try, and lives happily ever after?

Romances are for women, adventures for men, or so they say. Even for feminists, the speculative fiction of choice, the dreams we seek to place ourselves in, is not set in different worlds and times but in a here and now, and our adventures deal not with rescue or first contact with alien beings but with relationships (which, come to think of it, often deal with different sorts of rescue and first contact).

Three popular, well-reviewed "realistic" feminist novels of the early 1980s suggested to me that the conventional lines between genres might not be useful in dealing with feminist fiction. Perhaps because it was written by Joanna Russ, veteran and celebrated sf writer, I immediately recognized *On Strike Against God* for what it was: heroic fantasy in the guise of a screamingly funny contemporary coming out story.

Maureen Brady's *Folly* and Jan Clausen's *Sinking, Stealing* were more elusive. In *Folly*, Carolina women textile workers, white and black, go on strike; in the course of the story, the title character comes out with her best friend and sister striker. The title character of *Sinking, Stealing*, a lesbian co-mother whose lover has been killed in a car crash, goes underground with her lover's young daughter, fleeing the custody claim of the girl's father. In both books, complicated situations ended with hope for the workers, the lesbians.

"Unbelievable," some reviewers pointed out, which both annoyed me and tipped me off. I could believe that, despite all the forces arrayed in opposition, the women workers could run the factory themselves, and the co-mother might at least share custody of the daughter she had helped raise. But then, as an f/sf reader, I was used to suspending disbelief and taking off for unknown times and places. Much "realistic" feminist and lesbian fiction is also speculative, extrapolating

6

as it does from familiar realities toward unimaginable communities, accomplishments, and, yes, relationships.

At the end of *On Strike Against God*, Esther the narrator quoted a graffito that first surfaced on a wall at the Sorbonne during the 1968 French student uprising: "Let's be reasonable — demand the impossible!" Feminism demands (or, at least, requests) not only the impossible but the *unimaginable*. Aided by theories, herstory, hearsay, and dreams, we create in our daily lives what no one we know has lived before. Perhaps speculation is so integral to our art as well as our politics that we don't need a separate genre? Our fantasies range both through otherwheres and whens and through heres and nows.

The imagination is like a muscle that needs regular warming up and stretching exercise. Deferred, it grows world-bound; if unused long enough, it atrophies. My own writing continually brings me up against the limits of my imagination, while giving me opportunities to expand those limits. Recently, my own writing delivered the following lesson.

One of my agendas as a writer is to explore in fiction what I've learned about the internal and external dynamics of fat oppression. Jamie, one of my fiction protagonists, seemed a suitable vehicle. I envisioned her fat, leaning against a post-and-rail fence at the small horse farm she manages — and before my eyes her outline would shrink to a sturdy size 16. When I forced her larger, she moved jerkily, according to my will, never her own. Finally I let her be.

Months later she arrived early to meet someone at the ferry (like me, she lives on an island) and spent the waiting time surreptitiously studying a fat woman sitting on a bench. This woman's bright roses and purples glowed against the dreary December dock. Beside her sat a canvas bag imprinted with the names of women artists. Jamie, who rarely encountered inklings of feminism in her rural community, fantasized various scenarios for this woman, trying to imagine how she came to be carrying that bag.

When the boat finally came in, this woman went to meet one of the passengers, a tall rangy woman with a tripod under her arm. From their embrace, Jamie knew at once that their relationship was not platonic. All her previous assumptions about the fat woman on the bench crumbled. Being a reflective person, she mulled over the incident in subsequent days and weeks.

I, the writer, had the vehicle to explore my agenda about fat oppression and physical appearance, without forcing my characters to do my bidding at the price of their own integrity. But I doubt that this woman, whose name turned out to be Carrie, would ever have shown up on that dock had I not struggled months before to create a fat woman protagonist. Expanding the imagination is like learning another language. For months or years one wrestles with vocabulary and grammar, frustrated by the inability to articulate the simplest thought, and then, in a quantum leap, competence comes.

Reading the many stories submitted for this anthology, I frequently sensed imaginations warming up. Situations might seem forced, and characters stilted, as if their creator were pushing them too hard. The bonds of centuries still constrict us. It takes practice to conceive women characters who can come to life and have adventures. Even more effort seems to be required to imagine those women in alliances, defending and challenging and loving each other, developing guilds, communities, and whole worlds together. The greatest challenge of all is to make it all seem effortless, as if the story couldn't have happened any other way.

For me one of the joys of reading women's speculative fiction is scouting out the cutting edge of our imaginations. Where do we go when we can go anywhere? And why, when even the sky isn't the limit, are so many of our female protagonists young, strong, beautiful, and rich, if not royal? Why do class hierarchies and empires prevail so often, not only in fantasy but in future space? "Internalized sexism, ageism, racism, classism, ableism, looksism," sure, and something more: failure of the imagination?

For this anthology, 180 writers sent me a total of 280 stories. All but two (Judith Katz's "The Amazing Disappearing Girl" and Hattie Gossett's "womanmansion/to my sister/mourning her mother") came in unsolicited, "over the transom," in publishing jargon. I could have filled two more anthologies this size and had good stories left over. Despite wildly differing styles and subjects, the top contenders all *moved* me — to wonder, engagement, laughter, and/or tears.

And they stayed with me weeks after I put them down.

They remain with me still. The colorful capes swirling under a Gelasian dome are part of my memory now, and so is the computer-enhanced grass-roots democracy in "Sign of Hope." Sambal Goreng is still out there fending off writer's block, spaceships *jump* hyperspace with a novel source of energy, and as for that harmonically conceived girl–child . . . she could be anywhere. These stories have enhanced my memories and stretched my imagination. May they do the same for you.

Many women contributed to my being at the right place at the right time for this anthology. Among them I want to single out Mary Farmer of Lammas Women's Shop for hiring me and letting me buy whatever I wanted; Carol Seajay, editor and publisher of *Feminist Bookstore News*, for supporting my f/sf column; Katharyn Machan Aal, former director of the Feminist Women's Writing Workshops, where I not only met Lorraine Schein and Shirley Hartwell but learned much about both my craft and my commitment; Irene Zahava, bookseller and editor, for recommending me for this job; and Elaine Gill of Crossing Press for letting me do it.

With all the money I've made in the last ten years of writing and giving readings, I could probably buy two months worth of groceries. Stamps, paper, and, especially, time to produce *Memories & Visions* have been financed by regular jobs as proofreader for the *Martha's Vineyard Times*, chambermaid at the Lambert's Cove Inn, and word-processor for a variety of clients. My funds have been greatly stretched through the generosity of Cris Jones, whose house has sheltered me, Morgana the computer, and my voluminous files for the duration of this project.

Finally, I want to thank all the women who shared their stories with me, especially the fifteen whose work appears here. Sometimes your generosity and trust were overwhelming. I hope you like the result as much as I do.

The Chaos Diaries

•

Lorraine Schein

Fractal — I am the Chaos witch, who lives at the edge of your dreams and gives them shape and shapelessness. You can discern me sometimes fleetingly in the dream under the dream, the forgotten one, almost remembered beneath it, whose memory's aura still envelops you, though the substance is lost. Lost on the tip of your memory, as a word is lost on the tip of the tongue, fallen into the silent remnants of the forgotten.

This is my Book of Shadows, black covered, pages edged in silver, and in here I write of Chaos, have taken notes on its fractals, and record my observations that offer clues to its forms and manifestations.

All witches are Chaos witches, and all women are closer to Chaos than men by the very nature of their being and that of the universe. But I have chosen to study Chaos and describe her very essence.

Fractal — *Flying Silence.* You have to know how to fly silence to find Chaos in this fractal. You have to follow the moment to its origins but not push. Women have always flown these silences. Gliding into these vaporous trajectories. It's what men don't value in us, but we do in each other. Watch the moment shift into a cloud, the cloud an emotion. Only she can see it now. Only I can see her seeing it.

Fractal — *Fate.* There must be such a thing as fate, since there is Chaos. Fate is Chaos manifesting its patterns in our lives. Free will is just the pattern not perceived, unnoticed, unadmitted to out of pride. The generative order, upon which our lives impose an order of a lower degree.

Fractal — Today I visited a woman of the future through a gap in her dreams. She did not know what was happening. For a fraction of a second she ceased consciousness. She struggled in fear against the void, the amnesia terrifying, a being trying to remember its name. Then her mind and existence snapped back into form.

I followed her through the day, curious, when she awoke. She dressed and went out, down a long blue-paved street that parted at its end to let her through. It closed smoothly and silently overhead, leaving her in darkness. There was light at the end of the corridor we found ourselves in; its rays, visible to my eyes, but not hers, cast a chaotic form.

We drew closer. I sensed her mind coalescing around a new thought, a disturbing one. The mind is a hologram cast by the brain, real yet spectral.

A small white cubicle stood before us at the end, glowing. The woman took off her clothes slowly and lay on the long white table inside it and started to scream. She screamed for many minutes, until I thought the street above our heads would cave in from the sound.

Then the silver machines arose, unfolding like flowers from the walls and floor and clamped her down. An orgasm shot was applied to her genitals. She moaned in pleasure, then started to scream again. Her mind pulsated in shattered fractals all around.

It was very interesting. I took these notes.

There are many manifestations of Chaos, and here in their secret lab, the Chaos researchers were examining a disorder of it — or rather, since there can be no disorder of that which is a new order in itself, a different order.

Fractal — The Mathematician. The mathematician in the Chaos lab is afraid of me, though he has only seen me once.

He flicked on the computer on his desk; the spiky stubborn geometrics of the Mandelbrot set flickered onto the screen. He sighed looking at it, and punched in its coordinates to do a fractal analysis, but wanting to know more. Wanting to know its secrets.

He turns from the screen for a moment to work on his calculations. When he turns back to the screen, he is startled. (I am there.)

There is the face of a woman on the screen. Her hair is dark and features irregular. Her eyes are dark formulae, laughing at his amazement.

Her eyes grow larger, spreading fractally, till they fill

up the screen. He leans forward, fascinated. Then he sees it.

In the center of each three-irised eye, where the pupil should be, is a small perfect shape. A Mandelbrot set.

The image fades, reversing chronologically back to that of the woman again. Then it blanks out; the Mandelbrot set he had been working on flickers back onto the screen, after a moment of black-out.

He will never forget me.

It appeared in his dreams that night. The Mandelbrot set a huge eerie mountain on an icy plateau under brooding clouds. The same repeating sinister forms endless before him. He stands before it, at its foot, begins the long wearying climb. Eons pass, time slows. New species are born and die. At last, he scales the summit, pulls himself over its edge with trembling hands, and surveys his surroundings. And sees through the mist again the same repeating relentless forms before him, endless above him in the distance, yet even more massive, glowing in the darkness.

He starts his climb again, and as he ascends this time, sees that there ahead is still yet another of the same familiar shape, exactly like this one, part of an endless enormous range of Mandelbrot mountains ascending beyond him, reaching to the sky, enormous, the last one large as Jupiter and jutting off into deep space . . . .

And he knows there is a woman whose eyes are dark swirling formulae beyond them all, waiting . . . .

Fractal — Last night I watched the sky experimenting with its clouds and colors and at night, with its stars. The universe is an experiment whose hypothesis only I know.

And today I talked with my friend Liane, a poet who lives in a cave by the sea. Poets can see the outlines of Chaos, and are not afraid of me. She certainly could.

We had tea and talked of our work. Richly worked tapestries hung on the cave's walls; a small fire in its center flickered shadows onto them.

Outside, it had started to gently rain. I showed Liane how I wove the shaped spaces between the raindrops. She laughed wih delight. Then I cast a spell for her.

The air around us grew charged and wilder; the rain was coming down now in long black sheets angled to the atmosphere's chaotic order. I took her hand.

"Liane," I said quietly to her, "close your eyes slowly." I started to chant in a low voice. The flames of the fire began to die down. A sudden draft of wind blew a strand of her hair across her face.

The storm entered the cave and darkened it, but we did not get wet. The rain was light and shadow flowing around us.

"This is a time storm, Liane," I said. "Empty your mind, do not fear it. I am here." The time storm flooded around her. Violet energy chakra waves began to pulse about her head, her brain wave patterns becoming visible to me. I cast back in the storm, searching, for 1119 B.C.E., finally locating the oracle at Delphi. The brain wave patterns of its priestesses glowed and arched fantastically before me. I brought them forward with me through the still raging storm, ready to instill and replicate their complex patterns into her brain waves. I went to work. Neurons hissed into place, finding their structure, sparking like fireworks.

Liane's head fell back. Angry red patches appeared on her face at the temples; her body tremored and shook convulsively. Her mouth opened and out of it came a sound like the hissing of snakes, like a great wind driving a ship to destruction and wreck on the bottom of the sea outside.

Her eyes, which were still closed, opened. At last, she spoke, saying in that voice that wasn't hers, that wasn't that of any mortal:

> "I am the mother of Chaos
> And I have seen the Way
> Follow the Goddess and her daughters
> And the moon that burns by day."

Then the Goddess power released her, the brain pattern subsiding and returning to the past. The red patches faded from her face, her head came forward and Liane smiled at me, saying, "I was in a poem, I became a prophetess. I felt it . . . surge through me. Thank you so much. But there is only one thing I want to know. What did I say?"

I had written it here, in this book, and I read her her words, and told her what they meant. The time storm had dissipated, there was again only the sound of the rain outside and the small fire that lit the cave. I stayed till nightfall, then said good-bye.

Fractal — *Fortean Phenomena* — Alien Abductions. Cattle Mutilations. UFOs. Glass Breakings. Mysterious Disappearances. Space-Time Vortices. Baffling Fires. Hauntings. Bigfoot. Talking Animals.

These are all unique fractal-events, for which you have not yet discovered the pattern. They are not as uncommon as believed, they occur with great regularity, but only the Chaos-sensitive can perceive them, I have found. Facts that don't fit the pattern of your reality, reality as you have constructed it and that the data I have gathered here prove wrong. One day I will leave this book for you to find, then you will understand . . . .

Fractal — *A Chaos Trap* — Here is my formula for making a Chaos trap:

— Draw a pentagram in the night air at midnight, blur and partly erase its edges.

— Cats, dark-haired women, and virgins are conductors of Chaos — even better is some combination of the above, a dark-haired virgin woman, a virgin cat, etc. Have one or more conductors for your trap.

— The blood of an anarchist, while not strictly necessary, speeds up the process so much that I have included it here as a necessary ingredient. The anarchist need not be dead; one drop will do.

— Construct the trap along the coordinates of childhood and stir with antimatter wands.

— Drop moonlight into a particle accelerator, add the anarchist blood. Have your conductor(s) stand nearby and ready, observing. Cover it with the purple silk that wrapped a deck of ancient Tarot cards.

— Spin it all at the speed of sleep.

— Just before opening, sprinkle in some freshly broken glass, flying powder, and 3.1 ml. of freshly fallen waterfall eddy. These will act as a fixative to that which can't be fixed; but can only be attracted to itself in its present free form.

I constructed a Chaos trap yesterday, according to the formula given above. Liane, who has dark brown hair that borders on the edge of black, that looks blacker than black because of the subtlety of its color, was my conductor. We had located all the substances needed, even the anarchist blood, and the trap's construction was going well.

Suddenly, just before the accelerator stopped, and Chaos was to be released into the supraluminal realm (for only by its release can Chaos be trapped), it all blew up in our faces! We had achieved an unqualified success — this was evidence of trapping Chaos on a higher level, rarely attained, though much sought after. We shouted in triumph; there was Chaos all over the room.

Portions of this diary were destroyed, pages rendered illegible and charred by the explosion. What I have written here is all that is left.

Fractal — I have left these remnants of my diaries for you to discover, under the dream beneath your last remembered dream, hidden by twilight, its pages riffled randomly by the winds of Chaos, turning themselves ineffably in your sleep, in your mind, turning, slowly turning. . . .

Itu's Sixth Winter Festival

•

Shirley Hartwell

(Excerpts from *Daughters of Gelasia*)

Itu had decided to spend this day, since it was the law that she spend it by herself, thinking of the first daughters she had met here upon her arrival six years ago. Six years. A lifetime. The first daughters. Lara, Shimmon, Tullia, Helice, Rohanna.

Rohanna. Assigned to Itu's initiation into the daily routine. Showing her something Itu had not seen even though she had already observed the city's day to day life: the nighttime baking, the polishing of the house baths, the sluicing of the courtyards, the cultivation of the gardens that extended in huge wedges from the backs of the houses, the replenishing of the water in the rests of the temple way and the forest way, the laundering of the tunics and trousers and breast sashes and their return to the balcony rooms. Parts of the routine Itu already knew. What Rohanna showed her was their combination. Hundreds of tasks performed hundreds of times each year by every daughter in Gelasia. At first doing only what Rohanna assigned, Itu learned from her how to see, feel, talk, and listen her way into making her own daily acts. Making them a part of the life-sustaining net of work called the routine.

Itu always marvelled when she remembered learning from Rohanna, not because Rohanna had been so young, but because Itu had since rarely seen such skill in any daughter of any age. Who made the assignment? Helice? Itu could not remember. Wise they were, she thought.

Helice. Itu pictured back not to that first meeting when Helice had been the priest she visited on Temple Hill, but to another time, a year later. I walked from the temple one morning feeling covered with grace and saw Helice walking near the library. I took a step towards her and the step felt different, as though I'd stepped through a magnetic field into a new place that looked the same. And so I had. That night I sat in the courtyard listening to the others. Lara said something wise, and Shimmon said something wry, and Helice laughed at both of them. I watched her lean forward to listen to Rohanna in that attentive way she has. I must have been staring at her, her laughter still sounding in my head like the voyage gong reverberating. And she looked different. I didn't have a name for how she looked to me. The courtyard chimes brought Itu back to the present with a start, telling her that it was time to end her day-long meditation. The early winter dusk tinted the pink walls silver. She began to dress for the festival.

Earlier this season she had helped cover the dome with its heavy winter transparence, winter skin that held the heat and let in the light of the day and the moon. All preparations for this evening had been made before today. Everything except the food and the capes had been placed on the triple-tiered ledges that rimmed the dome; on their deep green, black-laced marble were now wine, cups, wands, drums, and bells. The food had been prepared and was stored in the library. The new capes were on the cape hooks of the temple entrance. Old capes, this year's embroidery completed, lay across balcony railings in every house. Nothing had been left undone. Every daughter could spend this day alone, preparing herself for the night to come, the most important festival of the year.

Itu went to the place on the balcony marked by her cape and watched the balcony fill with the daughters of her house, stood with them in silence until every daughter but two appeared. Finally, she saw two thirteen-year-olds, Rohanna and Sancia, dressed in padded satin festival coats that they would never, after their caping, wear again, cross the courtyard and open the massive arched doors of the harbor entrance. The waiting daughters reached for their capes, removed them from the balcony railing, turned. The balcony seemed to shift. Down the six circular stairways they filed, six single files that met in the courtyard, met in a procession six daughters wide, still silent.

The procession, made from a day of solitude, erupted

17

through the harbor arches. Itu flashed her eyes at Rohanna, and once clear of the entrance, swung her cape high over her head. Indoors, capes were never worn with any other garment, but now that she was outside, she let it fall over her festival clothing. All around her she saw other capes flying through the air, showing their twilight colors.

Itu could do many things with her cape. She could make it ripple and spiral and float and leap, but right now she kept its warm blueness around her. As her house joined the other houses, she saw ahead of her daughters running along the rim of the basin way, their capes held high and streaming behind them. Itu ran, making the cape call, a loud sustained chant interrupted with fast pats on the mouth. Other daughters took up the chant in different rhythms and tones. Some started the cape trill, vibrating their tongues on the roofs of their mouths. This is a wild procession, thought Itu, as she thought every year. She loved it. They were moving fast when they reached the temple hill and snaked up its spiral way.

Itu left her cape on its hook in the entrance cape room, smiling to herself as she carefully arranged the folds of the other capes it touched: to think I watched a caping ceremony without even knowing what it meant! I didn't think it had to mean anything, except itself. Then when I started wondering and asked Rohanna, she just looked at me and said, I have not yet been caped. So I asked, well what does it mean *not* to be caped, then? It means I haven't been caped yet, she answered with that blank expression of hers that is so like Helice's, that makes me angry and gives me such a feeling of exhilaration at the same time, as though I am on the brink of something Gelasian that is right there if only I can see it.

Itu felt more like a precious insect than a daughter as she stepped into the swarm of daughters inside the dome. Wild trills and chants had subsided to a low buzz of talk. She made her beginning visit to the center, turned towards the edge, felt the space begin to open as the gathering rearranged itself along the three-tiered rim. Except for the babies, who were held, all of the not-yet-to-be-caped, even the littlest females, climbed to the third tier and began handing down the drums and the bells to the already-caped, who were taking their places on the first two tiers. The sound of the bells as they were clasped around ankles and wrists filled the air with a light tinkling noise. Itu could almost breathe in the sound. Soft drum beats began.

Itu stomped her feet lightly on the green marble floor to hear her own ankle bells, clapped her hands to the drum beats to hear her bracelet bells, arranged herself on the first tier and relaxed against its warm marble, looked around the temple at the three tiers. As she did so the twilight ended and flames appeared on the tips of wands held by the not-yet-to-be-caped. With the ring of fire this winter night began, and twelve daughters were still standing. Three circles around twelve daughters, who stood waiting to be caped.

And there Rohanna stands, my She-to-be-caped.

Itu began to fidget a little as she waited for the encapement performance to begin. Each daughter chosen to encape tonight would demonstrate her cape dance skill. Itu would perform after Querida.

Suddenly, or so it seemed to Itu, so lost was she in the first few performances, she saw Querida come through the temple doors doing the Leaping Cape, tossing the peach silk up with her left hand so that it leaped in a high arc. Querida caught the descending rush of cape with her right hand; she threw the cape again and again as she moved from the temple doors to her She-to-be-caped.

Although no two capings occurred at the same time, the performances overlapped; halfway through Querida's dance Itu, having gone to wait at the temple doors, entered doing the Spiral Cape, her nervousness become performance.

She spun through the doors, flared the turquoise of Rohanna's cape wide open and high to begin the first spiral, dipped the cape as she turned, deepened the spiral by bending her knees so that the cape barely cleared the floor. Just as it was about to brush the marble, she started the spiral up, then down again. She felt the drum beats coming inside of her, heard only the bells on her own ankles and wrists as she whirled along her path towards Rohanna. She saw the turquoise around her and she saw it where she had been: a spiral corridor behind her that led to her own She-to-be-caped. The last shoulder-height movement swept the color around Rohanna's shoulders. Only then did Itu hear the drums as separate from herself, hear the others' bells again.

Itu sat and watched the remaining encapements. Rohanna remained standing, encaped. Soon all twelve were caped and it was time for the next-to-last cape dance.

Helice did her dance alone, without overlapping the previous one. The drums were silent. She slid through the temple doors, carrying a silver cape and wearing her own, which rose about her like a flying ruby disk as she turned. Into the air she threw the cape of her She-to-be-caped-again, twirled it into a spinning cone. She kept both capes moving and began circling the temple floor.

When Helice was halfway around the circle, the drums started. Who is She-to-be-caped-again this year? Itu had never figured out how that twice-recognized daughter was chosen. Probably Shimmon this year, she thought, if Helice was the encaper. But Helice ended her turns in front of Lara. She poised the twirling cape above Lara's head and let it go, and Lara stood just in time to let its silver circle fall upon her.

Later, while the food and the drink were being set out, Itu asked Helice, now dressed in her sarong of gold cloth, How is it decided who will be named She-to-be-caped-again?

I don't know . . .

Oh, not that answer again, thought Itu. She's probably going to tell me she doesn't know until she knows.

. . . how others have chosen, Helice continued, but I chose Lara because she brought you to Gelasia, Itu.

Itu waited for the last cape dance. She reached behind her for wine, turned, and came face to face with Rohanna in her turquoise cape.

Thank you for being my encaper, Itu, Rohanna said, and then added more formally, In my name, Rohanna, I thank you for caping me.

Now you are She-who-is-newly-caped.

Itu heard her words repeated: She-who-is-newly-caped, come to the center. The priests were sending the message through the gathering.

I didn't know that phrase was really a name, Itu said to Rohanna.

It wasn't a name until you said it. How do you think names get to be names? Rohanna teased, not formal now at all. Itu watched her as she answered the call and moved to the center, Rohanna with her cloud of black hair, Rohanna whom she had first seen as a spidery little female of seven coming towards her at the bottom of the temple way, Rohanna, now caped. Newly–caped. Who with the other newly–caped would soon perform her first cape dance.

Lara left her place in the triple circle and walked slowly towards the center, singing:

> you have many times heard the song
> you are about to sing
> but never have you sung it for yourselves
> tonight you will sing the song
> say the words of mystery and honor

The ring of newly-caped began their turn-the-circle dance; Lara began her twice-caped dance, moving counterpoint to their direction. Five circles around the center: the third tier of daughters holding light, the two tiers of watching daughters, a circle of dancing daughters, the circle described by She-who-is-twice-caped.

> What is the song, Lara asked. Sing the song.
> I dance for you, my first lover, came the response.

Itu watched Rohanna's gaze fix upon Sancia and remembered how she and Helice had looked at each other during her own first cape dance.

> I dance for you my first lover
> I look at you across the circle
> I turn the circle with you
> and ten others looking at each other
> six gazing paths we make each to a lover
> where our gazes intersect a fire burns

Lara turned before them, her silver cape brushing those of the turning circle.

> you have found a mystery
>> what cannot be described
>> what cannot be explained
>> what cannot be told
>> only known
> you have found it with your selves

The wheel slowed, softening the sound of the dancers' bells; flying capes of turquoise, peach, amethyst, rose, leaf green, pearl fell and softly swirled about the dancers. Lara, too, slowed her dancing pace to barely seeable motion. She continued in tones that sounded loud in the muting of the bells:

> You have sung honor to the one with whom you found a mystery. You named her lover. Now sing honor to your cape sister.

Twelve voices chanted softly.

> I tell you, my first lover, that when you name another lover, I will name her my cape sister. We may have cape sisters through the other.
> *Say honor to your first lover.*
> You will always be my lover. I say so with my name.
> *Say honor to your time together.*
> Our time will finish.
> *Say the honors.*
> I say you will always be my lover and our time will finish. Your lovers will I name cape sisters. In my name do I say so.
> *Say honor to your sisters through the cape.*
> I say that when your lover names another lover, she will be my sister through the cape. Your lovers will I name cape sisters. Their lovers will I name sisters through the cape. In my name I say it.
> *Say honor to the web made through the cape.*
> I say that I will never take back from you the name of lover. I say that if I do, I will lose my cape sisters and all my sisters through the cape. I say that I will keep the web and keep my name. Always.
> *Say honor to the keeping of the web.*
> I say I will find my way to keep the web. I say I will be a part of your finding your way. I say I will do the same with all the daughters that I ever name as lovers. We will keep the web. In all our names, we will keep the web.

They continued softly:

> so goes the web of desire
> we will hold the web
> with all our names

we will hold the web
May it ever hold,
Lara said in a louder voice, moving faster.

May it ever hold,
the newly-caped repeated.

May it ever hold,
they sang, spokes of desire wheeling them faster and
faster around the burning center.

Itu as encaper was among the first group of tiered
daughters to join the dance. Then came the lovers and cape
sisters of the encapers; the remaining daughters seemed to
rise in unison as they saw in the dance a lover, a cape sister,
a sister through the cape.

Itu heard her own bells magnified by other dancers
following the same rhythm, heard different rhythms sounding too. Strong and various they were. The gathers of her
ripe-plum velvet tube fell from beneath her bare breasts and
brushed her ankles. A glimpse of turquoise lit her eyes. Capes
flew in the air around her. Garments of every hue clung
to the dancers' bodies. The undulating spinning swaying
movements, the bright colors, the gleaming skin, the fire
of the wands, and the flashing eyes of the dancers was a
dazzling kaleidoscope that would have blinded Itu had she
not been a part of the blaze.

[Itu had heard of armored daughters but had never met
one. Armored daughters had always lived inland and had
never been seen in any voyage city. When they began to enter
voyage cities, their appearance there was called a wave.
There were three waves of armored daughters. The first wave
— of only five — escaped to a voyage city from the band that
had captured them as children. They were pursued there by
their own band and other bands, who became known as the
second wave of armored daughters. The second wave
destroyed the voyage city but did not find the three armored
daughters hidden there. A Gelasian trading ship discovered
the devastated city and offered refuge to the first wave of
armored daughters. The newcomers declined to become a part
of the life of the city and eventually settled in a lightly forested
area surrounding the great houses and gardens of Gelasia.

23

Itu helped to greet the first wave of armored daughters. She did not like their shiny armor or their eyes that did not shine or their voices that were missing whole octaves. But most of all she did not like about them something that the other Gelasian daughters could not see. Most of all she didn't like that she did not know what that something was.]

The Third Wave of Armored Daughters

Itu never remembered afterwards what part of the daily routine she was about to begin when she looked out the harbor window of her balcony room and saw two ships coming through the harbor mouth. It was not until she was standing on the basin rim, having run there in a rush of daughters, that she knew why the ships seemed so menacing as they loomed larger and larger towards her, why her heart pounded, why the rushing of her blood thundered in her ears.

There had been no voyage gong. The sound of the gong she did not hear frightened her beyond speech, as it must have the other Gelasian daughters, for they all stood there silently watching the ships move in, anchor right in the middle of the basin, lower small boats to the water, row them towards the rim near the temple.

Only then did several daughters start towards the silence of the voyage gong. The rest went to the boats and did as Gelasians had always done. These armored daughters that they welcomed were heavier, older, than those who had left for the forest belt.

More armored daughters, Itu said to Rohanna. Why do we welcome them. I know. Your Gelasian way.

Your way too, Itu.

I feel not Gelasian around armored daughters, Rohanna. I have broken our way with them before.

So have I, Itu. But I am Gelasian. How could I not be, even when I break the way? And you too. Gelasians make the way.

I did not want to do this welcome, Rohanna.

That does not make you not Gelasian, Itu. It does not.

Rohanna seemed alarmed, so Itu did not say, I do not

feel Gelasian now. I feel something else. Instead she joined the welcome, helped arrange for groups of visitors to go to various courtyards for food and drink, which offer was accepted without a hint of the fear that had kept the forest armored daughters on their ship.

Itu helped serve the guests of her own house, watched them smile, listened to them talk. Entirely at ease, not silent and withdrawn like the first two waves of frightened armored daughters, they strode about the courtyard, filled it with their flat unmusical tones.

You haven't had many visitors like us before.

Itu realized the challenge was aimed at her. Before she had a chance to reply, she heard Tullia say: Yes, we have. There have been two groups of armored daughters here before you.

And where are they, the visitor asked Tullia.

Don't tell them, Itu thought. She remembered the hard glint of metal all around her when she had listened to Maslin on the deck of the Gelasian ship, listened to Maslin warn her: We will not help you find the lost city daughters. The bands would trace us through you. We have already discussed it. We did not escape to be found and recaptured. Don't tell them, Tullia, Itu thought, and interrupted, trying to deflect the question with another. Do you call yourselves armored daughters? she challenged. She couldn't worry about that now. She saw the startled look on Tullia's face and thought, she either realizes the danger of what she's said or is shocked that I've ignored their question. And a small confusion rippled in waves from Tullia to the other daughters of the house.

What brings you to stop here? Itu asked another visitor, not caring about an answer. They must not find out about the armored daughters in the forest. Why am I protecting them, she wondered. Why not let the visitors take their armored daughters back, and be done with all of them.

We have heard such wonderful stories of your city that we wanted to come and see you for ourselves.

Us? Why us? Itu asked, surprised into a true question.

We heard how beautiful you are.

Itu's mind reeled. Her vision of the courtyard shattered in her eyes like an exploded mosaic.

And where have you come from, she asked, thinking

of the ships that had loomed into the harbor. And when she heard the answer the courtyard fell hard back into place and she knew whose ships they had. The stolen daughters of the devastated voyage city must have been carried from their sister city in their own ships. And where were they now.

Itu looked around at the faces of the house daughters she had lived with all these years. Surely she could read them. Did they know what she now knew? But as she looked all she saw was the courtyard different, the faces of the daughters of the house unreadable to her.

She continued her serving mechanically, as though what she was doing was separate from herself, and she began to see why the faces of the house daughters were unreadable. The hospitality they offered had become false. They would not offer more, Itu was sure. She watched as Tullia sat instead of replenishing empty trays of food, watched Rohanna and Lara set jugs of unpoured wine aside, watched the movement of all the daughters in the courtyard stop, heard their voices fall silent. Until Lara substituted for the usual Gelasian offer of lodging an offer to escort the visitors back to their boats.

Itu did not go with them but waited in the courtyard for their return. She sat there feeling someplace else.

Itu wore her cape, blue like a wild flower, to the temple. She waited until the searchers spoke. They had not found the voyage watcher. And then she rose to speak. She began her story of her conversation with the smiling human, but paused in astonishment at the word. I know that's what they are called, she finally said in answer to the puzzled faces turned towards her. Only Helice's face appeared unpuzzled.

Itu continued with her story, felt something else pushing through. She repeated the words of her courtyard conversation. But when she began to tell how she had felt during the exchange, how the courtyard had shattered in her eyes and come together in a different way, how her blood had thundered in her ears at the basin rim, this she was not sure she could make clear, because after all, she heard herself say, though I am Gelasian now, I once knew captivity. I do not know if the rest of you will understand what I am

26

saying.

But they did. It was like the testimonies Itu had read in the library. One by one the Gelasian daughters stood and told their stories, how they had felt. The courtyards had shattered in many different ways that night, and they had all come together hard.

Helice in her ruby cape stood to speak. The story has been there all the time, at the seventh level of the library. I was sent to it by my last night's dream. Humans, she said. They have slaves.

Slaves, Itu said. I was made a slave, and I escaped. I have stories to tell you, stories I heard before I was taken from my mother, who was a daughter.

Look! Sancia's cry interrupted her. All attention turned from Itu, who looked with the others through the temple netting, and saw shapes that were not of the grove, and lights that were not of the moon, but torches. The temple skin began to flame.

Helice ran out of the temple first. She ripped her knife right through the temple skin where she was standing and ran through the shredded opening. Itu ran hard after her, knew where she was headed. Helice raced towards the library, passing the procession of humans carrying more torches.

Don't go into the library, called Itu to Helice, both of them leaving the slowly moving file behind. Inside the library Itu pushed past Helice and blocked her way down the central stairwell that spiralled seven stories underground. They will burn this library, Helice. She held Helice's shoulders, the ruby cape bunching in her hands. Pornography, they call it. The writing of prostitutes. Prostitute, they will name you, Helice. They will burn you alive.

Itu saw daughters fall in flames, saw the torches reach the door.

Into the first level came the humans. Itu clung to Helice at the stairwell as down into the maze of counters the humans filed, to set fire to the wooden boxes, to set fire to the soft cloths covered with their pictures, to set fire to their words and their stories.

Itu was screaming now. You will burn! Helice easily broke away from her and started down into the maze. She screamed at the other daughters who entered with the humans, having escaped their torches. Help me stop her. They will burn her.

Instead, some daughters followed Helice down. Others clustered around Rohanna, helped her move Itu out of the building. Our memories, Rohanna hissed at Itu. Save our memories.

Our memories are down there with Helice.

Our memories are right here too.

Itu looked through the doorway, screamed again for Helice to leave.

She cannot hear you.

I am going after her.

Rohanna blocked her path. She has one thing to do, Rohanna said fiercely. You have another. Don't go back.

She will burn, sobbed Itu.

You think I don't know that, growled Rohanna. Do you think I don't want to get her too? And the others? The others, Itu? And do you think they'd come with either of us? Helice will not come back with you, Itu. Rohanna stood aside. Go, if you want. Go. But you know what you have to do, and you can't do it if you burn.

The humans erupted from the stairwell and moved swiftly out the door and off the hill.

First came the terrible smoke, then the tips of flames shooting up from the seven levels below.

I will never see her again, was the most Itu could manage to think as she watched the points of fire shoot higher and higher, watched them lick the ceiling. And then came the flames in waving sheets. The first level collapsed. The roof exploded. The sheets rose again in points and wide tongues of fire from seven stories deep licked the sky.

Itu saw nothing but fire, heard nothing but fire.

She is in the flames. She is in the flames. Itu screamed at Rohanna: She is in the flames. But Rohanna could not hear her over the blinding roar.

Helice was in the flames. She stood, burning, on the invisible plane where the floor of the first level had once been, and she turned towards Itu. They looked at each other through the fire.

Itu watched her burn. Helice burned and burned, until Itu thought she must disappear into the flames. But instead Helice began to shimmer, points of light flashing dark and light so fast that Itu couldn't tell whether the light was flashing or the dark was flashing, until Helice was all darkness, darkness flashing through the flames. She looked straight at Itu one last time, threw her head back, raised her arms in their ancient gesture, twirled above her head a cape that was not there, its ruby darker than flame. Helice arched her feet, moved her body into the sound of silent drums, and stopped, poised forever at the beginning of the spiral cape dance. Silver bells echoed; their clarity pierced the roar of the flames, and Itu listened to them.

That night the survivors sat together at the rim of the basin, now empty of the looming ships, and felt the spirits of sisters, lovers. cape sisters who had died in the flames. Never will we be without you, were the words that were not spoken. Never will you be without us, came the silent response. The next day the daughters took the bodies, all but one, and gave them to the sea.

Then they took Helice's body, ebony poised in dance, to the place where the voyage watcher had disappeared.

Itu set her into place. We will come back to you, Helice, to remind ourselves of the lesson you've left for us to see. You were always better than anybody else at teaching lessons. We will come to you to remind ourselves that everything ends and that nothing ends, that we always dance the eternal dance.

Womankind

•

Rosaria Champagne

The train came to a fast halt and my shoulders lurched forward, ahead of my breath, and then returned to me.

"You're a woman," the man to my left commented softly, his face hidden behind a late edition *Tribune*. His manicured nails sat pompously on fat, red fingers, which held up his newspaper in front of his face like a shield. I hated him immediately.

"You are," he repeated.

"No I'm not," I said as gruffly as I could.

I felt myself begin to sweat. Why did this man suspect me? I was in drag, as usual. What gave me away?

I glanced around the cabin. There were twenty rows of grey vinyl seats separated by a grey tile floor. Two men sat in every double seat, each wearing navy blue suits and white shirts. Their hair was held in place with hair gel and they each wore brown horn-rimmed glasses on their grey vinyl faces. Each of their small brown eyes pierced through the financial section of the late edition *Tribune*.

The man to my left turned the page, brushing my cheek with his right hand as he exaggerated the movement. "Why don't you give yourself up? They might go easier on you," he said.

I had had a rough day, and all I wanted to do was get home, get out of this god-awful blue suit, wash my hair, and take a long, hot bath. I was in no mood to be hauled down to the courthouse for being in drag, nor am I of the proper disposition to be horse-whipped for being a woman "out of place." Then I'd be returned to my husband in the suburbs where I'd have to pamper his ego and fake orgasms again. Nobody likes being in drag all day, but it certainly is less burdensome than faking orgasm.

I stood up, cornered now between the window on my right, rows of men in front of me, and rows of men in back. The man to my left stood up, too. "If you give me a blow job, I won't turn you in." He smiled, showing a space between his front teeth.

I had reached the limits of my patience, and I guess I lost my temper. I pushed him down on the floor and kicked his briefcase into the middle of the aisle. His newspaper fell from his hands, and his shoulders and red face converged forward. I unzipped his pants, considered, Is it a snap off or twist off? then pulled off his penis. It stretched at first, like taffy, and the purple vein protruded more than I had noticed purple veins protrude in the past. It came off in a snap and sounded as if someone had just unsnapped a child's pajamas. It shriveled up immediately and I stuffed it in my pocket.

I ran out of the cabin, away form the frozen stares of the other passengers and into the vestibule. As I reached the door, someone screamed "STOP HER!" And I realized I had to act fast.

The steel doors in the vestibule were locked because the train was now flying forward. I frantically pushed all the buttons, but none would release the doors. An alarm screamed. With my stolen penis, which had grown in length and width from the excitement of my escape, I bludgeoned down the window part of the door and stuck my hand into the cold air. In my open palm, wind slipped through my fingers, and I could feel the wetness of freedom. Then, a cold hand grabbed my arm. I wrestled to get it back, but he rubbed it back and forth on the jagged glass until my hand popped off at the wrist. I forgot to bleed.

The doors flew open, and the momentum from the blast of air sucked me below the train. I clung desperately to the railing, but was shot beneath the train by the power of the wind. I gripped the bottom platform of the train; my body stretched across the tracks like a bridge. With only my left hand attached to my arm, my body flopped against the train tracks like a sack of sand. Finally, I just let go, hoping the speed of the train would crush my useless body flat as a penny, and I would go fast.

I released my hand, hit the ground, and felt my body split in half. I squeezed my eyes tight, amazed at how painless death had been. I remembered I had a cat at home to feed, and I felt a little irresponsible, dying like this. Then I heard voices and I realized I was not alone. I opened my eyes and saw hundreds of women, maybe more. I had no idea where we were. I checked my watch and realized that time had stopped.

How they found this place, and why we were allowed to live free here, I'll never know. I should have asked, but the only appropriate time for such introductory questions was now, and I missed my chance, still contemplating the sad plight of my cat left at home. The women seemed settled, as if they had lived here all their lives. Some were cooking, some singing, some nursing, some writing. Like me, each held a stolen penis and used it to write or paint or stir the pot of soup on the fire.

Are we dead? I asked the woman to my right, a short Jewish-looking woman who was breast feeding a baby.

Of course not, she said. You were just born.

I asked her how I got here. She said I walked, of course. Her baby stopped sucking, and she wiped the dribble off her breast with her sleeve. I just walked? I said.

I met Elaine over there. She writes poetry, too. She shared with me some paper she had collected from the flat stones the track kicks up with the fire. The paper was heavy and rough, and she told me if I wanted finer paper, I'd have to ask Kerry, and she would give me the finest paper in the world. This is fine, I said. Paper was scarce, and I loved her for sharing some with me. I didn't have a pen, but squeezed the juice out of my penis for ink. It served me well as a pen. In fact, it worked better as a pen than it did in any other capacity, I thought.

Eventually, it became very hot and the air thick. My hair had grown to my waist, and my underarms had puffs of thick brown clouds below them. It was summer, I thought, and we took off our clothes and used them as pillows. We sang a lot. Tina played her guitar, and I sometimes played it, too. I asked her once if she feared the men would find us out, singing as we did, but she said no. She said the men could never hear us, no matter how loud we sang or cried. She said that I shouldn't be afraid of men ever again because remember, we have their penises and they are lost without their penises. We don't have them all, I said, but Tina didn't hear me. She was singing with joy and it was my turn to sing the harmony. So I did, and felt loved and happy.

Elaine and Tina and I became lovers. We were children again, bathing each other, and gently, under the bubbles, inserting tiny fingers in tender places.

One day, Elaine and I were sitting on our suit jackets. She was reading to me a poem she had written, and I suggested she use parentheses instead of commas (I love parentheses). She said I was being bossy again, and that I would never just listen and accept. She said I was just like a man when I acted so bossy. In fact, she said, maybe you *are* a man, and pulled off your own penis just to spy on our community and make love with the women. No! No! I said. But it was too late. The others heard our quarrel and they too began to wonder whether I was really a woman.

Here, take it! I said, giving to Elaine my penis. If I were really a man, I wouldn't just give you my penis willingly, I said.

But what will you write with? she asked, genuinely touched by my selflessness.

I'll find something, I said.

Here, take mine, she said, handing me her penis. Only women can trade penises, she said, and was convinced, finally, that I am a woman.

As I reached to accept Elaine's penis, Kerry intercepted it. She snatched it out of my hand and held it tight. Prove you are a woman, she demanded. I looked to Elaine, wondering how I was to prove such a thing, but Elaine just looked away. Prove it! Kerry demanded. By now, everyone was staring at me. I was really in a predicament. How could I prove something so obvious — and yet so important? Not knowing what else to do, I pointed to my breasts and vagina, but Kerry said that wasn't good enough. In this day and age, people wear breasts and vaginas like they do raincoats when it rains, she said.

Kerry said that if I were really a woman, I'd know what it is that women have that men cannot even imagine. A divine gift, she said, something extraordinary, and if I couldn't explain it, I obviously was an imposter. Quite frankly, I had no idea what she was talking about.

33

Are you going to defend yourself or admit to your guilt? she demanded, her fists digging in her hips.

You're the goddamned imposter, not me! I yelled. The other women agreed with me, and shouted, Yeah! Yeah! You're right! Kerry turned to them, saying, How can you believe her? I've been leading you for so long . . . But the others yelled back, telling Kerry she was wrong. She looked around wildly.

Everyone was cheering now and hugging and kissing me and telling me I was right. Elaine told me that she loved me, then stuck her tongue in my ear to substantiate, I suppose, her support.

But I knew I wasn't right. I had just done something terribly, terribly wrong, and I knew it. When I had condemned Kerry, I condemned the whole system. As soon as my hateful words were uttered from my mouth — maybe even before, when they were focusing in my brain like swept dust on a kitchen floor — I had killed the system. Me! I had destroyed it with words, and it was too late.

I was crying now, and Elaine was stroking my hair and telling me that it would be all right. She held my head to her breasts, and I lay there in my own wet tears, in the softness and warmth. It will be OK, she said. Kerry will get over it. No, I said. It will never be the same.

We all became very sick after that and died very slowly. We didn't know what to do with the dead bodies, so they stayed wherever their owners had died. It made it so the living couldn't breathe without inhaling the foulness. I remember the day my fingers fell off my hand. I tried to pick them up, but I couldn't control both stumps. The blood gushed from the holes where the fingers had been, pouring forth in beautiful fountains of red. I watched it, in awe of my possessions. Then Elaine's fingers fell off, and all of our neighbors' fingers, too. We couldn't write anymore without fingers, so we put our penises in our mouths to write. Once in our mouths, they grew hard and excited, and so they, too, were useless to us.

Our eyeballs fell out, and we begged for death, thinking we could no longer endure any more pain. But our eyes, although separated from their sockets, continued to see. Without eyelids, though, they could not protect themselves from fire and rain, sharp objects and heavy boots. From hazards we never knew were so deadly. Once, while asleep, I curled a little closer to Elaine and accidentally rolled over on her eyeball and crushed it. She screamed with the intensity of rape, and her eyeball burned the flesh off of my hip. She died the next morning.

They are all dead now, I think. It is very difficult to tell when your eyeballs continue to observe and relate things to you that you know are not really happening to you, but to them. It is hard to let go.

Everyone else died when her eyeballs were destroyed, like Elaine. But mine fell out in a pasture, I think, because I see a lot of green and I don't know where I am.

The Rational Ship

•

Caro Clarke

I don't like writers on my ship and as I saw this one coming
through the bar doors I knew I was adding another onto
a long hate list. She was the usual goods, her hair cropped
short, no facial tattoos save for the Writer's Line vertically
down the eye from brow to cheek,the plain blue skin-suit,
and above all that snooty, remote expression of someone
who thinks she's too good for her company.

She saw me at the bar and came over.

"Captain Mintrell?" she asked, and when I nodded she
said, "I'm Writer Strocall — Writer Stroc'."

Another thing I hate about writers is that they never
give you their full names, reserving such precious knowledge
for their own Guild-members.

"Cantance," she ordered from the bar. A long hose
snaked out; she tucked the neb into one corner of her mouth
and took a few puffs.

"I hope that's just recreational," I said sourly.

She looked at my glass. "I hope the same of you,
Captain."

"I run a rational ship," I said. "We don't go mystical.
Let me tell you: I don't like writers and I keep the numbers
down to one. That's hard work for you, but it means bonus
payments. It also means you won't get script-happy with
your writer-buddies and will pay attention to my orders.
Understood?"

"I know this already," she smiled one-sidedly around
her neb. "'Mintrell the Merciless.'"

I could feel steam rising but it was increasingly hard
to get writers for my ship and I couldn't afford to lose this
one with less than three hours to plose.

"Listen," I said. "I wanted to see you alone to explain

how I run my ship. The rest of the crew has been with me for years but I've never had the same writer twice. I keep it mechanical and I don't want any involvement. Right?"

"I'll give you what you want," she took the Cantance neb from her mouth and looked me over lazily. "When do I go aboard?"

"I'll take you now," I threw two gold wafers on the bar; as much as I hate writers, I'm still the captain and I pay for my employees.

Over at the star-harbor my loading crew were busy clearing away the last of the pay-freight. The *Mintrell's* faceted sides gleamed iridescently in the harbor's evening light-bands. My ship. I could almost feel it warm up as I approached.

"Dok, Hallram," I nodded to my loaders. "Writer Stroc'."

They lifted their ears politely but said nothing. None of my crew likes writers either, except for my star-searcher, and he's been getting odder.

"This is a Thrhad-class ship, isn't it?" Stroc' asked.

"The *Mintrell* has been completely redesigned." Didn't the idiot have eyes? "It was a Thrhad-class ship when I bought it but since the overhaul it's been designated as a Captain-unique."

"So," she threw me a measuring look. "An illuminating fact."

"What's *that* mean?"

"Why you restrain to one writer, for instance."

A typical writer remark. They're so sure their brains run the galaxy.

"Let me tell you," I said. "It's not your business how I treat my ship. Keep your speculations till you're off-looped."

She shrugged.

We fetched a renitence disc and lifted to the crew portal. When I stepped in one deep note rang: the ship's way of greeting me. *Mintrell's* sweet, metallic smell and its warm currents of home-dense air filled me with content. My ship.

Our reunion was broken when Stroc' impatiently shifted behind me.

"I'll take you to your shell," I said. "I'm going that way. About an hour to plose you'll be called to meet the crew; it's a custom of mine."

She said nothing so I took her up the slide-tube to her shell.

"You'll be familiar with everything inside: it's the standard set-up," I explained. I'd found writers fretful about their living quarters.

She hoisted herself on the grip-bar and slid feet first through the dilator. A wave of release swept over me. Even though a writer might be on board, she was now encysted, held in limbo until I was forced to summon her.

My own command shell wrapped round me like a cocoon. I automatically strapped myself down and bonded with the ship. It was a good feeling. I could sense the precious pay-freight in its hold, the fuel waiting to go — go — go, the nerves of the Core Analor ticking and humming. The plates were right, the stanchions were right. Under its crystal skin the *Mintrell's* steel bone and chemical pulse were sound and orderly. This was a unitary ship.

Time to call the crew. Unlike most ships, the *Mintrell* had been provided with a common room; I liked to see my crew and I reckoned that it provided a stronger bond. For two of my crew it had: two years ago, Fvas, my engineer, and Nihiitilis, my second S.D. operator, had signed a life-pledge. We'd fitted them a special double-shell as our gift.

I opened my whistler and ordered them to assemble. They'd been waiting for it and soon we were together.

"Everything all right, captain?" Cradge, my Combat-Mechanical, shared my dislike for writers just as she did my love of orderliness; I never saw her components except clean and polished.

"I got a writer," I said. "Name of Stroc'. Are we ready to plose?"

"Loading is completed," said Dok.

"Sustention deck buttoned down," said Legted.

"Guns loaded," said Cradge.

"And I've finally sobered up," Braieder, my star-searcher, grinned from his hook on the wall.

"You'd better be," I scowled in mock-anger. "I don't want you pointing us into the Empress's back garden."

"Oh, I'll get you to the right neighborhood," he began to swing a little, his arms dangling loosely past his truncated torso. "You'll just have to tack back."

"With your wages paying the extra fuel," said Ajam, my money-rider.

"An hour to plose. Take your ease before we batten

down," I said. "Then I'm going to call the writer."

"That should bile me," Loader Halbram muttered.

When they'd finished eating, I sent Cradge down to fetch her. She entered the common room as cool as an ice-cap, not feeling or not caring about our obvious antipathy.

"Writer Stroc'," I said and introduced my crew. "Listen, if you want to eat, Nihiitilis will supply you."

"I don't eat before a plose," she shook her head.

One of these taut-belly types. She'd take Cantance but shied away from food.

"As you wish," I said.

"Can't you be persuaded?" Braieder swung hand-over-hand across the ceiling-grips, his support cables trailing behind him. "The *Mintrell* boasts one of the finest galleys in the Hegemony. I myself do not partake, as you can understand, but I assure you that — "

"Space it," I growled. "If Writer Stroc' doesn't want anything, she won't be given anything."

"The captain's will be done," he winked at Stroc', who said nothing and looked bored.

"Perhaps you'd like to return to your shell, then," I suggested, nettled. Braieder could be tiresome but she had no right to disdain him. This was my crew.

"Very well," Stroc' seemed unconcerned.

"She should stay and talk to me," Braieder complained. "We need to know each other."

"You'll link when the time comes," I said.

"I'd rather be sociable. Most writers are sociable, aren't they?" he asked her. "Some ships have whole decks of writers being very sociable. Are you one of them?"

"Not often." Stroc' paid little attention to him.

"I'm disappointed," Braieder chinned himself on a ceiling bar. "Give me lunacy; I'm deranged, I'm disarranged, myself."

"Writer Stroc' prefers to go to her shell," I said, and she looked at me and left.

Peteliter, my second engineer, made a face. "Writers!" he said in disgust. "If you were stranded in space with them for your whole life, they'd never get to know you." I wasn't surprised; that's why my crew stays with me.

We plosed from the planet Hocklujtt within acceptable time and vectored past the sun in a close tuck. The *Mintrell* is a big ship, one of the largest on its run, and it needs plenty of time to ladder-up to light-speed. We were all strapped into our shells, save for the writer, who had no duties until the kick-over. As usual, I locked into Braieder during ladder-up for company.

"Good evening, Captain," he said in mind-lock. "Once again we take you through the melodies of the spaceways," and began to mind-sing one of his strange compositions. We were heading for the planet Kred's Skylight, a customary port-of-call for the *Mintrell,* so when Braieder stopped singing to scan the stars it was only as practice. Since he'd signed up under me, he'd never pointed us wrong even by a filament.

The *Mintrell* needs two Imperial days to ladder-up to the kick-over, but I never felt the time passing. The ship sings to me more sweetly than Braieder, the heavens whisper around its hull; I am alone in the command shell, hard on my Board, feeling the ship's skin as my skin, its sensors as my eyes and hands.

At last we were going as fast as the vastors could propel us. It was time to chain before I got hooked on the threshold between space and praeterspace. I could sense it vibrating closer and closer to my heart as the ship chimed me to remembrance. Reluctantly, I opened my whistler.

"Prepare for kick," I told my crew. "Braieder, start tracking. Writer Stroc', get up here."

I always put my writers as far away as possible from the command shell, but Stroc' was at the dilator in quick time. I was strapped in, skull wires tapped, buffer-band across my forehead, and elbows and thighs tightly bound to the Board. I barely registered the pressure of the straps; I was the ship, skipping and yawing on the edge of time. Then my mind was half-pulled to myself as Stroc' slid down the length of my body, her weight evenly against me. While she reached for her own chain-wires I wrestled with my hatred. Chaining is best done with a harmonious mind but the most I could manage was to force my instincts under lock and key.

With a shock like ice water we were chained mind to mind. Another person shared my ship, shared the awareness of myself; I was the ship and no one could have it. Stroc' and I assessed each other, the touch of our naked flesh together less important than the raw jolt of another I. Through the chain I sensed all Writer: the pride, the

40

remoteness, the arrogant imagination, the reach spanning praeterspace that sets a Writer above all other ultra-psis. At the same time she had been probing me. I hoped she found a dedicated captain, a superior ship. She made an angry noise in her throat, mind-spoke,

"Mintrell the Merciless,"

and fastened her mouth on mine with a breath-gasping kiss.

At some point Braieder triple-chained on us from his shell. He was in the slight delirium that came with flinging out his senses to find our port.

"I'm happy," he crooned to himself. "I'm happy, happy." He was taking giant strides across light-years, across parsecs.

I was feeling like a dead fish on a cold slab. Stroc' lifted her face from mine.

"I'm not going to help you, Writer," I taunted. "You're going to have to work — work — for it."

I couldn't see her face in spite of the lights in the shell, my eyes were now the ship's eyes staring at black space. She didn't answer; she began to overture. For the first few minutes I was able to judge her performance cold-bloodedly. She was a fast learner, noting my reactions and playing them well. Her mouth was on mine again, then on my throat, then tantalizingly down, while her hands kept moving. I felt a light sweat break across my body: caught at last.

"Turned on," I mind-spoke to my star-searcher, speaking from that cool pocket of reason only captains could maintain. "Have you got it?"

Braieder was still crooning. "Yes, Captain, I have it. Oh, it's pretty. Pretty as a pearl. A pearl whirling."

"See it?" I asked Stroc', still in mind-speech.

"Yes," she didn't pause.

"Keep pointing," I told Braieder, then couldn't say any more as Stroc' hit a vital region. Our minds flickered together, I saw her script: a blazing white line her imagination painted over a three-dimensional fantasy of praeterspace. That's how she saw it, that's how I saw it now. My job was to kick this ship over that gap, following that fiery line to the whirling planet Braieder pointed us to. He pointed, but at the kick it would be me, Stroc' at the ship's wheel, me.

Her hands were between my thighs. I could feel heat, pressure, mounting. My head rocked back, I gasped for air.

"Come on, you juicer," I mind-spoke like a shout. "Power me!"

My hands, free from the elbow, clamped onto her flanks, her breasts, urging her head down and down. She resisted, fought me, played me like a kite on a string. Her script flared before me, my line dictated. I was the ship, bucking and shuddering under her tongue. I had to jump — jump! I arched up, riding the burn, riding the speed, I was faster than light, I was beyond space. We hung — we were there — she pushed me home, I vortexed, we kicked over the gap — I was — I — Endless instant, suspended eternity — I floated in radiant streamers above Time, knew somewhere that I was flying, flying alone on a ticket she'd written for me from space to space. Then we sank, I sank, we fell, the gap was crossed, we were slowing down, we were back in time. Her script ran straight and true, Braieder sang,

"Home to rest, home to Kred's Skylight,"

and linked-out of our three-part chain.

Stroc' lay heavily across me, sweet as Cradge. Although I'd done nothing for her, she was sated and weary. The Board was wet from both of us. I hovered peacefully between myself and my ship.

Stroc' stirred and turned her head. Although we were still, disinterestedly, mind-chained she murmured aloud,

"Mintrell,"

and lifted herself to look into my face where I was strapped against the Board. She kissed my eyelids, stroked my cheek. "Mintrell, nobody can take your place. You are the captain. You are always the captain."

I get soft after a kick-over. I held her as best I could between my hands and kissed her in return.

"Your script was good," I thought to her. My mind was sluggish and replete. "A good kick. A clean kick." Her skin was moist and musky. I wanted to lick her dry, wanted to bear her weight forever, feel the nuzzle of her breasts. "Stay with me."

She laughed in my ear. "You'll wake up soon, Mintrell. Let me talk while you're still able to listen. Writers are on their own. A captain commands a crew but the writer has to be free to write the script. We fear the Board, we don't want it."

"I want you," I said. "I need you with me."

I felt the faint stirrings of re-awakened lust as I mouthed her.

She broke the mind-chain and pushed herself away from me so suddenly that I jerked against the Board-straps.

"Stroc'!" I pleaded.

"No, Captain, you'll kick the ship over an unscripted gap if you don't watch it."

"Please," I said.

"There's no pleasing you."

I opened my eyes. In the dim light of the command shell I saw her crouched over me, her face tired.

"You need something, Mintrell. Not a person: you'll bond tighter than a ship and kill them. Maybe you need to command a whole fleet, diffuse your loyalty. I don't know," her hands stroked me lightly, regretfully. "I don't often turn on during a script, but you're too perverse for a mere writer."

I hardly heard her, watching her lips, her eyes, wanting to touch her spiky hair. She reached for the grip-bar and pulled herself out the dilator before I could think of anything to say.

Then the commonplaces of the ship flooded me. Fvas was reporting, Legted was reporting. Somewhere I could feel Cradge, moving like an unwilling turtle in her metallic casing; like me, ready to fight the world.

The Core Analor picked up Kred's Skylight on its monitors. Braieder heard the blip and, his job done, turned out into his usual sleep-world. I could feel myself cooling down. Rational again. I got angry over all the musty drivel I'd said, all the involuntary responses I'd made under Stroc''s skill. That's what it was to be captain of a ship, to be expertly handled: flipped on, pressured, released. A human thruster.

I swore and commanded the Board to unstrap me. Writers always left you limp and doubting. They didn't need to but they always did, made you feel tawdry. All they could do was lay down a script, a stupid bloody script.

We reached Kred's Skylight well within margin and so got clearance to land without waiting. I took the ship straight down to the prepared berth in the Harbor, kept vacant for me by the Harbor Proctor.

"Safe splash," I told my crew. "Let's get going. Dok — the freight. Fvas — pipe up new fuel. Legted — get the spores and cultures out first."

They humored me after a kick-over, accustomed to my anxiety. I want things done right, especially where people could see us.

I waited until I saw all operations begun, then slid from the command shell, washed and dressed. In harbor the captain has no duties; the money-rider handles the business. I craved drink and sleep and went to get them. As I lowered myself down the slide-tube, I ran into Writer Stroc', uniformed and ready to disembark. She looked shuttered.

"Good flight, Captain," she said.

"Your payment will be at the counter." Why didn't she leave? Forget the drink. I wanted sleep, all I could get, and I didn't want to waste effort jawing with a writer.

"You ought to take a break," she said. "Sell this ship, maybe."

"Get out of here," I didn't hide my disgust. "You've done your job. You don't understand anything."

"Oh, everything," she shrugged and went out the portal.

I let her take the waiting renitence disc and called up another. Writers think they own your souls.

In the end, I managed to have a drink sent to my room. I sat on the edge of the bed-flow and sipped it. An idea was floating around my head. Could I have a second ship? Would this betray *Mintrell*? I might be betraying it by limiting myself. I couldn't decide. But it could wait; I needed sleep.

Lying down across the bed-flow, I remembered what I'd overheard two writers say once long ago when I first became a captain.

"That Mintrell," they agreed, "a real hardcase and a pain in the ass but you'll surely get there."

Where was that?

I fell asleep.

The Amazing Disappearing Girl
•
Judith Katz

On the edge of the rock and moss cliffs that border Willa Kaufman's country land is a tiny cabin with an army cot, a wood stove, and a stack of warm blankets. The cabin was already nestled here when Willa Kaufman bought the land. It was called then a hunting cabin but no women who came to it ever hunted. Instead they came from the town of New Chelm for solitude, or else for trysts, secret and otherwise.

Nadine Pagan knew this cabin as well as anyone, for she and Rose came to the land often and made magic. Sometimes in winter they lit fires in the stove, sat on the squeaking bed, smoked joints, painted each others' faces. Sometimes Rose tried to make love with Nadine here, but as much as Nadine loved Rose she could not bear to be touched by her. She was afraid that under Rose's fingers she would surely fall apart at every seam.

After Willa Kaufman fell in love with that weasel, Sara Webber, even though neither of them ever used it, Willa declared the cabin off-limits and no women were allowed to come there. Sara reasoned that some day they might *want* to use the cabin, and a bunch of lesbians would be inside it, having a slumber party, and then where would that leave them, the true owners. Willa Kaufman reluctantly agreed. She went herself and put a padlock on the cabin door. She dusted her hands off when the job was done.

The little cabin sat and sat for many months empty. Rose came from time to time to tend her secret marijuana patch which was planted nearby. She peered in through the cabin's grimy windows. Then she sat with her back to the locked door, looked out onto the woods below, and thought carefully about times gone by.

It is toward this very cabin, this padlocked cabin way

up on the high cliffs of Willa Kaufman's land, that Nadine Pagan comes walking when she creeps out of Audry Schaefer's bed in the middle of three in the morning. She is driven, but she does not know what drives her, though the whole long way as she walks on achy legs and throbbing feet she sees only Micky Robbins stepping hard on the wedding glass and her sister Electa falling deep into his arms. She sees the flames she made out of two movie theatres and a drive-in. The whole long way, as she walks on unsteady feet down the middle of Main Street, up onto the highway, and under the light of the moon, kicking at pebbles on the back roads that lead to Willa's land, she is wondering, what can one of these events — my sister's wedding — have to do with the other events — these fires I have made.

By the time she comes to the land, night has turned into morning and still it is Micky's foot she sees and still there is the smell of gasoline in her nose and still she cannot make these things together make sense. But here she is at last on the dirt road that takes her up through the birch forest, past the rocks as big as Lot's wife, up she goes, into the woods. She carries nothing, she leaves nothing behind.

Nadine pries Willa Kaufman's padlock off with a strong branch. She closes the door behind her, wraps herself in a big red blanket, falls back onto the bed and she cries. She cries until her teeth ache and her eyes swell, and then she sleeps without dreaming, she does not know for how long. When she wakes it takes her a minute to remember where she is, and then she cries again.

For the next days she sits without moving, barely breathing, barely marking when the sun comes up and when it goes down again. The chickadees come to the cabin window and sing to her but they do not bring her pleasure. When she absolutely has to, she goes outside to pee, but she does not linger and never does she venture out into the deep woods.

Then one morning she wakes and it is a new season on the land, the air is crisp and cool, the sun is lower in the sky. Nadine pulls the blanket close around her and walks out of the cabin down toward the river that crosses Willa Kaufman's land. The water runs swiftly. Nadine Pagan dips in her hands and drinks and drinks. She washes her face in the chilly waters, but when she sees the reflection of her own eyes she barely recognizes herself, and again starts to cry. She howls like a dog, like a wolf, like a *vildachia,* because she looks like an animal to herself in the water, she has made herself an animal, and because of this what can she do but howl.

Nadine closes her eyes by the bank of the river, and when she does she sees burning. Then she sees her sister Electa in her white wedding gown dancing slow with her sister Jane. She closes her eyes and touches the warmth that is Audry, wide shouldered, soft lipped. She closes her eyes and Rose is before her, who winks and whispers, "I know you set the fires, Nadine, all three of them, yes I do. And I know why."

As if to put herself out, Nadine Pagan jumps into the river and swims, first to one side and then to the other, again and again, side to side, until she can swim no longer. She drags herself out of the river, wet and shivering, back to the cabin. She peels her clothes off and leaves them to bake dry in the early autumn sun.

When she sleeps, Nadine dreams of police cars. When she wakes she searches for food. The days go by and the days go by, and on the night of the full moon, Nadine Pagan has this dream:

> I take a knife and with my right hand I slice off my left handed fingers one by one. These I place in a big black kettle. With my bloody stump I hold an onion, with my right hand I chop; with my stump I hold a carrot and this I also chop. I slice I dice I rice I chop stalks of celery, cloves of garlic, green beans and tomatoes. These I throw into the pot with my fingers and begin to make soup, which I stir with a wooden spoon on an open flame. When it bubbles from boiling I ladle it into wooden bowls. In each bowl I am careful to put a finger, and of these bowls I give one to Jane, one to Electa, one to Rose, one to Audry. The biggest bowl, the one with my thumb in it, I give to my mother who is at the head of the table saying a blessing over the candles. My *Zayde* Yitzkach is on the ceiling playing a *froelich.* "Why is she lighting the candles?" I whisper. No one answers. Instead they sit each of them smacking their lips, eating me alive. "But why is she lighting the candles?" I whisper again. *Zayde* Yitzkach jumps down from the ceiling and

pats my stump gently. "Happy New Year," he tells
me, "It's *Rosh Ha Shana*."

When she wakes, Nadine Pagan moves not a muscle
and counts the days. Her *Zayde* was right. It is *Rosh Ha
Shana,* the Jewish New Year. She must go down to the river
and let go her sins. She takes with her a charred stick and
a scrap of paper she finds under the stove. She pulls on
her shoes and to the river she walks. At the water's edge
she scratches the words, *Ha Bayita,* the Home; the Fire,
Ha Esch; the family, *Ha Mishpocha,* and these she throws
into the river. She takes from her pocket her wallet and the
few dollars she has, and these she throws into the river as
well. From the pocket that sits over her heart, she lifts out
a notebook, her musical journal filled with stories and lies,
and also this she throws into the river, and with it her guilt,
her shame, the sound of her mother's voice. She picks out
of her vest pockets little pieces of lint and balled-up cookie
fortunes, thirty-seven cents in pennies and dimes. All of this
she tosses and watches as it drifts, sinks, and spins on the
choppy waters flowing south. On an old playing card, the
three of spades, she writes the words, Audry, Rose, and pyro-
mania. This she throws into the river and after that the
charred stick, her pen. She wishes to throw her violin to
the waters but this was her gift to Jane on the night of Electa's
wedding, and is no longer hers to throw away. Last of all
she takes from her neck a tiny six-pointed star given to her
by her Aunt Miriam so long ago. It reminds her of her
Grandmother Minnie and all she could not be to her, and
she throws the star also into the water at her feet.

And when she divests herself of all her goods, Nadine
Pagan sits on the bank and watches the river flow, gentle
waves lapping on muddy shore. She sits on a log stump
and thinks, "All my life drifts before me, and after me who
will stand up for me, who will love me after all I have done?"

In the chill of late September, in this spot in the woods
where summer's smell still lingers, Nadine Pagan unties her
heavy boots which have carried her so faithfully from one
spot to another. She takes them off and places them by a
rock on the river bank. Then she takes off her socks and
these she tosses into the river. She unzips her jeans, climbs
out of them, and these she throws in also, and then her

matted vest and tattered shirt, her cotton underpants, and finally the tee-shirt she wears that has on it three women dancing, until naked she stands shivering at the water's edge.

And for the sin of her inability to know love when she sees it, Nadine Pagan throws herself into the river, leaving behind only those fine brown hiking boots with their thick rubber soles to stand attention, side by side, while Nadine falls into the river, so sweet and yellow, how warm as it carries her down down into the deep of it, the sweet water tumbling over her as she falls down down down.

She flies and then she stops flying, the weight of her body in the swiftly flowing river pulls her further and further down into the river bed, pulls her slowly through layers and layers of clay and sand, through muck and mire she pushes and pushes, pebbles and shells stick in her mouth. She feels she is suffocating but still she breathes, she breathes and she feels fingers pull on her, hands grasp her ankles, pull her down down through leaves and twigs which lodge in her throat. Her neck feels like breaking, her lungs are collapsing but she pushes still, she knows that if she does not come out the other side of this she will never breathe again. And so she thrusts herself further, her cheeks full of pebbles, her nails packed with clay, she scratches the sediment walls as down she is carried, butt first, certain she will never breathe again, so certain, deeper and deeper into the mud, and then suddenly the sand breaks and there is more water rushing, and on the crest of this rapid she is carried at last to a grotto, where she can swim and rest and breathe at last.

Nadine swims toward the shore. When she stands, her feet touch slippery rock, solid ground; she is up to her shoulders in these waters and so swims, then walks, to the water's edge.

Nadine is met here by another woman, naked, round-muscled. Her breasts are large, her shoulders wide, her eyes are brown and golden. This woman at the water's edge, Nadine's height, no taller, a head full of wild red hairs, holds out her hands as Nadine slips and slides on the grotto floor. "Come," says the woman, who holds now a lantern, "follow me quickly, we have much to do."

Nadine glances down at her feet on this unsteady floor, sees now salt boxes tied to them with rags. Her legs are wrapped also with rags and the floor of the cave is no longer limestone but covered with icy snow, which cracks and bites into Nadine's feet. She is no longer naked, but wears a heavy cloth coat, bulky, two sizes at least too big. On her head, what's this, a little cap, and long *payisim* brush against her cheeks. *Tsitsits*, religious fringes, hang down to her waist.

On either side walk people dressed as she, some older, some younger, some women with shawls on their shoulders, some men carrying bundles, some have real shoes on their feet and some only rags. "Where are we going?"

The woman who met Nadine wears now a long white beard, a wide brimmed hat, and a heavy wool coat. The old man touches a finger to her own wrinkled lips. "Shh, little one, these woods are full of danger. The soldiers from the Tsar's army, may they rot in hell, would just as soon run you through with a knife as look at you . . . and they like to do it on holy nights like this, just to make us crazy. But we can't be bothered with that now, come along, follow me."

The stranger leads the way through crusty snow to a clearing. In the middle of it, sticking up out of the snow, is a heavy wooden door made from rough hewn boards. A big rusted ring is the handle. The stranger and some other men pull the door open. "Here," she says, "climb down." All the people do as they are told, all but Nadine who hesitates on the edge and peers into the cellar. "Get in, little boy," the stranger tells her, "God will protect you." Nadine looks into the old man's eyes. "It's safe, be a good boy, climb in."

In the underground chamber, torches hang on damp walls. Children like Nadine are huddled around women whose heads are covered with dusty babushkas. Some weep, some sing, others stand and pray. There are a few men, very old, who sit along the walls and bob their bearded heads over prayer books and chant.

At the end of the chamber is a door, but there are no windows. Nadine looks around helplessly. There is no one here she knows or trusts but everyone looks familiar. Here she belongs to no one, she has no family, there is no one to pay her special attention. Her eyes fill with tears. Then a woman holds out a piece of black bread to her, and a ladle full of water. "Little boy, little boy, eat this. If, God forbid, those barbarians find us, you will at least be big and strong." Nadine takes the bread and looks into the woman's face. She pinches Nadine's cheek. "How old?"

Nadine shrugs.

"*Bar Mitzvahed* yet?"

She shakes her head.

"Is your mother here?"

"No," Nadine tells her.

"These are my children, Rivke and Shmuel," the woman says. She puts her arms around the sleeping bundles at her sides. "You don't know where your mother is, we don't know where their father is . . . went off to Cracow and never came back . . . did he leave me for another woman, did the Cossacks tear him to pieces, either way I'm an *aghuna*. Come sit by us, it's warmer to sleep that way. You have to rest when you can. You never know when they'll find us and we'll have to start running again." The woman pats the space between herself and her Rivke. Nadine curls into it gratefully. She falls fast asleep, the little piece of black bread still in her hand.

When Nadine wakes, everyone around her is asleep. The torches on the walls are turned down low. The sounds of uneven snoring and shifting bodies replace chanted prayers. Nadine closes her eyes and tries to sleep again, but she cannot. Gingerly she pulls away from Rivke and the mother. She tiptoes over sleepers who toss fitfully on the cold floor.

Nadine stands before the door at the chamber's end for a long time. A glass lantern sits barely burning near a prayer book. Slowly, Nadine pulls at the door and picks up the lantern. It is dark and cold out there, but something on the other side calls to her. She looks back in order to remember all she sees here, then steps into the darkness and closes the door.

Limestone drips. Her lantern is dim. The path under her feet is cold and damp. Nadine is close to running water, she feels it, smells it, a river roaring madly, the cold spray tickles her face. She needs to wade through but she isn't sure — if the water is deep, she'll be swept away. The foam splashes up against her naked body, the current is so strong she will surely be knocked over. She lies back against the slippery rock that banks the river, turns down her lantern, and Nadine Pagan sleeps again.

When next Nadine wakes, she is starving. She looks for the black bread, gift of Rivke's mother, but Nadine is naked now, no pockets full of bread. She dips her hands instead into the rushing river and swallows what she can. Someone taps on her shoulder. Nadine turns and sees neither the old man nor the stranger who met her at the grotto, nor any of the people, women or men, from the underground chamber. She sees instead a woman, tall and familiar, with eyes like Rose and a smile like Audry Schaefer's. The woman stands with her hands extended, holds out to Nadine a blanket, and says, "We have been waiting for you, Nadine, follow me."

The other woman is not naked, wears jeans and a heavy jersey, on her feet sturdy shoes. She blows out the lantern and leads the way with a flashlight whose beam she holds toward the ground. They walk along the white water's edge to a place where the banks narrow and then jump to the other side. "It turns to dirt here, you'll feel leaves and mud underfoot, be careful not to snag your toes."

Nadine tiptoes behind the other woman, who is sure and steady on her feet. "Just over this ridge and we're halfway there." She holds Nadine by the elbow and lifts her up over the rocky path. "Watch the roots . . . that's it . . ."

At the top of the ridge the woman aims her flashlight straight ahead and blinks it on and off. From out of the darkness, three dots of light return. "When the boat comes, you'll have warm clothes."

"Thank you," Nadine whispers. She can say no more. She hears a faint sound in the water, oars pushing gently. The woman at her side again flashes her light and three stronger dots of light answer. Soon a small boat appears out of the darkness. A woman Nadine thinks she knows is at the helm. "Get in," that woman says, "quickly. The patrols are out — come ahead, don't say a word."

Nadine takes her place in the back of the boat, feels down to her sore toes and realizes once again they are wrapped in rags. She is wearing her little cap and overcoat. The two women with her are now very old, stooped, wrapped in shawls and babushkas. The woman at the helm moves her lips in silent prayer, just a whisper above the whoosh whoosh of oars.

The little boat slides through the darkness and in a

short time reaches the other side. The old women hitch up their skirts and step out. Deftly they pull the boat to shore. While one ties the vessel up to a log the other throws Nadine over her shoulder. "Be very still, child. I'm going to pass you off for a sack of potatoes."

Nadine giggles.

"Be serious," the woman is stern, "pretend you're a sack of potatoes and we can slip past the guards. Otherwise I can't be responsible."

So Nadine the small boy goes limp in the old woman's arms and is carried down a street that smells of onions and tar, of salt from the sea.

The old women walk stooped over, speak neither to each other nor to anyone else. Their pace is grandmotherly but the arms that hold Nadine are strong.

At last they stop in front of a tumble-down house that sags under its own weight. One woman knocks. The door creaks open. A woman asks, "You've got the child?"

"This sack of potatoes. An excellent imitation, yes?"

"Bring him in, bring him in. You weren't followed?"

They bolt the door behind them. The old women take off their shawls, but keep their babushkas tied to their heads. Someone unwraps Nadine's rags and rubs her feet. "You're a good boy, very brave," she tells her, and touches Nadine's cheek. She sets a piece of honey cake and glass of sweet wine at Nadine's side. "You've had a dangerous night. This will help you sleep." She swaddles Nadine in a soft blanket and lays her on a mat of rags by the stove. "Not the most comfortable bed, but at least you'll be warm. Eat now," she tells her, and kisses Nadine's forehead. Before Nadine swallows half the honey cake she is fast asleep.

Nadine Pagan wakes in a place where the stench is human, human refuse, burning humans, humans rotting alive in their own shit and blood. On her feet are wooden clogs which scrape against her bones. She wears a dress made out of wet cardboard, in the rain as she stands now it becomes heavy and heavier. The shoes stick deep into the mud. She has no hair, her eyeballs bulge. Nadine picks through a garden of human fertilizer. She sweeps the bones from a giant oven, pushes them out, and gags to remember that one of these sets of bones is her sister, her mother.

In another part of this desecrated planet is her father, her brother-in-law. She sweeps, she cries, she makes this lamentation:

> My bones your bones
> all of them the same bones
> I'll shovel them up
> until I drop
> then someone other
> will shovel up mine.
> My bones your bones
> in a minute I'll drop.

Nadine wakes up on a plush velvet couch. She hears the scratch of pen to paper, sees bent over a small writing table the back of a woman with hair very dark and curly, piled high on her head and tied with a ribbon. She is wrapped in a shawl, a candle burns at her side. Through a closed door, Nadine hears the muffled voices of more women talking. For a minute she thinks she is in the back room of Lechem V'Shalom, the women's restaurant.

"Excuse me," Nadine says in a voice so clear she surprises herself, "what place is this?"

The woman writing finishes her sentence then turns her head. "Rest quietly, Nadine, I'll get you some tea."

"But where am I?" The woman comes to Nadine's bedside and touches Nadine's forehead with the palm of her hand. "Rest, darling Nadine, soon all questions will be answered." The woman walks out. Nadine watches her, this woman in a green silk dress. Who is she and what is Nadine doing here on a couch in a satin bathrobe, a fire in the fireplace, women talking in another room? She watches the shadows from the kerosene lamp flicker on the ceiling. She feels like she's been run over by a truck. When she tries to lift herself off the couch, Nadine can barely move her head.

The woman in green comes back with a little teapot and a china cup. She puts them down on the night stand and tucks the blankets around Nadine. "Warm enough?"

Nadine tries to speak again but the muscles in her throat close all at once and the best she can do is nod. The woman pours tea and holds it to Nadine's mouth. The steam envelops her.

"My name is Magda," the woman says, and Nadine

swallows the tea. "I live here with my three sisters. We are very glad to see you alive. Some of us wondered what took you so long to get here. You must rest now and recover quickly because there is much to be done and many women wish to talk with you." Magda holds Nadine's head as she lays the pillows flat against the couch and then gently lowers Nadine down. Then Magda turns the kerosene lamp down low.

"But where is this place?" Nadine asks again.

"You'll know it tomorrow," Magda tells her.

Nadine falls fast asleep to the gentle voices of the four sisters meeting in the next room.

In the morning Magda pulls a square table up in front of the fire. Her sister, Esther, whose hair is wild and red, follows with a tray full of breakfast. A third sister, Shula, drags in two chairs. Nadine sits up and takes notice. "So look at her, she's a regular wide awake woman!" the fourth sister says, "I'm Etta. You're looking good."

None of these sisters looks anything like the others. They have not even the same color skin. All wear clothes from different times. Esther produces a deck of cards and a box of tiny cigars.

"Not before breakfast."

"Why not?"

"We have company."

"Who's company. This is how I am in real life, Nadine. I smoke before breakfast and in the old days, once or twice I lost my shirt in a poker game. Before breakfast."

"She doesn't know from the old days."

"Don't you?"

Nadine shrugs. She has been so many people and things in the past hours she isn't even sure she knows who she is right this minute.

"Esther means in the days when she was walking up above . . ."

"The poor woman is barely conscious and you're telling her above. She has no idea what you're talking about. In the meantime, the food is turning to ice."

"So you won't play cards."

"Later, Esther."

"'Later, Esther,' she says." Esther tucks the cards into a drawer but she doesn't extinguish her cigar. "Come sit at the table, Nadine. Maybe you'll have some fun with me one of these days."

The other sisters roll their eyes. They help Nadine to a chair and watch her eat. As she spoons up mouthfuls of egg and black bread, the sisters talk. "Let's get one thing straight. First of all, we're not really sisters. We're a family, we live together, we have the same way of saving the world in mind, but in our blood we're not related."

"Also, we are not all of us from the same time."

"Though all of us have seen what the others have lived through."

Nadine stops eating and looks from one to the other. She thinks she knows what they are talking about but she isn't sure.

"Where are we?"

"This is our house."

"When I came here, I came through a grotto. I was naked then and then I was a little boy from a time not my own. What am I doing here now? Am I really myself?" Nadine's voice was clear and strong. It pleased her to be able to speak with such fluency.

"You're more yourself than usual, Nadine."

"How do you know me?"

"You're world-famous, my dear. Everyone knows you."

"Esther, you sound like a Zen master. How is she supposed to know what that means? It isn't important this minute, Nadine, that you understand everything. You have come along way to be here, and we are very, very happy to have you. Things will change often. Sometimes you will wake in a different bed than the one you fell asleep in. Sometimes you will feel like somebody else entirely. But all the time, while you are there, the people you become will always be you. You have come to do important works, you have information we sorely need."

"What work?"

"You're done with breakfast? Then come."

The sisters lead Nadine into the next room. They sit in a comfortable chair. They bundle her up, then blow the lamps out.

On the wall now is a screen, on the screen there are images: of women dissected, splayed on poles and spears, tied up with their legs open and their mouths shut, tied up with a knife to their throats. The women in the pictures are black, yellow, red, brown, white, and each of them is bleeding. The images move, there are men in the movies, the men pull the women's eyes out, then their guts, fuck them in the head while other men watch.

"This is a form called skull fuck," Magda tells Nadine in a soft voice. "It is part of the cinematic genre known as 'Snuff.' It is an example of a particular way some men have of looking at women and the rest of the world."

The films flicker like tiny flames. "We don't mean to show you this so early in the day, but you must know what we are up against, and we want you to know why you are here."

"Is it not true that you've done work against this kind of thing?"

"It made me sick," Nadine says, "it made me so sick it killed me."

"You're not dead," the women tell her all at once.

"I'm not?"

"No," says Esther, "of course you aren't. Nadine, my darling, you're merely underground."

Killing Color

•

Charlotte Watson Sherman

For Beulah Mae Donald, a Black woman who won a $7 million judgment against the Ku Klux Klan for the murder of her son Michael, who at age 19 was strangled, fatally beaten, and then had his body hung from a tree in March 1981. Mrs. Donald was awarded the United Klans of America, Inc., headquarters property in Tuscaloosa, Alabama. She died September 17, 1988.

They say there's trees over seven hundred years old down in that yella swamp where even the water is a murky gold. Bet them trunks hold all kind of stories, but ain't none of em nothin like the one I'm gonna tell about Mavis. Now, I'm not sayin that Mavis is her real name, that's just what I took to callin her after seein them eyes and that fancy dress. Mavis had so much yella in her eyes it was like lookin in the sun when you looked right in em, but a funny deep kind of sun, more like a ocean of yella fire. You was lookin on some other world when you looked in Mavis' eyes, some other world 'sides this one.

I first saw Mavis leanin up against that old alabaster statue of some man my Aunt Nola say is George Washington, but I don't think that's who it is cause George Washington didn't have nothin to do with the Spanish-American War, did he? But anyway, I don't like to talk about that statue too much cause it just gets Aunt Nola to fussin and I always was told it ain't right to talk back to old folks so I don't, I just let her think she's right about things even though I know better; but that's where I first saw Mavis and seem like didn't nobody know where she had come from, we just looked up one day and there she was leanin against that alabaster statue of not-George Washington.

Now I ain't never been no fancy woman or what some might call a hell-raiser, but I know a woman full of fire when

I see one, and if somebody hada struck a match to Mavis, she'da gone up in a puff of smoke. Mavis had that honey-colored skin look like she ain't never had nothin rough brush up against it, and she musta had on genuine silk stockins with fancy garters to hold em up that ain't nothin like these old cotton ones I keep up on my leg with a little piece of string tied round my thigh; plus, she had on some kind of blood-red high-heel shoes! Now she had all of this on right here in Brownville, in the middle of town, in the noonday sun when all you can smell is heat rising, so you know I stopped and got me a good look at this woman leanin up against that statue with her eyes lookin straight at that old magnolia tree standin in front of the courthouse.

Most of us folks in Brownville try our best to look the other way when we walk by that big old barn of bricks, in fact, old Thaddeous Fulton who I likes to call myself keepin company with, but I call him Tad, he won't even walk on the same side of the street as the courthouse cause most of us know if you brush up against the law down here, you shonuff gonna get bad luck. But Mavis was lookin at that old courthouse buildin full on with them yella eyes never even blinkin and she did it with her back straight like her spine was made outta some long steel pole.

When Tad came around that evenin I tried to tell him about Mavis standin up lookin at the courthouse, but he just shook his head and said, "Sound like trouble to me," and he wouldn't talk about it no more which got me kinda mad cause I like to share most of my troubles and all of my joy with this man and I don't like to see his face closin up on me like he's turnin from a bad story in a book, but that's just what he did when I tried to tell him about Mavis. That man had something else on his mind for this evenin and I could tell by the way his eyebrows was archin up on his forehead. Now Tad is as slow-footed as they come and was born with only half his head covered with hair so the front of his head is always shinin like a chocolate globe, but can't nobody in all of Brownville match that man for kissin. Seems like he tries to gobble up most of my soul when he puts those sweet lips of his on mine and sneaks his tongue in my mouth. I almost fell straight out on the floor of the porch the first time he gave me one of his kisses and it wasn't long before we got started on one of our favorite pastimes — debatin about fornication. Now we always waited til Aunt Nola had dozed off in her settin chair before we slipped out onto the porch and started our discussion.

"Now Lady (he likes to call me Lady even though that ain't my given name), I done lived a big part of my life as a travelin man, and you know I lived in Chicago for quite awhile before I come back home and things ain't like they is in Brownville everywhere else, people is different and I knowed quite a few women that was good women, good decent women, but we wasn't married or nothin; we was just two good people tryin to keep they bodies warm in this cold, cold world. Now what's wrong with that?"

"Well, the Good Book says that those who are dead in sins livin in the lusts of the flesh are by nature the children of wrath."

"I done seen more of life and people than could ever be put in a book, and I ain't never met nobody that died from lustin with their flesh, what I did see was folks full of wrath cause they wasn't gettin no sin."

"Well the Good Book says . . ."

"Lady, I don't believe there is no sucha thing as the Good Book cause I know there's lots of ways of looking at things and you can't put em all in one book and say that this is The Good Book."

"Watchout now Thaddeous Fulton, you can't come around my house blasphemin."

"I still don't believe in no such Book, but I do believe in a good life full of love, now come on over here and give me a kiss."

Then I'd start gigglin and actin silly even though I left my girlhood behind fifty years ago, it just seem like I never had a chance to be a girl like this and then Tad would start ticklin me and nobody passin on the road woulda guessed that the muffled snortin lovin sounds was comin from two folks with all kinds of wrinkles all over their bodies.

"Well, if it's really the Good Book then shouldn't everything that feel good be in it as a good thing to do?" Tad always asked.

"That depends on what the good thing is cause everything that feels good ain't good for ya," I always said.

"But Lady, look at all the bad that's out in the world, folks gotta have some things that make em feel good. Things gotta balance some kinda way don't they?"

And I'd always agree that there needs to be some kind of balance to things good and bad and then Tad always starts talkin about how good I make him feel just lookin at me and listenin to me talk about the world.

"I try to show you how much I 'preciate you with my lips," he'd say and give me one of them devilish kisses. "Don't that feel good?" he'd ask and then keep on till all we was doin was whisperin and kissin and what the Bible calls fornicatin out on the porch.

The next day I went to town and there Mavis was standin in the same spot by that statue lookin at the courthouse. Folks were walkin by lookin at her and tryin not to let her see them lookin but Mavis wasn't payin nobody no mind cause she wasn't studyin nothin but that courthouse and that magnolia tree.

By Sunday, everybody was talkin about her and wonderin why she kept on standin in the middle of town lookin at the courthouse everyday. Then Reverend Darden started to preach against worryin about other folks' business and not takin care of your own, so I started to feel shamed, but deep inside I was still wonderin about Mavis. I decided I was gonna walk up to Mavis and talk to her and find out what she was up to.

Next day, I got up early and went on into town and walked right up to that statue. I waited for her to say something but she acted like she didn't even know that I was there, so I started talkin about the weather and about how that old sun sure was beatin down on us today and wasn't it somethin how the grass can keep stayin green in all this heat? Then I fanned myself for a couple of minutes but Mavis still didn't say a word. After I'd stood up there for about twenty-five minutes, Mavis turned her head and put them yella eyes on me. Now, I've heard stories about people talkin with their eyes and never even openin up their mouths, but I'd never met nobody like that before. But Mavis had them kinda eyes and she put em on me and told me with them eyes that she'd come for somethin she lost and then she turned her head back around and fixed her eyes back on the courthouse. Well, it was plain to me that she wasn't gonna say no more and I was ready to go home and sit in some shade, so I did.

That evenin when Tad came by to visit, he was all in a uproar.

"Why you messin around with that woman?" he asked after I'd told him that I'd stood up at the statue with Mavis for awhile. "I told you that woman sound like trouble. Folks said she rode off with old Ned Crowell yesterday evenin and he ain't been heard from since."

"Where she at?" I asked. For some strange reason I was scared for her.

"She still standin up there like she always do, layin back on that statue. Somethin wrong with that woman, I told you the first time you told me about her, somethin wrong. You better stay away from her before you get tangled up in some mess you'll be sorry about. You know how them folks is, you know."

"Don't go and get so upset your blood goes up Tad. Ain't nothin bad gonna happen around here." I tried to make Tad loosen up and grin a little, but he was too worked up tonight and decided he was gonna go on home and rest. I wasn't gonna tell him about Mavis and her talkin eyes cause he'da probably thought I was losin my mind.

I let three days pass before I went to town to see if Mavis was still standin at that statue, and sure enough there she was. I went and stood next to her and started talkin about nothin in particular. I fixed my eyes on the courthouse, but I couldn't see nothin that hadn't been there for at least fifty years.

"You know they keep that buildin pretty clean and old Wonzell Fitch picks up around the yard every evenin, you might wanna check with him about findin somethin you lost," I told Mavis softly.

She turned her head and told me with them yella eyes that she was lookin for somethin that belong to her. She didn't even hear what I said. I didn't say nothin else just stood up with her for awhile and then went on home.

Tad came by later on with his face all wrinkled up like a prune, but I didn't make fun with him cause I could see that he was troubled.

"Seem like three more of the Crowells and one of the Fitzhughs is gone."

"Don't nobody know what happened to em?" I asked. "It don't seem possible that four grown men could disappear without a trace. What do folks think is happenin?"

"Don't nobody know for sure, but some folks say they saw at least two of the Crowells and old Billy Fitzhugh go off with that crazy woman late in the evenin."

"Does the sheriff know about that?" I asked.

"No, and ain't nobody gonna tell him either, they like to get locked up they ownself."

"Well that sure is mighty strange, I didn't think she even left that spot at the statue to go relieve herself. She just stands up there starin, don't never see her drink no water or nothin, just standin up in all that heat."

"Well it looks like come evenin she sure does find herself one of these old white men and goes off with him and don't nobody see that man no more. You ain't goin around her is ya? I'm sure gonna hate to see what happens when the sheriff finds out about her bein the last one seen with them missin men cause you know well as I do what that means."

Me and Tad just sat together real quiet and still on the porch holdin hands like old folks is supposed to do.

Next day I had to take Aunt Nola to evenin prayer service so I decided I was gonna sit outside and watch the statue from the front steps of the church.

"You gonna miss service and then have the nerve to sit on the front steps of Reverend Darden's church?" she fussed.

"I'm gonna do just that and can't **nobody** stop me, neither."

"You gonna sit outside when you need to be inside bad as the rest of us?"

"Yep," I replied and then just stopped listenin. I'd already made up my mind about what I was gonna do and even Aunt Nola's fussin wasn't gonna change it. So after all the folks had gone inside, I sat down on the porch and watched the sun go down and Mavis keep standin at the statue lookin at that same buildin she'd been lookin at for almost a month now.

When the shadows had stretched and twisted into night, I saw the lights from some kinda car stop in front of the statue. Mavis jumped in the car with what sounded to me like a laugh and the car eased on down the road.

"No tellin where they goin," I thought out loud as the car moved slowly past the church. I could see the pale face of old Doc Adams at the wheel. Mavis never even turned her head in my direction or anyone else's, her yella eyes was lookin straight ahead.

"Another man gone," Tad said when he stopped by the next day.

"Was it old Doc Adams?" I asked scared to hear the answer.

"How'd you know? I done told you and told you you better stay away from that woman. God only knows what she's up to and I know I sure don't want no parts of it whatever it is. You askin for trouble, Lady, foolin around that woman. You better go on in the house and read some of that Book you always tellin me about, I know it don't say nothin good about killin folks!"

"Now how you know any of them men's been killed, Tad? How you know that? The men's is just missin right, don't nobody know where they at, right?"

"You don't have to be no college professor to see what's happenin! Those men are dead, just as sure as we're sittin here, they are dead! Now you better stick around home with Miss Nola cause this town gonna turn upside down when they go after that woman!"

That night I turned what Tad had said over and over in my mind. Could Mavis have killed all them men? How could she have done it, she ain't even a big woman; how could she kill even one grown man, even if he was old? And why wasn't the sheriff doin anything about it, couldn't he see Mavis standin right up in the middle of town leanin on that statue, just like we see her everyday?

I could feel a pressure buildin up in my stomach, a kinda tight boilin feelin I always get when somethin big is about to happen; so I decided I better go on up to town and tell Mavis she better be careful cause folks was sayin and thinkin some pretty bad things about her not cause of the way she was dressed, but cause of her bein seen ridin off with all them white men that ain't nobody seen no more.

Well, there she was standin in her usual spot with her eyes burnin holes in the courthouse. I didn't have time to mince words, so I didn't.

"Folks is talkin, Mavis, talkin real bad aboutcha, sayin crazy things like you tied up with the missin of some old men around here and how you musta come to Brownville to be up to no good."

Mavis didn't say a word, just kept right on lookin.

"This town'll surprise you, you might be thinkin we's all nothin but backwoods, country-talkin folks, but we got as much sense as anybody else walkin around on two legs; and don't too many people sit up and talk this bad about somebody they'd never even laid eyes on a month ago, without some kind of reason and some pretty strong thinkin on the situation. Now I don't wanna meddle in your business none, but I think you got a right to know folks is callin you a murderer."

Mavis turned them yella eyes on me for so long I thought I might start smokin and catch afire, I mean she burned me with them eyes that said, "I come for what is mine, somethin that belongs to me and don't none of y'all got a right to get in my way."

I stepped back from her cause she was lookin pretty fierce with her eyes all alight, but I still reached out to touch her arm, "I just hate to see bad things happen to folks is all, I don't mean no harm." And I turned to walk away, but it felt like a band of steel grabbed my arm and turned me back around lookin at the yella eyes that said, "Now you listen, listen real good cause I want all of y'all to know why I was here after I'm gone and I'm not leavin til my work is done. Way back when, I lived back out on what y'all call Old Robinson Road. Wasn't much to look at, but we had us a little place, a little land, some chickens and hogs. We growed most of our own food right there on our land and didn't have to go off and sell ourselves to nobody, not nobody, you hear me? We was free people, livin our own lives, not botherin nobody, not messin in nobody's business, didn't even leave the place to go to church; we just lived on our land and was happy. Now some folks right here in this town got the notion in their heads that colored folk don't need to be livin on they own land, 'specially if it was land any white man wanted. Old Andy Crowell who looks like the devil musta spit him out, got it in his head that he was gonna take our land. Well, I don't know if they're still makin men like they made mine, but he knew and I knew wasn't nobody gonna get this land, not while we was standin and drawin breath. So we took to sleepin with a shotgun next to the bed and one by the front door and my man even carried a little gun in his belt when he was out in the fields and I kept one strapped to my leg, under my dress. We went into that courthouse right there and tried to find out about the law, cause we knew there had to be a law to protect us, one for the protection of colored folks cause see slavery had been over for a while now, wasn't no more slaves that we knew about. We went on up to that buildin and explained to that man callin hisself a clerk that we had got some kinda paper tellin us to clear off our land. My man had the deed to that land cause he got it from his daddy who got it some kinda way durin slaverytime and nobody bothered him about it cause he didn't let nobody know he had it. But it was his and we had the paper to show it and that ratfaced gopher callin hisself a clerk looked at the paper that was the deed to our land, our land I'm tellin you, that clerk took the deed to our land and crumbled it up and threw it on the floor and told us to get out of his office. My man was just lookin that clerk in his face, wasn't flinchin, wasn't blinkin, was just lookin; but his eyes, oh his eyes was tellin that man a story, a story that old fool didn't even know he knew, but he did and my man told that clerk all about it with his eyes, then I picked up the deed to our land and we left. Well, it wasn't too long after we had gone to the courthouse before they come for him one night. You know how they do. Sit up and drink a bunch of liquor to give em the guts they don't have on their own and then they posse up and come riding for you soon as the sun goes down. You know who it is when you hear all them horses on the road, then you look through the window and see the tiny flickers of flame comin closer and closer, growin bigger and bigger till it looks like pieces of gallopin suns comin down the road and then they all in your yard holdin up their torches till it's all lit up outside like it's day, but you know it's the night of the devil, you can smell him out in the yard all tangled up with flint and sweat and liquor, I'd know the stink of evil anywhere and then my man picks up his gun and steps out into that red night and tells em to get off his land or he'll shoot and I could see the claws of the devil pullin on my man and I tried to pull him back in the house but he pushed me back inside and his eyes told me how he loved me like he did his own life and then the devil's fingers snatched him and his tongue wrapped around my man's arms and drug him out into the middle of satan's circle, where they all had white handkerchiefs knotted around their faces from their red eyes to their pointed chins and then they knocked my man down with his own shotgun and then they kicked him, each one takin a turn. I picked up the shotgun standin near our bed and ran out the house screamin and fired a shot. Two of em fell to the ground, but some of em grabbed me from behind and beat me in the head. By the time I opened my eyes, my man was gone. It was Aunt Nancy who came around and found me layin in the yard and cleaned me up and nursed me. I musta laid in the bed for over a month before I could get up and go to town and find out what happened to my man. And what I found out is this: that evil can grow up outta the ground just like a tree filled with bad sap and turn every living thing to some thing rottin in the sun like an old carcass. Now you tell them folks that's wonderin why I'm here and what I'm doin and what I'm up to, you tell them that I'm cleanin that tree right down to the root." And that cold steel band slipped from my arm and Mavis turned her eyes back on the courthouse.

When I got back home I sat on the porch even though it was in the middle of the noonday sun and thought about what Mavis' eyes had told me. "I must be losin my mind," I said to the listenin trees. How in the world could that woman tell me any kind of story without her lips movin and no sound comin outta her mouth? What kind of woman was she? And what kind of woman am I? And what would God say about all of this? I went inside the house and reached for my bible, surely some kind of answer could be found in there.

After reading for a while, I still hadn't found the answer I was lookin for, so I went into the kitchen and started cookin instead.

"What's for supper, daughter?" Aunt Nola asked.

"Oh, I'ma fix some squash, fry some catfish, some salt pork, make up a pot of blackeye peas and a pan of cornbread and probably some peach cobbler for dessert."

"Tad must be comin by, I know you ain't fixin all that food just for me and you."

"Yeah, Tad did say he was comin round here later this evenin, maybe I'll take you on up to prayer meetin before he gets here."

"Umhum. Y'all gonna get me on out the way so you

can sit up in this house kissin, while I'm gone. You oughtta be shamed of yourself, old as you is."

"I might be gettin on Aunt Nola, but I ain't dead yet," I told her and kept on cookin.

I decided I was gonna get Tad to help me watch and see what Mavis was up to that evenin after we dropped Aunt Nola off at the church.

"You want me to do what?" Tad almost screamed after I told him what I wanted to do. "I ain't goin nowhere near that woman and you ain't neither. You wanna get us both killed behind her don't ya?"

I patted his arm and talked to him as soft as I could to try to calm him down, no sense in his blood goin up over this foolishness.

"Tad, I just wanna prove to you and everybody else that Mavis ain't killed nobody and she ain't doin none of us no harm by standin up by that statue. She can't even talk and look how small she is. How she gonna kill a big, old man?"

Tad gave in even though I could see he didn't want to do it, and drove the car about a block away from the statue and parked. We didn't haveta worry about whether or not Mavis could see us, cause she wasn't lookin at nothin else but that tree in front of the courthouse.

"Now look at her, you know somethin wrong," Tad said.

"Don't go and start workin yourself up, we ain't gonna be here long cause it's already startin to get dark and you said she usually leaves about this time didn't ya?"

"I don't know when she leaves, cause I ain't been here to see it. Folks just been sayin she leaves around this time."

"Well, we'll wait a little while and see."

Sure enough, before too long, an old red pickup pulled up next to Mavis and she ran around the front of the truck and jumped inside. Even from where we was parked we could hear the sound she made when she got in the car. It wasn't no laugh, like Tad said, it was more like a high-pitched cryin sound mixed with a whoop and a holler. It made the hair on the back of my neck stand straight up and Tad said it made his flesh crawl. Anyway, the truck pulled off and we followed a ways behind it. Couldn't see who was drivin on account of that big old rebel flag that was hangin up in the back window. But we followed em anyway; out past the old poor house, past the pea and okra shed, past the old Lee plantation and out past Old Robinson Road. Tad started gettin mad again cause he wanted to turn around and go back home.

"You know we're goin too far from home. Ain't no tellin where that crazy woman goin."

"Hush, and keep drivin. We gonna prove somethin once and for all tonight and put a end to all this talk about murder."

So we kept on drivin, but it was so dark now til we couldn't really make out what we was passin by.

"I don't think we're in Brownville no more, you can tell by the shape things make in the dark," Tad said after a while.

I didn't say nothin, just kept my eyes on the truck's red lights in front of us. A few minutes later, the truck pulled off the road we was on and went into the trees. When we reached the spot where they'd turned off, we couldn't see no road, no lights, no nothin, just trees.

"Well, I guess this is the end of the road for us, ain't nowhere to go now but back home," Tad said. "They probably went back up in them woods to do their dirty business."

"What dirty business, Tad, what dirty business? First you was callin her a murderer, now what you callin her?"

"What kinda woman drive off with men in trucks in the evenin, what you think I'm callin her?"

"Let's just walk a ways in there to see if we can hear somethin."

"I'm not walkin back up in them woods, now you go on and walk up in there if you want to, I ain't goin nowhere but back home."

While we was standin up in the trees fussin, a car pulled off the road next to Tad's car. A skinny-faced man leaned his head out the window.

"You folks havin trouble?" He asked.

"I musta made a wrong turn somewhere back down the road and we just tryin to figure out the best way to get back home," Tad replied.

"You sure musta made a wrong turn cause ain't nothin out this way but trees and swamp."

"Is that right?" Tad said.

"Yep, that's right. That big old yella swamp is about two miles into them trees and it ain't nowhere no human man or woman needs to go. Ain't nothin that went in that swamp livin come back out that way. Nothin but the shadows of death back up in there. You step through them trees and it's like you done stepped down into a tunnel goin way down into the ground. Ain't nothin down there not yella. Them old snakes hanging down from them trees like moss is yella. Mosquito bites turn a man's blood yella. Yella flies crawl on the ground where worms come up outta the yella mud and twist like fingers broken from a hand. Shadows come up and wrap they arms around ya, pullin ya down into that yella mud where the sounds don't come from this world. Ain't nobody livin goin down there and comin back the same, 'specially if they heart ain't right."

Me and Tad thanked the man and got back in the car and went back home, the skinnyfaced man's words burnin our ears.

"Now don't you try to get me to run around on no wild goose chase behind that woman no more. I don't care what she's up to, I don't want nothin else to do with her."

Next day, I went to town to talk to Mavis first thing. Sure enough, there she was standin next to that statue.

"I been thinkin about what you told me about the evil way back when, and it seems to me that it might be better just to let things lay, to just let em lay and forgive the ones that did it like Jesus would."

Well what did I go and say that for? Mavis whipped her head around and shook me with them eyes. "Who are you to forgive all that blood? Who are YOU? Put your head to the ground and listen. There's an underground river runnin straight through this town, an underground river of blood runnin straight through, just listen." And then her eyes let me go and she turned back around. When I turned to walk back home, I saw some old dried up mud caked around the bottom of that red dress she wears everyday; mud that was yella as mustard, but dried up like old blood.

Not long after Mavis shook me up with them yella eyes of hers, I took sick and Aunt Nola, poor thing, had to tend me as best she could, bless her heart. Tad came by and helped when he could but I'm the type of person that don't like folks to see me hurtin and I sure didn't want Tad to keep seein me with my teeth out and my hair all over my head, even though he claimed I still looked good to him. Aunt Nola acted like she didn't hear him, but I could see

70

her eyes light up. Once I got to feelin better and was almost back up on my feet, Tad started hunchin up his eyebrows so I knew pretty soon we was gonna get out on the porch and get to arguin about fornicatin, which to tell the truth, I'd rather be fussin about than that foolishness about Mavis. But Tad told me that Mavis wasn't standin up at the statue of not-George Washington no more and nobody knows where she went to. She just disappeared as easy as she come. The sheriff never did find out about her. It turned out that all them old missin men had been tangled up with the Ku Klux years back and had spilt plenty of blood out in the yard of that courthouse, hangin folks from that big old magnolia tree.

Sometimes now, I think about what Mavis told me about evil growin up outta the ground and that old underground river flowin with blood and I put my head to the ground and listen, then I go and stand by that statue and look at that old courthouse buildin feelin Mavis in my eyes.

O's Story

•

L. Timmel Duchamp

And after the others (each claiming an early start in the morning) had departed en masse, she hunched forward and fixed an intense scrutinizing gaze upon me. Since I like her wore a fairly full day-mask I had to wonder what she thought she could make from my eyes and mouth, the set of my head or perhaps — though sometimes one *can* make out signs of telling significance there — the demeanor of my throat. (I myself tend to concentrate on hands and body language, though most people embrace the delusion that eyes reveal something more than their owners wish them to do. *Her* eyes gleamed amber through the narrow dagger-shaped slits of her mask. I made only this of them: that where she came from not even the wealthiest families on her planet pattern the irises. It's true that her eyes suddenly looked more excited than they had all evening, but considering how still her hands lay even as she leaned forwards I took the excitement as a cumulative by-product of whatever it was she had been sniffing.

"I always forget how rare physical murder is in most parts of the galaxy," she murmured low in her throat. "Though what I personally found most disturbing in Ellu-itre's story was the murderer's apparent lack of motive." She sat back in her chair and rested her hands on its arms. "Violent as Arrigans are, Captain, they at least have *reasons* for their violence."

A party at a table on the other side of the room exploded into a loud chorus of guffaws that irritated me. "Arriga is unique," I snapped at her. "Which is fortunate for the civilized portion of the human species. I doubt if one can talk about *reasons* for extreme violence. Most people I've met from Arriga left precisely to escape such irrationality." I had naturally assumed the same of *her*, and since she had just referred to Arrigans as *they* I continued to assume it. "It's beyond human comprehension that such savagery can be endured or sanctioned." In my opinion the Combine had been inexcusably slow to correct the situation. But then perhaps they had been deceived by the planet's long history of violence and hadn't noticed that the smouldering fire had heated up and been fed with volatile chemicals until the entire planet, reaching combustion point, had burst into possibly unquenchable flames. The anti-Combine faction sententiously argues that the Combine had cynically tolerated constant factional warfare on the planet because it had allowed them to manipulate the Arrigans as they pleased — thus ensuring the Arrigans' preoccupation with fighting one another rather than unifying to oppose the Combine. Such "explanations" fail to take into account the Combine's desire not to dominate internal politics on any world, no matter how primitive. Granted, Arriga's civil wars had motivated the Arrigans to mine the materials the Combine so greatly desired since the export of those minerals financed their wars. But if, on the other hand, the Combine had refused to sell war materiel to any of the factions — and to its credit the Combine sold to *all* factions, impartially, at identical prices — then the Arrigans most likely would have poured their *entire* energies into producing war materiel and have stopped mining anything not directly contributing to their wars. Thus the Combine had — for a few decades at least — saved Arriga from itself. In my judgment, the single grave error the Combine made with respect to Arriga was in allowing a minority to dominate. While one cannot care much what primitives on some relatively isolated backworld do to one another, the situation alters drastically when that same planet and those same primitives unify themselves into aggression against the Combine in particular and the Civilized Universe in general. From everything I've seen and heard — and starship personnel *do* get around — the Arrigans are anti-Civilization. If it weren't for their minerals, I'd say space the primitives, let them isolate and suicide all they want. But we need those minerals. Not that most of Arriga's minerals can't be found elsewhere. But some of them are more abundant and more easily mined on Arriga than anywhere else . . .

"I know little about what you call their 'savagery'," my Arrigan companion remarked in a pointedly mild tone of voice. "I haven't been on Arriga for a long long time."

I snorted. "And you were just now saying that Arrigans have *reasons* for their violence?"

"You're referring, I think, to the war. I could argue that they have reasons for fighting the Combine, but since I have no particular attachment to Arriga or Arrigan values, I won't." Her jewel-studded lips curved into a smile revealing creamily smooth teeth. When backworld primitives make their genetic decisions, they often follow fads centuries obsolete on the civilized worlds. I myself enjoy running my tongue over the vertical ridges on my teeth, the very slightness of the ridges makes the sensation delightfully subtle. The difference between her parent and mine lay in taste and imagination — or the lack thereof. Not that she should be blamed for her parent's shortcomings . . . "But what I was specifically thinking of," she continued, "was a contrast to the story of mass murder Elluitre told us. In his story, a Jannisetian murdered four people chosen at random. Though one does now and then hear stories about murder, most of them are ancient or invented tales repeated on occasions like the one tonight in which a group of near-strangers, sitting in a bar on some barren culturally deprived space station, swap anecdotes. The story Elluitre told us, I think it's safe to believe, actually happened, and recently." She smiled again, but now her eyes pierced me with such an opaque intensity that my neck prickled in that way it does when I'm about to engage a partner I suspect will go past the bounds of ordinarily defined decency (bounds we starship personnel tend to flout on dull furloughs like this one); yet I could cull nothing sexual or even sensual from her eyes or manner, nor could my own physical response be described as sexual. Whatever lurked in her eyes made me uneasy, and for a few long seconds I considered getting up and walking away from her.

"As I understand it murder is quite common on Arriga," I remarked in a tone I intended to be marginally offensive, with the hope that *she* would walk away from *me*. I seldom back down from even the most perverse propositions or awkward situations, for since my first years working starships I've prided myself on the diversity of my experience, the ruggedness of my psyche in having what it takes to taste and chew and even digest the most strange and alien and threatening whenever and wherever I encounter it (provided I'm off-duty). I preferred, then, to stave off this challenge to my equanimity (especially since I knew of no rational reason to find this backworld woman in any way frightening) by driving her away before she could lay on me the poison I saw waiting in her eyes . . .

"At the present, I think it is true that political murder is common on Arriga," she murmured. She stared broodily at the boisterous party as they struggled to their feet and staggered out of Plumpers' presumably en route to an environment more a match for their own mood and spirit. "Some people would find the rates of political murder on Arriga not much worse than the rates of wiping practiced on, say, Anaconda or Frogmore." Her eyes returned to mine and I saw that a somber gravity had replaced whatever had been in their amber depths that had made me uneasy. "I suppose people accustomed to forced washing and wiping of minds never realize there's not much difference between killing an identity and killing the whole human being." Her tongue worried at one of the jewels in her lower lip. "I do believe that apart from the political uses of murder, other instances of it — private individual against private individual — are not at all prevalent. But that when they do occur, they usually involve strong motives." She smiled — and brought that thing back into her eyes. Cold spread through my body, tensing me up. "I've heard of only one instance on Arriga in which four people died in personal nonpolitical violence though I've thoroughly researched murder on Arriga, scouring the public documents for its traces. I've carried a strong memory of this one particular case with me ever since I first learned of it — more than twenty-five standard years ago, shortly after its occurrence."

"And did it shock and rock Arrigan society?"

But she did not take the bait. "I've no idea," she replied. "I heard the story *after* I'd left Arriga."

And she had just been talking about people telling ancient stories most likely apocryphal! "Then how do you know it's true?" I demanded, seizing on this point of contention (though it bore not at all on my original grievance, I'm afraid my rational processes were already a bit muddled by that point).

Her smile distilled icy splinters of disquiet that drove straight into my spine. "My source was impeccable," she said.

I slipped a fresh vial out of my pocket and busied myself opening and inhaling from it. A long deliberate look around the room as I consumed most of the vial revealed that only five other parties besides ourselves remained. By this hour of the morning most people had either found partners or gone on to some livelier surround. People tended to patronize Plumpers' Lounge in groups under six, mostly when they wanted a slow indolent evening of quiet intoxication and talk. The management of Plumpers' *guaranteed* their entertainment to be strictly noninteractive and nonintrusive. (Which is why, I suppose, most of the clientele were mature starship personnel — I know I never came much to Plumpers' during my first few dozen furloughs on this hole of a transfer station.) "What possible *reason*," I said when I'd had enough from the vial, "and I mean reason that any rational civilized person would recognize as such — what possible *reason* could one human being have for physically annihilating another?" I, fortified, returned to the attack.

"Ah, reason," she echoed. The amusement I scented in her voice provoked me, but I said nothing, only waited to hear the story she so obviously wanted to tell me. "Reason is a peculiar thing." One of the ancient wheezing servers (probably as old as the station) creaked up to the table and set before her a glass of something pungent, steaming, and mildly intoxicating to judge by the whiff I got of it. "Most Arrigans consider the routine annihilation of psyches to be savage and irrational. Why save the body while destroying the person to whom it belongs?"

"Only authorities and experts have the power of wiping a human psyche," I reminded her. "Whereas a sufficiently determined individual can easily kill another at will."

She wrapped her hands around her glass as though to draw its heat into her flesh, and I wondered — staring fixedly at the shiny ovals of chrome grasping the glass — if my chilliness were not of physical rather than psychological origins. "But your argument favors 'authorities and experts'," she chided.

"They are certainly better qualified to judge than any private individual," I retorted. "And when it comes down to it I'd rather have *them* determining our individual fates than any individual who decides to take such life-and-death decisions into their own hands."

She lifted the glass; half-burying her nose in it she inhaled deeply and then drank. I watched her throat as she swallowed a full third of the concoction (I never drink those sorts of things myself, they look and smell like foul solutions such as might be used to preserve any number of naturally corruptible objects) before taking the glass from her lips. "And what if your authorities are driven by excessive self-interest and self-aggrandizement?" she countered.

"I didn't say that authorities and experts need not be regulated," I pointed out. "But a few black holes does not a universe of anti-matter make."

Her mouth grimaced. "That must be one of the most abused metaphors in the standard language." She picked up her glass again; this time when she took it from her lips she had finished off its entire contents — excepting the drop that clung to one of the tiny jewels ornamenting her upper lip, making its deep green facets shimmer and gleam even in Plumpers' seedy gloom.

"I suppose in your story the authorities were corrupt, etc?" I prodded, impatient to get on with it. If the others had still been with us the story would have been told straight out without all this testy sparring — or else shuffled aside by another story more easily forthcoming. But of course she hadn't told the others this story — and I intuited even before I heard her tell it that she wouldn't have told them, that she had chosen me as her exclusive audience, that she saw or sensed something in me that had made her choose me. I think now that it was my half-conscious recognition of this that made me so uneasy, that chilled me to a clenched-teeth shiver.

"Of course the story depends largely upon the context within which it unfolds," she said. "Ever hear of a place on Arriga called Elsinore?"

I shook my head. "I've never been *on* Arriga's surface. That's one kind of wild environment I can do without."

Her smile intimated some secret source of pleasure, irony or amusement. "Elsinore is a cold, windy, mountainous place," she said. "Sparsely populated. Its major industry has always been the mining and refining of a half-dozen or so heavy metals that are often found in proximity to one another. A very overcast gloomy sort of place. Oh, and large parts of it are permanently covered with glaciers. Most of its inhabitants are either dour and depressed or ascetic and work-obsessed. But in such harsh environments that's typical, wouldn't you say?"

"You sound as though you once lived in this charming place," I commented.

She laid her palms flat on the table, thereby giving me a long steady look at the thin ovals of chrome with which she had at some point in her life replaced her fingernails. The effect was one of coldness, especially given the icy colors of her clothing. "I don't know if I once lived there or not," she said. My eyes jumped to hers; their shivery opaque intensity made me stupid, for not immediately grasping the implications of her words I asked her how it could be that she would not know if she had ever lived in a place whose mood she could describe with such particularity. "Thirty standard years ago," she said in a voice peculiarly flat, "your experts and authorities wiped whatever psyche lived in this body." She lifted one of her hands and tapped her sternum with her chrome-tipped fingers. The gesture riveted my gaze. "I've no way of knowing if I've ever lived in Elsinore." Her fingers dropped from her chest; I lifted my eyes to hers, only to find them — as before — inscrutable. "After wiping they tell one very little about the past history of one's body." Her jewelled lips curved and parted, revealing the impossibly smooth cream of her teeth. "But just before sending me on my way they told me this story about Elsinore . . ."

Horror crawled over me, engulfed me, nearly strangled me. Murder, she had been declaring the "story" to be about, *murder.* And why else would they tell her such a story if it weren't her own particular story, a cautionary tale they wanted her to carry forever with her, a warning about what might lurk in her very chromosomes (no one really knows for *certain* whether behavioral tendencies are strictly a product of environmental forces), or even in areas of her psyche at such deep levels that not even wiping could touch it . . .

"So," she continued, apparently not noticing my violent repulsion, "I had as clues to my previous self only that story and the semipermanent markings the previous inhabitant of this body had left behind — the jewels in my lips, my chrome finger and toenails, the tinted skin of my belly and thighs and buttocks . . ." For a crazy instant I felt an urge to ask her what color that skin had been tinted — for in spite of my feelings of revulsion her mentioning these body alterations conjured in my mind an image of what she might look like naked. I do not think I am misremembering if I say that such an image even at that point tantalized me despite my wish to be finished with the encounter and away from her. Desire can sneak up on one, can intrude itself in flashes at the most unexpected junctures. "Oh, and then there were certain dry facts," she added. "The fact, for instance, that all the therapy had been paid for — sparing me the necessity of spending a couple of decades of my life working to repay the costs of the radical therapy that had been forced on me; the fact that I had — and still do have — an income from a trust fund which would enable me to live more than comfortably without working if I so chose; and the fact that I am permanently barred access to the surface of Arriga, and have had my Arrigan citizenship stripped from me and replaced with a nominal citizenship on Anaconda." She leaned forward. "These *facts*," she half-whispered, "tend to confirm my guess that the story they told me is *mine*."

Her eyes glittered at me. It occurred to me that she strongly desired me to believe that this was indeed her story, that in fact she had a great personal stake in convincing me of it. This insight exacerbated my uneasiness. Unable to make sense of her motivations and desire, I drew on an anger towards her I hadn't (until that moment) known I felt. "People who have been wiped are always willing to believe anything about their pre-wiped selves they are told or think they have pieced together — so desperate are they for a past," I said in a cuttingly patronizing tone of voice. She did not flinch, however, and her continued steady regard rendered me ashamed almost as soon as I had spoken. While she had broken the taboo by telling me this about herself, *I* had equally transgressed by taunting her with her loss.

"There is a woman in the story, named O," she said softly after almost half a minute of staring unwaveringly at my face (my eyes, not so steady, had moved from her face to scan the room and back to her face again two or three times as she continued to stare). "Which, as you know, is *my* name," she added quite unnecessarily.

"Do go on," I said, certain she was hoping to nonplus me. I would thwart her, I determined — indignant (as I came to read it later) that she had marked me for an easily discomfited audience. Even then I knew she wanted to shock me, and I sensed that she had chosen me as her audience not because I alone had stayed behind after Elluitre's story of mass murder had been told, but because she had decided that of all of us in the party my responses would be most satisfying to her. Already I had begun thinking of myself as her marked prey.

"The story can be synopsized quite simply," she said. "But at a cost to comprehension, so I'll elaborate as necessary. Elsinore had a Governor. A hereditary Governor." Her lips curved slightly. "They don't have hereditary governors in advanced societies, I know. But on the backworlds, families are not confined to one member per generation, and stability is drawn from their sprawling size and of course their members' loyalty to the honor and prosperity of the family."

"I might have known," I commented with disgust. "Where there's violent savagery on a backworld one can more or less count on its proceeding out of primitive animal practices CDS sanctions on the grounds of demographic need."

"So that bothers you, does it," she murmured. "I consider your wiping savage, while you consider horizontally sprawling familial structures savage. Well, I must confess that I, too, find such familial structures distasteful — but then my deepest values were formed not on Arriga, but within the bosom of a therapy team."

If that were so, then how could she contest the legitimate use of forcible therapy? Articulating this question for myself increased my discomfort, for it suggested that she had somehow managed to slip the constraints that most forcibly reconstructed individuals never challenge in even their most private secret thoughts. Never had I heard of a radically therapized person proving incorrigible, never.

"So. Imagine this Governor of Elsinore with two brothers and a sister. These four siblings, said to be close, live in the Governor's Tower. And the Governor produces children, a son and a daughter. Because the world is Arriga, it is expected that the Governor's son, H, will succeed his father who, it is also expected, will rule Elsinore for many many years to come for he is only fifty-five standard years old, you understand; his own father, the previous Governor, having died violently at the hand of an assassin from a rival territory, had left his son to succeed at a quite young age. In due course, the children of this Governor go off to Pleth for the final years of their education. While they are away the Governor dies quite suddenly and mysteriously, it is thought by suicide, though he leaves no note and no one can think of any reason for why a powerful prosperous honorable man of fifty-five standard years should want to end his existence. When the Governor's son and daughter learn of their father's death, they return at once to Arriga. Upon reaching Elsinore they discover that C, one of the Governor's brothers (on Arriga they have a term for such relations, the brothers of one's parent are known there as uncles), is now Governor. C greets them warmly, but then asks them why they left Pleth, why they disrupted their education. Their father, he tells them, would have wished them to finish. He urges them to return to Pleth, and his remaining brother, P, now his chief adviser and minister (as C had been for his brother the previous Governor) and G, the sister, also a close adviser and confidante of C (as she had been for her brother the previous Governor), add their voices to C's to encourage their niece, O, and nephew, H, to return to Pleth. And so one Arrigan month after their return to Elsinore, H and O make starship reservations for their return to Pleth.

"But they grieve, Captain." She paused; her eyes seemed to inquire of me whether I could comprehend such grief. "They grieve, for they were as close to their parent as exclusively vertically-propagated generations are. Perhaps you don't believe me, but I assure you I speak the truth." She leaned back in her chair and fingered the empty glass still sitting on the table. (The servers in Plumpers' do not come unless one summons them — and now as I saw her toying with the dirty glass it occurred to me that her neglecting to summon a server to take it away suggested that dirty used objects must neither annoy nor disgust her.) The tips of her chrome nails pinged lightly against the glass. "Their grief drew them more closely together than they had been since preadolescence. Sexuality is a difficulty for siblings, a thing someone unfamiliar with the sibling phenomenon probably does not realize. H and O, now in their grief, accepted in one another what they had years earlier first tried to ignore, and then finally despised." I remember distinctly and clearly that it was at this moment that she first touched me: as she said the word "despised" I felt the calloused bottom of her bare foot on my ankle. Startled, my eyes leaped to hers — and, assuming that the touch had been accidental, waited for her to draw her foot back. But her foot instead slid up my calf as staring straight into my eyes she smiled. The sensation, the spread of physical excitement up my leg into my groin through my body shocked me: not that I hadn't been intermittently indulging speculation about whether or not her intentions towards me were sexual, but between my definite hostility towards her and the matter of our conversation the sudden interjection of a blatantly sexual element struck me as somehow perverse . . .

My mouth dried. I looked at her, I watched her — and didn't move my leg. It was as though she had dared me; perhaps I suspected she would taunt me with fear were I to reject her perverse advances. My powerful sexual response only compounded my fear. Apart from my sense of her being beyond the ordinary bounds of decent control (though never did I think of her as being out of her *own* control), I felt as though she knew exactly how far to push me to the edge of what I would or could tolerate, that despite all my experience in ordinary sexual perversion and daring there was this craziness in her unrestrained by the normal inhibitions of our society (she may have been reconstructed in the values of civilization, but one felt her to be as primitive and savage and uncivilized a person as one could find anywhere on human inhabited worlds) that threatened everything I knew or understood (or rather *thought* I knew or understood) and valued in myself.

It is not often that one allows a sexual encounter to entail such a degree of risk. I'm convinced now that only the fear of seeing myself as a coward kept me from jerking my leg away from her, rising to my feet and beating a hasty retreat.

"In this shared and intimate grief," she continued, "they

became partners, partners of the most intense sort. In fact, one could use the anachronistic term *lovers* to describe their relationship. H and O became lovers." She slid the tip of her tongue through barely parted lips; I watched mesmerized as it played against the tiny jewels. A wave of dizziness washed over me, I wondered how those jewels would feel were she and I to culminate this evening in partnering . . . (The mouth truly of all parts of the human body is the most savage and primitive organ. Consider its functions, its attributes, its very shape and features. Yet it serves variously, consistently, the functions of the body, the will of the brain . . . .)

"These sibling lovers concealed their relationship from everyone, including their uncles C and P and their aunt G," she resumed. "And because they did not wish to be parted, they put off their return to Pleth. When they announced this decision to their uncles and aunt, they declared that they would both change universities so that they could remain together. Between themselves they had decided that it would not be fair for either of them to change to the other's school, that it would be best if they started out somewhere else, both of them new, without ties other than to one another." Sighing she withdrew her foot from my leg, leaving me feeling once again cold — and instantly anxious for further physical contact with her. You may be wondering why I did not myself take the initiative, why my attitude towards her had become increasingly passive. But anyone experienced in bizarre encounters must know that each situation takes on a dynamic of its own — especially if the encounter is with one of those few who (like, I think, this O) must repeat again and again and again the same specifically structured encounter with each new partner that comes along, in which the dynamic is one deliberately manipulated by them. If I had at that point attempted to take an active role, the entire thing would have fallen to pieces, would have gotten away from me: she would have lost interest in pursuing me, would have vanished into the night, perhaps to find another partner, perhaps simply to write off the evening as a nonrecoupable loss. Perhaps all this sounds contradictory — for before that infusion of intense sexuality into the encounter (catalyzed within me by the sensation of her foot on my leg) I had still had sense enough to incline towards disrupting whatever she was up to. Now I couldn't — now I fervently desired that she go on with whatever it was she had to get through, now I longed to sink down into whatever abyss of madness she wished to lure me. I knew that if I said straight out "let's partner" or if I reached across the table and touched her or groped with my foot to recontact hers that I would be violating the dynamic of the encounter. This, after the fact, is how I make it out to have been: as though at that moment I still retained enough sense of external reality that I *could* have disrupted it if I'd chosen to. In other words, I think that I hadn't yet at that point succumbed *entirely* to her madness.

"Of course C, P, and G tried to persuade them that it would be best if they did their waiting on Pleth — that at their age Pleth was the place to be — that they could vacation in the mountains of Pleth, or on an ocean beach, somewhere infinitely pleasant by comparison with Elsinore," she continued (as though that other level of communication were no longer of interest to her). "But H and O dug in their heels and refused to return to Pleth until the beginning of the next academic year. Reasons for their intransigence were never offered to me," she remarked, reminding me with a shock of how she had come to know the story — and that she meant me to understand the O in the story to be herself. "But I have always thought that the sibling lovers wished to remain on Elsinore because Elsinore itself, in all its gloom and in their shared experience of grief, provided an essential background for their love. I think that each of them must privately have suspected that returning to Pleth would break the spell, would make their love seem hideous, awkward, absurd even . . . and thus they each probably feared that a return to Pleth would mean a plunge into a loneliness and alienation they in their youth could only dimly imagine . . ." Her eyes and mouth suddenly appeared cold, remote, inaccessible; the thought came to me that she must herself at that moment be contemplating such alienation and loneliness — which is when it first occurred to me that one deprived of all knowledge of one's childhood and youth must know such regions well.

"The rest of the story goes quickly in any telling," she said. "C feared that the longer H and O stayed the higher the odds of their stumbling upon the truth of their parent's death. What he did not know was that his victim's personal attendant, disturbed at C's taking over as Governor — which, as you may recall, should according to Arrigan rules not have happened, since H was next in line to the governorship — when preparing the Governor's body for disposal extracted the permanent supplemental memory from the corpse and saved it with the intention of giving it to H at an appropriate moment. Now ordinarily this might not have gotten H very far, but the Governor had several years earlier — bearing in mind the assassination of his own father at a fairly early age — put into the attendant's safekeeping all the codes necessary for going into the permanent supplemental memory should anything happen to him, the Governor." She smiled. "You are thinking, perhaps, that the Governor trusted his attendant too far, and perhaps you're right, but Arrigans, I have been told, have an entirely different system of loyalty and honor. Never had that attendant been tempted to traffic with C, or with any other coveter of the governorship."

"What I am thinking is that H somehow learns that C killed his father, and then in turn kills C. And perhaps G and P as well," I interjected, eager to get to the end of the story. As far as I was concerned the story served merely as a vehicle for partnering — a vehicle she required for constructing the precise scenario that would satisfy certain erotic conditions she had. Obsessives care little for the person they partner and everything for the details. I kept trying to imagine what the parts of her body hidden by the table would look like (what colors, for instance, the skin of her thighs, buttocks, and belly had been tinted), I kept wondering whether alterations not yet mentioned by her had been made to her genitals . . . in short, I was paying little attention to her story, I had come to assume since her mentioning the sibling lovers that she had been wiped on account of the incestuous relation — as well as to spare her the most direct memories of H's murder of his uncles and aunt . . .

"You are jumping to conclusions, Captain," she rebuked me. The chrome tip of her index finger pointed accusation (or was it warning?). "Yes, H did eventually piece it all together — but it took him months. First, of course, he was quite preoccupied with O. And secondly, the information didn't immediately leap out at him, for at the beginning he had no suspicion that his father had been murdered. True, the cause of his death had never been satisfactorily explicated. But H was slow to suspect his uncle. Even on Arriga it is said that blood is thicker than water." She laid her hand on her left breast. The flat feral yellow of her eyes reminded me of holo-simulations of ancient untamed beasts long extinct. As though her brain, her eyes, her head had nothing to do with it, she absently stroked her breast. My gaze vacillated between her eyes, her mouth, and the movement of her fingers (flashing chrome ovals moving over nubbly frosted raspberry and brown fabric which showed little of the shape of the breast beneath—leaving all to my imagination — which by now waxed prodigious). If earlier I had been cold and shivery, now my body burned with fever, throwing off heat, prickling with sweat melting through my pores . . .

"Finally," she said, "H figured it out. But he had no proof that would stand up in a court of law. He talked about it with O, for weeks they discussed it. H grew more and more distracted. He expressed open hostility to C, he could not help himself. He dropped veiled hints that he knew, risking C's retaliation. G and P, however, chided him for his ungratefulness to C (who, they told him, had only H's and O's best welfare at heart), accused him of ambition, of wanting to be Governor himself although he at that time was not at all fit to rule Elsinore, and of being unwilling to be C's heir. Finally, driven by frustration and outrage, H told G and P that C had murdered his father (their brother). G and P went straight to C and told him of H's accusations. Subsequently, C, P, and G renewed their attempts to persuade H to return to Pleth. Once H returned to Pleth, C told P, G — and O (for the three of them had taken to talking to O about H, not knowing that O went straight to H with everything their uncles and aunt said to her about him) — H would relinquish his insane obsession, an obsession they claimed he had developed purely out of a heightened sense of guilt sons often feel when their fathers die."

"Which is why in civilized worlds generations usually alternate by sex," I put in, unable to resist jabbing at this backworlder sensibility she seemed to expect me to take seriously. I was bored with her story. I wanted to say to her, "get on with it, get on with it, I can hardly wait to get out of this place and into a privacy booth" — but of course I refrained from doing so precisely because I *did* want to get on with it.

"The story has it," she went on (ignoring my remark), "that H grew more and more disturbed, and absolutely paralyzed. The time approached for H's and O's return to Pleth. He began to talk about postponing it yet again. O worried. She noticed that his interest in her had slackened, only occasionally flaring up in violent partnerings that while outstripping their previous intensity had nothing of the love in it that had originally characterized their relationship. She could feel him beginning to hate her, as though he had begun projecting onto her all his negative feelings for C. The time for their departure drew closer and closer, until finally it lay only a local week away. It became clear that H had no intention of leaving. 'I should kill that bastard,' he began to say. 'I should kill all three of them. They are all guilty, C for directly murdering him, G and P for allowing it to happen, for simply rearranging their lives around C as though my father never had been.' H's bitterness shocked O. For a day or two she waited, half-terrified her brother would murder C. Three days before their scheduled date of departure, O demanded of H a commitment to return with her to Pleth. 'No,' he said. 'You must go alone. We're through. I don't care if I ever see you again.' And to O's devastation and desolation, she saw that he meant it. When she told him that if he did not go she would not either, he reviled her, flinging at her every scatological and sexual insult he could summon to mind.

"O was crushed, she saw that she had lost him, lost him to the poison C in killing O's father had distilled." She paused and placed both hands palms down flat on the table and I saw that her fingers were shaking. I looked at her face. Her lips trembled, her eyes glittered. When she resumed her voice emerged strained, hoarse, shaking. The excitement she exuded whipped up even greater sexual excitement in me — I could feel the wetness between my thighs, the whole thing had suddenly escalated, I have no idea how. (Obsessives are driven by their own timetables, dragging their victims in hapless tandem.)

"O saw that she had only one alternative: and that was to solve H's problem. She could not go back to Pleth without

87

him, she could not bear his rejection of her. If only, she thought, C were dead, H would then forget all that, H would return to her, H would again love her. To put it tersely: O secretly seduced C — and introduced into his ear a tiny deadly insect she knew would eat into his brain and destroy it. Elite Arrigans, you know, have almost as many means of restoring their lives as do Jannisetians and Evergreenians and Plethians. When one murders, one needs must destroy the brain. Two days later—the day before O and H had been scheduled to leave Elsinore, C died." She smiled at me with tender derision. "O thought the problem solved. She believed with all her heart that H would now come to his senses, would come to her the lover he had once been. Never did she dream that H would upon learning the truth revile and denounce her — and then kill himself."

"*O* killed C?" I — slow to take it in — numbly reiterated. "But —" I stared at her aghast, and the shock of what it was she thought she was telling me cut through the sensual haze that had ensnared me. "But if you are O," I said stupidly (my voice now matching hers for hoarseness and quavering), "then you are saying they wiped you for *murder?*"

"Why else did they bother to tell me the story, Captain?" she whispered, her eyes alight with the smile that suddenly felt horrifically evil to me. *This* was what she was getting off on, it was the sense of herself as a *murderer* that so excited her: my fear and horror had been what she had been after all along — my peculiarly *sexual* fear (and I can see now that it would have *had* to have a sexual timbre for her to have been able to get off on it). You may well ask whether I feared her physically harming me. After all, we sat there in the open lounge of Plumpers' (though I had fully intended going somewhere more private with her as soon as she had reached the appropriate point in her scenario), and I am well trained in self-defense skills and quite a bit larger than she (though clearly she wanted me to know that she knew how to use devious methods, that anyone with a mind to it could perpetrate murder). No, I don't think physical fear of her touched me. I would call it instead a peculiarly *sexual* fear. The fear of betraying oneself, of losing something, are fears that sometimes arise in sexual situations, I suppose because the sexual encounter heightens and intensifies one's concentration on the moment to such an extent that the smallest quivering of one's seemingly naked self becomes magnified to the point of taking over one's entire perception and being . . .

"They wiped me thirty standard years ago," she said in an almost ordinary voice. "They've felt no need to wipe me again. Surely you aren't concerned, Captain?"

Her smile mocked me, it sent my eyes skittering over her face — only to recoil at the fragmented distorted chrome reflections of myself curving over her nose cheeks forehead. "The way you speak of wiping," I said, my own voice far from ordinary quavered and shrilled unpleasantly in my ears, "one can only think you've somehow evaded it, which is supposed to be impossible!"

Her eyes lit up as though my words deeply thrilled her. "I am myself," she said silkily, touching her fingers lightly to her sternum. "I am myself. I have myself."

I don't know why I thought of it at that moment, but suddenly I recalled that one thing I had known about her all evening (apart from her origins on Arriga), namely her occupation. The thought of the helpless cocooned bodies of passengers in this woman's control appalled me to the point of nausea. *O secretly seduced C — and introduced into his ear a tiny deadly insect she knew would eat into his brain and destroy it.* "How can they allow you," I cried, glaring at her, "to be a cold storage medic?" My voice shook. "How could the Board ever certify you in the first place? You're sick, you're out of control, it is absolutely outrageous that —"

She leaned forward, stretched her hand across the table and laid her fingers on mine. "Calm yourself, Captain," she interrupted my denunciations. "I've been performing that job for seventeen standard years and have had not a single casualty over that entire period of time." Laughter cascaded from her mouth, startling and unsettling me. Unthinkingly, I snatched my hand away. "Let me tell you about the greatest temptation that ever came my way." Her smile broadened to a grin. "It happened four standard years ago that there came under my care Daniel Sayles, a representative of the Council for Developmental Strategy. He was on his way, Captain, to Arriga — where he would take the newly imposed function of Temporary Outside Governor, a position which gave him absolute power over all governmental and Combine structures operant on Arriga." Her laughter rang out. "Not only did I not kill this man whom I knew would shortly be dictator over all Arriga, but I *partnered* him, Captain, I *partnered* him." Her smile taunted me, provoking the thought that she wanted me to know she had partnered this scion of one of the most powerful and wealthy Janniset families, she thought such a tidbit would sharpen my desire for her. "Before going into cold storage he requested that I revive him not when we reached Arriga's orbital transfer station, but a dozen hours before we were due to connect with Arriga's Net. Which meant that unlike most of the other passengers, he would remain in cold storage for only a very short part of the trip." The point of cold storage, of course, is to spare passengers not only the ship's popping in and out of system, but the longest part of the journey as well — namely the transit through the system between the pop-point and the orbital transfer station or appropriate moon. Few people choose to waste their conscious and biological time on through-system travel. "Sayles said he wanted to connect with the Net as soon as possible so as to get as good a data grip as possible on the current situation on Arriga before making planet-fall."

Yawning she stretched her arms over her head. At that hour of the morning fatigue and sleepiness would not be unusual, especially since our intake of stimulants had fallen sharply with the onset of our exclusive tête-à-tête. But it seemed to me she stretched merely to exhibit her body to me, that she yawned merely to show me her tongue and her teeth, to flaunt her jewelled lips at me. "I told Sayles everything I've told you," she said when she had subsided back into her chair. She leaned forward, her feral yellow eyes peered at me through the slits of her chrome day-mask, intense and passionate, intent and suddenly focused: as though announcing she was ready for the kill. "Perhaps I even told him more, Captain." Her tongue touched one of the jewels in her upper lip. "There are public baths just up the street from here," she roughly stated. "Will you join me?"

Her abruptness took my breath away. For what had seemed an interminable time I had been waiting for something of the sort, but now . . . I opened my mouth to refuse her, but at that moment her foot slid over my leg, shooting the most exquisite streaks of sensation up into my (I confess it) wet throbbing vulva. Dumbly I nodded, and made a feeble gesture towards the door. She smiled, withdrew her foot from my leg and rose to her feet. I trailed her out of Plumpers' barely conscious of anything but her: I a mere zombie led mesmerized to the slaughter. I've told you several times she was an obsessive, and thus you can imagine for yourself what partnering her was like. Obviously I lived to tell the tale. But I'm left with a question I've never been able to resolve to my own satisfaction: she may have been an obsessive, but was her story true? Had she even been wiped? Frankly I find it easier to believe she partnered Daniel Sayles after telling him that story than that she could be the person she is after having been wiped. If she lied about being wiped, then one must wonder about the sanity of people certified by the Board to hold jobs which place others in their life and death dependency. But if she did tell the truth about that, then we must all worry, mustn't we, about the efficacy of wiping which we've always believed to be absolute. Unsettling, isn't it?

It may have been a one-night stand, but I've never been the same since. My advice is to stay away from Arrigans. They're nothing but trouble. It's no wonder the Combine has begun a serious debate over abandoning and quarantining the planet (despite Daniel Sayles' best efforts). Probably it would be best if the same were done to that woman, O. But as in the case of the planet, one suspects they'll wait until the worst happens. And then, of course, it will be too late. Most people don't believe backworlds and their inhabitants are a threat to civilization, but that's what all civilizations have believed about the savage barbarians that eventually and inevitably destroy each civilization. Beware the Os, my friend, beware. Learn from my story — or you'll be doomed to repeat it — as she wishes it. It's always that way with obsessives, always.

Conversation with a Legend

•

R.M. Meluch

I flew in from Greece yesterday wearing a thin cotton dress and summer sandals. It was already cold here in the British Isles. First thing I did on landing in London was pull a pair of socks out of my bag and put them on. The second thing was to get out of London. It's too bloody big, if you'll pardon my saying so. Do you suppose there are as many people in London as there were in the whole world of 342 B.C.E.? Why that date? Alexander the Great was fourteen years old in 342 B.C.E.

I hopped a fast train to Scotland where I chunked all my Greek cottons and bought wool things, a pair of proper shoes and this umbrella. I don't guess the rain bothers you. No. Of course not.

I took a room on the outskirts of Inverness, rented a car and drove down here. So here I am on the shore of your loch. Cold, do you think? Lovely, in a dreary sort of way with the mist spilling over the braes and ghosting over the water; raindrops on the heather. It's what I expected Scotland to be like. I'd have been disappointed if the sun were shining.

Rain seems to have driven all the tourists into the pubs. It's just you and me.

Do you understand what I'm saying? I somehow think you do. I think you can sympathize with me. May I tell you my tale?

This is difficult. I'm a modern American woman; I'm not supposed to believe in reincarnation. I'm not supposed to believe in *you* either for that matter. So.

It's in Plato's *Phaedrus*, this theory of reincarnation: We are, all of us, souls who have lost our wings and dropped from the orbits of our gods in their winged chariots and fallen to earth where we have come to be born in mortal houses. When we die, we go to a place like heaven or hell for a thousand years according to the life lived, then we reincarnate to a better lot if done well, a worse one if not well. It takes no less than ten thousand years for a soul to regain its wings and return to the place of its beginning, following in the train of its god. The truly remarkable soul with a strong memory of divinity — a memory of Beauty — can take flight in only three thousand years.

There it is, stark and quick. There are some pretty words in *Phaedrus*. I remember reading it aloud in the shadow of a mountain, a pair of luminous eyes fixed on me. It's a wonderful piece. About rhetoric and love and immortality and the nature of the soul.

However, I have always had some problems with the idea of reincarnation. One is that there are more people alive today than there ever were. So there must be a great deal of first-time souls among us. You, my friend, are at least a second-timer if you have a soul at all, since one can't be an animal in one's first incarnation.

My other problem is that whenever you meet people who think they are reincarnated, they were always Somebody in a past life, like Ruth — *the* Ruth in the Bible — or Mary Magdalene's mother, or one of Napoleon Bonaparte's generals. No one is ever a third world villager who died of malnutrition at age seven.

But then I guess you could argue that the ones who remember the past are the ones who have something *to* remember. A friend of mine said I was probably Alexander the Great, because of my near-fanatic interest in him. I said no way in hell. Alexander would not have put on socks in Heathrow Airport because her feet were cold. Alexander would be coming in on Air Force One, or something to that effect.

I have my own corporation, am considered a brilliant young success, but I'm hardly a star of the first magnitude. I'm not very charismatic as Alexander was, and I can be outright antagonistic without much provocation. I've been called Attila the Hun's granddaughter — though I have to say that was spoken in semi-admiration by an underling. Friends are few. And for that I feel like jumping out a window sometimes. Memories of Beauty and divinity are very elusive these days.

But. See this? This is a reminder. This is Beauty. No,

you can't eat it. It's silver. There's one like it in every jewelry store in Greece, which is how I was able to smuggle this one out of the country. On my wrist. In plain sight. Replicas of Macedonian bracelets with opposing lion heads are fashionable this year. This one's not tarnished so nobody thought twice that it might be a genuine antiquity.

— Whoa, no, you can't have that either. That's not trash. That's my dinner. I know they're funny here; they wrap their carry-out food in newspaper. Here, see? Fish and chips. Hey.

Well, why not. It's probably cold by now. You like cooked fish? I wouldn't have guessed. Let me have the other piece at least. Here, the chips are soggy. *You* take 'em. I've got my bottle of Greek wine. This is all I have for dinner sometimes anyway. Naoussa. Good wine. Brought a few bottles with me.

Where was I?

Greece. I went to Greece to find something. Beauty, I suppose.

I went north, where tourists and English speakers thin out. I came at last to a town in western Macedonia where tourists and English speakers disappear altogether. Most people coming to Macedonia go to Vergina to see Philip's tomb, or to Thessaloniki to see Philip's gold, or to Pella to see the ruins of the palace; the Greek tourists go to the waterfalls in Edhessa.

I came to Naoussa to find the Garden of Midas.

The Garden of Midas is where young Alexander and a circle of his lifelong friends and future generals went to school, people like his best friend and soulmate Hephaistion, and maybe Ptolemy, the founder of the Egyptian dynasty. It was the only peaceful interlude of his life. Sometime around 342 B.C.E. Their tutor was Aristotle, who was incidentally a pupil of Plato. They almost had to have read *Phaedrus* in the Garden. And maybe talked about reincarnation.

The Garden of Midas hasn't been found yet, not by archaeologists leastwise. Some say it's by Vergina, near the royal tombs. No it's not. That area around the old palace is an uninspired place, like Pella. I can see why Alexander never went home again. At any rate, the Garden is not there. The guidebook is wrong; it was just a guess on their part anyway. The Garden of Midas is a place you'll never find by archaeological means. You find it with your guts and your heart. And your soul. And by God I found it.

It's where it's supposed to be, at the foot of Mount Bermion. Near the town of Naoussa as it happens.

The area is known for its apples and wine. I had a stock of both with me as I went driving up town (literally — Naoussa is on a mountain) grinding the hell out of the clutch of a rented car.

I'm so lost in this century, do you know? Yes, I suppose you do.

I was stopping traffic. Not just because of my driving but because I was female, blonde and alone. Ignoring all the staring Greeks I was in the grip of a possession to go up this hill. *Pothos.* That's Alexander's word. A *longing.* Something was drawing me up that hill. The back of my mind was telling me Midas' garden was up there.

I had climbed past the town, past the last buildings, and was driving into forest when I passed a sign. I knew the word. Turns out it's the same in both ancient and modern Greek, but I just couldn't remember it. I knew it; I knew I knew it; but the meaning was not coming to me. *Stratopedon.*

Then I came to the chain link fence and the guardpost. I remembered the word when I saw the guns. *Stratopedon* means "army encampment."

End of the line. I turned the car around and coasted down the hill in defeat and nagging emptiness, disappointed and so alone. I parked my poor car and set out on foot looking for a place to eat. There were cafeterias aplenty, but cafeterias serve just that, *cafe* — coffee — and they are full of men. It was sundown, and the only women on the streets had a half dozen children in tow. All the men were in the cafeterias and I was a lost soul on the outside looking in, with a sense that I have known what it is like to be on the inside.

Finally I found the only restaurant in town, and I ate dinner with a cat. There doesn't seem to be any health regulation against animals in the eating places. In fact it just isn't dinner without a cat around.

You're not a cat, but then I didn't get much of my dinner either come to think of it.

It was in the restaurant that I found a guide. We met because we were staring at each other. *Lots* of people were

95

staring at me, but this time I was staring back. You see, she was a young blonde woman too. She was an American, hired to teach the schoolchildren English.

She and her companion joined me at my table. She told me that Greek women in the traditional back country do not go out unescorted, and they don't drink — not in public anyway. The locals even cut *her* off after one glass of wine.

This she told me while I was sitting there polishing off a whole bottle by myself — much to the fascination of everyone in the restaurant.

I told the teacher I would have made a very bad Greek. But that's not exactly true.

Do you know that all the time I've been crouched on this rock talking to you I've just *assumed* you were male? I'd have made a good Greek.

I told the teacher that I had wanted to go up the mountainside but I had run into the guns.

She told me the road continued past the army encampment. I had merely to stop at the guardpost and the soldiers would let me pass by.

Suddenly life was interesting again.

I asked her if there was anything up the hill. She said yes. My heart positively sprang. The short hairs were prickling up my back and arms. *Yes?*

"Beyond the army camp the road forks three ways," she said. "The one road goes up and over the mountain, I don't know how far; it gets very bad. Another one goes nowhere. But the one on the far left goes to a nice little sort of park."

"A *park?*" I'm fairly shrieking by this point. A *park?* A Garden perhaps?

Morning found me coaxing my 1.1 litre engine back up Bermion past the army camp to the park.

I knew this was it before I got there.

The park is an expansive grove of venerable plane trees. Dry wild grape vines hang in long strands from the branches. It's an open stand, easy to walk through, grassy underfoot. Bunches of cyclamen spring up in all the sunny patches, their pink petals pulled back like butterfly wings. Heaps of ivy crowd over the rocks and strangle some of the trees, some near to death. Mount Bermion is a place famed since antiquity for its wild roses, but this isn't the season for roses. There's clover and chicory. The wild carrot is in white flower. I didn't expect crocuses this late.

I wandered about in a kind of enchantment. Being there made me feel young. The trees are magnificent. The old ones broaden in contorted shapes; from squat beginnings several trunks rise with mottled skin and spreading boughs. You can see the blue mountain peak through their turning leaves.

I strayed from the cleared area toward the denser wood, accompanied by the constant harassment from a fly — the reincarnation of Eumenes you don't suppose?

The forest floor is covered with a bed of brown leaves. The sun was warm. The air was warm-cool, pleasant, only a few white puffs of clouds in the sky.

I heard running water. I'd heard it since I'd parked the car. One never quite loses the sound anywhere in the glade. I followed the sound off the path through bramble thickets, clumps of mountain box, and chestnut trees with ripening spiny green balls. Then the underbrush broke and I was standing over a deep streambed hidden in the forest. I don't know if I can say what the sight did to me. I just stood there frozen in wonder. My throat was tight. I couldn't have spoken if I had to. I couldn't move for a moment. It was just a stream, so natural and familiar. Healing and home. I had been here before and I had been happy.

Running waters had worn a little glen into the ground; sunlight still touched the higher ground, but within its deep banks is cool and shadowed, smelling of moist green bracken, fallen leaves and damp earth. I slipped down the mossy rocks, holding onto the bared roots of an ancient tree. Mud slicked on my palms. I frightened a tiny brown lizard. It scurried on the leaves, its little sides heaving in terror.

I followed the stream up a little ways, to where its white bubbling rush is joined in from a side streamlet, splitting and tumbling over the little falls into the brown pebbled stream bed in a cheering lively spate. The water is icy cold, clear and clean. Conglomerate rocks around its edges are worn smooth, and footing is tricky. The planes shade it with a yellowing autumn canopy, their twisting roots exposed and undercut by the current. I came to an enormous one, a plane tree, ten men thick at its base. I found in one of its several knotted trunks a place to sit.

On the other side of the stream was another aged tree with a hollow way up, big enough for a boy to crouch in.

When did I know who I was? An argument could be made that I had known all along. But I would contend that I didn't know until he called my name.

"Hephaistion."

I think that I held my breath. I turned my head to see him where there had been no one before, on the other side of the stream. You would know him even if you hadn't known him in life. Most of his representations catch something of him. If nothing else, you can't mistake those eyes. Eyes gray blue like the sky at overcast dawn. A fair leonine look in all his portraits, called idealizing, but that is the way he was, especially in the Garden of Midas.

I told you I *knew* I'd found it.

Young. He was young. When I'd last seen him in life he was thirty-two. But now he was here as I had known him here. Like I said, Pella and Aegae are dreary — he had never gone back — and I was not about to revisit the place of our last parting as it is now, not without the 82nd Airborne behind me. Of course he would come back to me here.

I don't know how he saw me — as you do or as I had been, another fourteen–year–old youth, tall, with a xanthous mane like his, more handsome, but lacking in his radiance and energy like the bursting star of the Argead House.

I don't know how he saw me because unlike him I was really there. He was not an incarnation; I would swear I could almost touch him, but he was a wraith. A shade on the wrong side of the river. I think he must have mugged the ferryman. He was not one to rest easy among the strengthless dead.

However it was he saw me, I had been feeling so wretched of late that I wondered what he had ever seen in me in the first place. I was nothing without him. Now the stream was all that separated us, and I wanted to dash across and throw my arms around him. But I knew somehow that the stream was more than a stream and I dared not.

Although the analogy is imperfect, there is a scene in the *Iliad* where the ghost of Patroklos comes back to the living Achilles in a dream. Achilles tries to embrace the ghost of his friend dearer than life and hold it; it disappears and he wakes with empty arms. I read that and cry every time.

We always cried. Every time.

I refrained from crossing the stream even though it was tearing my heart out.

He looked so lifelike. His blue chiton was even torn at the border, and thorn scratches criss-crossed his legs. How could he not be real? He had big hands, like a boy who is not done growing, but he was never as tall as he wanted to be. I was destined to be the kingly looking one.

I couldn't even say his name. I tried. My throat clotted with an unrelenting lump, caught among disbelief, long felt sorrow, and inexpressible joy. Truth was I was afraid to speak, lest I break some spell.

Finally my voice came stumbling out bald and weak as a bird just out of its shell, "Alexander."

He bade a gentle greeting. I knew the sound, a boy's changing voice, making a graceful drop because it hadn't too far to go. I don't know what language we were speaking. Macedonian I think. Funny how I can't say. Must have been Macedonian. Alexander wouldn't have had any way of knowing English.

He said he missed me.

I could not believe he was not gone yet — back into the orbits of the gods in their winged chariots with the other fortunate souls who have regained their memory of divine flight. I thought he would be one of the remarkable ones. I thought he had gotten it right the first time.

No, he said he was not perfect.

"I thought you were," I confessed.

"I know *you* thought so." He smiled and threw a chestnut ball across the stream at me. It missed. It was supposed to. Then he was pensive again. "You could make me believe so. O Hephaistion, I am missing my right hand."

"That's better off than I am," I said. "I'm a right hand without a head. I'm so lost without you."

"I am here."

I sputtered, struggling for understanding. I had been a rational American near as long as I had been a half mystic Macedonian, and I needed this to make sense. "How? Why?"

"Waiting for you," he said. Simple. Alexander says it's so, so it is. "I am not going to move on without you. Like you did me."

He was hurt when he said that. There was reproach

in his voice.

In our past lives, I had died before he did. It devastated him. Of course I don't remember that part. I had to learn from history books that Alexander was unhinged at the death of Hephaistion. We had just conquered the best part of the known world, were setting up to organize a central government in Babylon, and there it ended. He did not outlive me long. Neither of us saw the far side of thirty-three.

He could not forgive me for leaving him. It burst out in a sudden rebuke, "What made you have breakfast, you big pig. Couldn't you *wait?*"

My last meal killed me. I'd had a fever. The doctor told me I wasn't supposed to eat. And no wine. I never listen. I'm always the expert.

Hostile historians say we both drank ourselves to death. This is not strictly true. But it's not entirely untrue either. Between the two of us we put down a lot, a lot, of wine. But it wasn't the amount I drank, rather the timing that was so bad. If patience is a virtue, I may as well go straight to hell and stay there.

"I'm sorry," I said.

"Do not do it again," he said.

"I wasn't planning to."

"Yes you are."

Suicide. I *had* been entertaining the idea lately.

"Do it and we'll never be together. You'll come back as a lizard."

Being a lizard wouldn't be so bad. Is it? I wouldn't have to think, which I do to a deadly degree, and I wouldn't be missing what I no longer have. But Alexander was demanding.

I cried at him, "Then you be there next time!" I don't know how much choice we have in these things. But then Alexander always created his choices. "If I'm to go through all this again, you had better be there!"

So he promised. "I swear . . ." He looked round for something to swear by. "By this plane tree."

And I started laughing. Phaedrus swore by the plane tree.

Just then I noticed he was wearing a bracelet. One. The Makedones wore them in pairs, symmetrically, one on each wrist, but he only had one. He took it off. "This is yours."

I remembered it. I had lost the bracelet in those woods. He had given it and its mate to me, and I had lost one. I'd torn this place up looking for it but never found it.

Only I can't say never, can I? There it was.

And we made a pact to meet again. To take on the world again. He bowed his head for a moment like a butting bull, his eyes shaded deep beneath his heavy brow, great solemnity on his young face, his fist closed round the bracelet of twin lions facing each other. He finished with a prayer to the gods of this place. I said, "Please mention me in your prayer, for friends have everything in common." He was the one who started laughing that time. A soul has a long memory, when it has something to remember.

Impulse seized me. I jumped down from the tree and into the stream. I wanted to hold him, just for a second.

And I was alone in the glen. The bracelet was still there glinting in the wet leaves. I cried my eyes out.

Aweel. I canna stay mair. (Did that sound Scottish?) This bottle is a dead soldier and I think I'm frozen stiff. This mizzling rain seems to be breaking up. The tourists will be coming out again to see Urquhart Castle and to look for you. You'd better go.

What? You want me to come in there with you? Not without a quarter inch of neoprene, thank you. Or a dry suit better still. I'm not suicidal; I have a chariot to catch.

Thank you for listening to me. I don't know how much you understood, if at all. You're the only one I can tell who wouldn't have me chased with a net.

I have only one problem now.

Who am I going to tell about you?

Signs of Life

•

Barbara Krasnoff

"Hell, Fran," the 'tender said, staring at her from the far reaches of a sparkling infinity. "Can't you manage to scrape a little more life into your face? We've got tourists coming in ten minutes; what the hell good are you to me if you're passed out?"

Fran squinted up at the man, unsure whether it was worth the effort to try to get his face into some sort of focus. From the worn futon on which she lay, it looked as though he stretched past the range of the ceiling and out to the edge of the atmosphere; his voice shimmered with distance. Vaguely, she wondered whether he actually expected an answer.

Apparently not. Impossibly long arms pulled her into a semi-sitting position. The hands vibrated as they moved; Fran giggled.

"Verisimilitude," Marty rumbled with disgust. "They tell me that they'll only send their tours here if my place has verisimilitude. Do you know what that means, Fran? That means I have to supply you goddamn pastits with enough shit to keep you flying without killing you off altogether. You have any idea how much work that takes?"

He finally managed to prop her up against the wall. Fran reached slowly over to touch the rainbow face and giggled again.

"I tell them, I can get actors, good actors, will look more like prosties and pastits than the real thing. What do they say? That they've got a list longer than the trade route of places better than mine waiting for a chance for tourist gelt. That if I want to stay on their agenda, I've got to have verisimilitude. Here. Drink this."

Something cold and liquid pushed its way past Fran's

lips. She swallowed obediently, enjoying the sensation of the fluid as it fluttered down her throat. Then gasped for breath as it suddenly burst into fire inside her stomach.

"That'll do it," Marty nodded, and stood. "Verisimilitude is one thing, but they're not paying to see you stare at the wall."

He moved away, probably to attend to the other pastits who camped against the walls of his bar, but Fran was hurting too much to notice.

The fire spread from her stomach into her skin; her clothes quickly became damp as her body tried to get its temperature back down to a reasonable range. She closed her eyes and clutched her hair, trying to hold on to the last residue of the drug that was quickly being flushed from her system.

"My god," said a distressed female voice above her. "Is she all right? She looks terribly ill."

Fran's eyes snapped open and she glared at the source of the disturbance. The woman was about twenty-five and dressed in the false-torn garb of the small group of City intellectuals who professed sympathy and solidarity with the residents of Downtown. She had crouched down until her face was even with Fran's, and her eyes glistened with what Fran had no doubt were sincere tears.

Fran's first instinct was to snap at the woman for interrupting her misery. Sympathy was all well and good, but it didn't buy her any flytime. However, as one of Marty's full-timers, she knew the rules. So she bared her teeth in what she hoped was a general approximation of a smile.

"She's fine," said another voice that Fran assumed was the tourguide. "Just coming down. If we let her alone, she'll probably be able to join us in a little while. This way, please." The young woman nodded, sniffed, stood, and allowed herself to be led away, not without one last glance back.

Fran sighed, and stretched her legs slowly out in front of her, trying to work out the kinks. Starlight might set the neurons free, but it curled the body into a semi-foetal position that played hell with the muscles. She studiously avoided looking at her surroundings, which seemed etched in clear, stark relief. This was always the unpleasant aftertaste of returning to reality: the world seemed uglier, more garish than it had before. Each laser-sculpted tile in the ceiling seemed to jump out at her, every stain on every table cried out for her attention, the pungency of her own scent drifted unpleasantly past her nostrils. A nap, she thought, would be really nice right about now. But Marty had customers, and Fran had a performance to give.

Marty's place existed exclusively for the use of the businesspeople who came to trade at Oppenheimer IV's busy spaceport, known to its inhabitants simply as the City. The City was a shining, landscaped and meticulously planned metropolis created and maintained solely for the comfortable transaction of business. Shuttles kept a steady traffic between the planet and the orbiting spacecraft that flocked to Oppenheimer, attracted by its reputation as a center of commerce. There were exquisite housing and cultural facilities for visitors, friendly communities for residents, and even licensed places of recreation for crews restless from long voyages. All the illegal, immoral, or simply distasteful social problems that necessarily accompany any urban environment had been carefully placed at a slight distance, out of official sight and mind, in the warren of hurriedly constructed streets and low buildings that was known simply as Downtown.

Unfortunately, the officials who ran the City found that most of their highly respectable guests couldn't resist a quick glimpse of the other side of the City — and some weren't returning. After the requisite amount of bureaucratic wrangling, carefully routed tours were arranged to give visitors a taste of Downtown — without exposing them to its dangerous reality.

Marty, a failed businessman on the lookout for opportunities, decided that this was his chance. He spent a considerable amount of money (most of it borrowed from the Corp, the syndicate which virtually owned Downtown) to bribe the correct officials, and to redesign an old, abandoned prostie bar. The new hangout was a paean to bad taste with just the right overlay of seediness. It was carefully underlit, overheated, and decorated with old crew luck-charms and faded holos of posturing men and women at various stages of sexual play. And as a final added attraction, Marty served up a disney of romantically depraved thieves, addicts, and prostitutes (along with overpriced food and watered drinks) to tour groups that were shepherded through three times a day, four on weekends.

His most valued commodity was his crew of pastits: Starlight addicts intent upon chemical self-destruction whose fashionably desperate presence drew the tourists like a magnet. It drew the Downtown addicts as well: a standing joke was that if you lived a good life, you went to heaven after you died; if you lived a very good life, you went to Marty's first.

Fran had gained access to this haven about two months ago. She had been in her usual spot in the large, heavily populated market square where most of Downtown's goods — sexual and otherwise — were sold. Hands plunged deep into the pockets of her loose jumpsuit, tightly cropped hair showing its first hints of gray, Fran watched brilliantly costumed prosties of all ages and both sexes coo at interested crew and frightened tourists. She didn't have the pull or the ambition to gain one of the more desirable perches along the low wall that surrounded the square's defunct central fountain, and she knew better than to stand too near one of the multitude of tiny storefronts that defined its periphery. Instead, she leaned against a shady wall in the least trafficked part of the square, sucking absently on a piece of hard candy in order to still the pangs in her stomach and occasionally scanning the daytime crowds for a potential client.

Once she had isolated a promising passerby, Fran would stare at her prospective customer with a casual sort of interest, as though she was about to ask directions, or wanted to know the time. This attitude, along with light hazel eyes and a thin, boyish face, usually attracted one or two customers a day — enough to earn what she needed to feed her habit without having to spend too much time at an occupation she considered supremely unpleasant.

"Hey, lady," murmured a deep voice at about the level of her waist. "Looking for a companion?"

Fran looked down at the small dark man who, it was rumored, had been one of the hottest holo artists uptown; when his work went passé, he had crashed badly. Very badly. "You couldn't afford me, Raul," she grinned at him, not bothering to move. "Anyway, I thought you didn't like skinny women."

"At this point, I'll take what I can get. Even you." He motioned slightly with his head, and Fran obligingly squatted down to his level.

"Listen," Raul said quickly. "I know I owe you for sharing your last couple of takes with me."

"Last three . . ."

"Last three, yeah. Want to pay up." He shook his head at her outstretched palm. "Not that way. Got something better."

"Something better? Right."

"No, really." He leaned forward until his mouth nearly touched her ear. "I can get you into Marty's. As a perm."

Fran's eyebrows dropped. "Not funny, Raul.

"Truth." He grinned. "Word is that Marty just lost a female pastit, and is looking for a replacement. Young, so that she'll last at least a year or so. And with an interesting story. Well, I thought of you immediately — hell, Fran, you were crew; the clients will eat you up. All you have to do is show up, and you'll be bedding down there tonight."

When Fran presented herself at the bar, the 'tender gave her a long, cold stare and slowly nodded. "Raul told me you were coming," he drawled. "Said you still had some personality left. Good to see I can still trust him."

He took her elbow and steered her past the seating area, which was crowded with tables that had obviously seen better days, to the back of the room where a layer of worn futons lined the wall. Most were occupied by a variety of semi-conscious pastits, their faces slack and expressionless as Starlight spun wonders inside their heads. "This blue one's yours," he said. "You get to fly twice a day, once before we open, once at night. You need anything else in between, you let me know. Two meals, and whatever you can get from the tourists — minus my percentage. I've only got two rules here: You only fly when I tell you, and you make nice to the clients. Keep them in mind, and we'll get along fine. You trip up, and you're back selling your ass in the square. Got it?"

Fran stared back at him coolly for a moment. Then, without changing her expression, she strolled over to the futon, sat, and held out her hand. Marty grinned, dropped a small blue pill into her hand, and left.

On her right, a large middle-aged man with an impressively thick beard stared at the ceiling, his head cradled in an artificial arm. On her left, an elderly woman wearing a patched shift and a worn pair of gloves stirred and smiled vaguely at her. "Nice to see you, dear," she wheezed. "You came just in time for dinner."

Fran swallowed the pill and leaned back against the wall. She was, she decided, home. At least, all the home she'd need for the rest of her life.

As usual, most of the day's customers perched uneasily on the stools that lined Marty's bar; those who couldn't find seats stood protectively together rather than occupy one of the empty tables. Looks like a profitable crowd, Fran thought, peering through the low lighting. About forty people, most obviously well-cashed, even though they had dressed down for the occasion. The usual group of business travelers; should be good for at least a meal. Three young people (including the woman who had stopped in front of Fran) who were trying to look as though they belonged there, and failing miserably. One sour-looking individual whom Fran had seen before, and who was already eyeing the prosties. And a few miscellaneous types: crew, probably, getting their bearings before striking out on their own.

Nearby, other pastits were also beginning to stir; it was time to earn their flytime. Fran pushed herself up onto her feet, waited a moment to make sure that her balance was secure, and headed for the washroom.

When she returned, hair still damp from the shower, several of her companions had already taken up their usual places. Siobhan, her elderly neighbor, was being grandmotherly to the students, while a large, overweight former fighter incongruously named Michel orated happily (if somewhat incoherently) to several amiable crew members at one of the larger tables.

Fran, happily, was under no obligation to make any first moves to the customers. Unlike most of her peers, who were obliged to be as pushy (within limits) as possible, she played the part of the Noble Space Traveler Who Had Seen Too Much. Which was nothing but a great deal of well-decorated crap, but since the role demanded that Fran look haughty and introspective, and lie her head off, she didn't mind.

She stalked over to the bar and pulled herself onto a stool, a couple of feet away from a stout man with large, curious eyes. "Marty," she said wearily, making sure the mark could hear her, "you got anything to eat that doesn't taste like waste recyclings?"

Marty smiled sympathetically at her. Seen without Starlight's special effects, he was a tall, well-built man with a rapidly fading hairline and a glib, plastic face. "No time for that now," he told her. "You've got a customer."

He nodded over her head toward the center of the room. Fran twisted around slightly and squinted through the haze.

A square-set woman with cropped hair and a sideways grin slouched easily at one of the smaller tables, legs stretched out comfortably before her. One elbow rested on the table, leaving her right hand dangling casually in the air, her fingers moving in an apparently random rhythm. Except to Fran's startled eyes: repeatedly, carefully, they spelled out two letters. H-I the woman signed, over and over, H-I.

There was a hardness in the pit of Fran's stomach; a hardness that she thought she had left behind long ago, along with her pride and her old life. The dark eyes fastened calmly on Fran's. Whoever the woman was, she obviously knew that Fran understood exactly what her fingers were saying.

Fran turned back to the 'tender. "No."

The man's eyes narrowed. "Now, listen here, Fran. You haven't been bringing in a whole lot of gelt lately, and the Corp upped their cut last month. If you want to live here, you've got to chip in your share. Now this mark comes in, she hands me a note says she's looking for an Interpreter with no connections and will pay well."

"Marty, I can't interpret. You know that."

"Why, because they kicked you out of the Guild? Hell, if the lady wanted a certified Interpreter, she could have got one in the City. She wants somebody who doesn't care where she goes, and who'll keep her mouth shut. You fit the bill."

Fran stared at the 'tender sullenly. His face hardened. "Would you rather try your luck on the streets again?"

"Bastard." But she immediately stood and pushed toward the table, ignoring the protests of several startled patrons.

As she saw Fran approach, the woman's fingers relaxed; otherwise she didn't move. She was somewhere in her late twenties, and her confident mien and the white scar running down one dark forearm showed that she was no tourist. Probably crew — although her clothing was bright and fashionable, it was practical enough for shipboard use. But the steady gaze and quiet face told Fran something else quite clearly.

"You're Hearing," she said bluntly, dropping into a chair. The woman's eyebrows raised.

"You don't know Sign," Fran continued. "Not really. All you know is how to spell, maybe a few signs. Enough to get by. Enough to communicate with a crew."

The woman grinned. "How did you know?" she asked, in a rich, deep voice.

"How about something to eat?"

The woman nodded affably, and Fran immediately raised a hand toward the bar. When she was sure that Marty had seen her, she turned back to her customer.

"Your face doesn't talk. And you were spelling, not signing. Now I have a question: how did you know I'd read you?"

"Just a hunch. And a bit of cash passed to your 'tender."

Marty dropped a plate in Fran's general vicinity; he smiled comfortably at the woman. "Can I get you something to eat?" he asked. She shook her head.

The 'tender lowered his voice. "If you want privacy for your talk," he continued smoothly, "just let me know. I've got a few empty rooms out in back. Fran knows."

Fran stared at his retreating back. "You know," she said casually. "He thinks you're trying to pick me up. Are you?"

"You have any objections?"

Fran shrugged. "Not in the least. I work both sides of the river. But I'm no prostie — which means I'm not as talented, and not as cheap."

"But considerably more interesting." The woman grinned again and shook her head. "It's a nice thought, one which we might discuss at a later date. Right now, I've got something else in mind. A different sort of proposition." Fran picked up her sandwich, glanced at the insides, and took a bite.

The woman laced her arms on the table and leaned forward. "My name," she began, "is Leisant Dima — you can call me Lee. I do tech for an independent tradeship called the *Beethoven*. Right now, there's only two crew — myself, and the pilot, Stu McDermott. It's his ship, and his business, but I get a considerable share for my part in the upkeep." She paused.

"We need an Interpreter. Tonight."

Fran swallowed. "You don't look so broke that you couldn't afford to pick up a freelancer in the City. How 'independent' are you?"

"Oh, we're legal as all getout. And believe it: if we weren't, I could hack our way past any difficulties." Lee shrugged. "But the problem is, we're heading into some delicate negotiations. And we need somebody who we can trust to interpret the proceedings."

"Right. Listen, if you're crew, you know damn well that the Code would prevent any certified Interpreter, even a freelancer, from talking about your business to anyone. You could kill fifty people and sell fifty more — confidentiality would still hold."

Lee snorted. "Sure. Well, let's just say that Stu, for one, doesn't have a whole lot of faith in codes on a planet that's owned by the local syndicate — the Corp, is it?"

Fran nodded.

"We need an Interpreter who isn't in anyone's pay — and right now, you look like the closest we're going to come." She cocked her head slightly. "I take it you're not certified."

"Not any more."

"Why? Drug use?"

"No," Fran snapped.

Lee waited a moment, then when Fran didn't offer any more information, she shrugged. "Well, I guess it's your business. Stu's a good lipreader, but we don't want our . . . customer to know that. So we need somebody who's fluent in Sign and can do a reasonably good imitation of a shipboard Interpreter."

That brought a sour smile. "Sure," Fran said. "I know the drill."

"Then you'll take the job?

Fran bit her lip and glanced at the bar. Marty was talking in a low tone to a young woman, a girl really, who had obviously been on the ground a bit too long. Fran remembered the street and took a deep breath.

"How much?"

Lee smiled. "Thirty-five for the first two hours; ten each hour after that. The usual rates for a low-grade Interpreter."

Fran considered another moment, then nodded.

"Fine," Lee said. "This evening, then. At eleven."

"No." Fran glanced inadvertently toward the back of the room. "I . . . I'm going to be busy until at least 11:30. Make it 12."

Lee stood slowly, her eyes shaded by dark lashes. "Listen, I'm taking enough of a chance with you. I don't want you showing up with only half your mind working."

Fran grinned up at her. "Shit, when I'm flying I can't even count my own fingers. Be here at twelve. I'll make sure my brain's up to it."

The woman nodded, and then looked past Fran toward the tour guide, who was making frantic, ugly handmotions indicating that it was past time to leave.

"Twelve, then," she said, and walked gracefully to the door.

Fran stared down at her sandwich, but her appetite was gone. She raised her hands to eye level and flexed them experimentally, trying to work out the stiffness of three years of disuse. After about ten minutes, she lowered her left hand and slowly closed the right into a fist, thumb out. A. Opened and flattened the hand. B. Made a half-moon of the fingers and thumb. C.

She smiled. "Well, what the hell," she told herself.

She ran herself through the alphabet, then through basic signs, sentence structure, idioms — all the lessons that she could dredge up from nearly forgotten memories. Her fingers slipped and she cursed, tried again; her world constricted itself to the space before her and the signs it contained.

Finally, after she successfully finished the Gettysburg Address, Fran stopped and looked around. There were no customers left, except for a few locals. Most of the pastits were finishing off what was left of the food or stumbling back to their futons to get in some flytime before the evening crowd arrived. The room felt airless, oppressive; Fran slowly massaged her hands and took a shaky breath.

"You hungry?" Marty had dropped into Lee's chair. The unfinished sandwich was still on its plate; he sniffed at it distastefully.

Fran shrugged. "You know what I need."

He grinned. "Sure, why not? You earned it."

He reached into his pocket and brought out a small metal box. "To tell you the truth," he said conversationally, tapping a combination on the small lock panel, "you would have been entitled to this even if you didn't take the job. I'm going to have you sit here signing every day — the marks thought you were some sort of starshocked Deaf crewmember; it was better than a sideshow."

"Forget it."

The 'tender stopped, a small object held delicately between his thumb and forefinger. Fran stared at the tablet impassively.

"I won't," she said, "play Deaf for you or anyone else. It's against the Code."

"Is it?"

Marty smiled, stood, and strolled over until he stood directly behind Fran's chair. One brawny hand slowly massaged her shoulder and neck; the other, she knew, still held the drug that kept her alive. So to speak.

"The Code is why you're here," he said, so quietly that only Fran could hear him. "The Code is why you came into my place, nothing in your pockets, smelling of the streets and looking for a roof to fly from. You broke their Code, and they broke you."

Fran tried to turn her head, but the warm hand against her neck held her firmly. "You're wrong," she told the empty air. "They had no choice. The Code is necessary. If there were no rules of conduct, no guarantee of confidentiality, the whole profession would die. They couldn't make an exception for me."

"Of course, they couldn't," Marty murmured, his mouth close against her ear. "Much better to kick you out and pretend you never existed. But after all, what did you expect? Pity? Flexibility? From a group of robots who spend their lives repeating other people's thoughts?"

That touched a nerve not quite dead. She pulled out of the chair.

"You don't know what the hell you're talking about," she spat, fueled by anger and frustration. "Interpreting isn't just repetition. It's an art, a way of communication, something you can't . . ."

A noisy group of students pushed their way into the bar, calling for drinks and whistling at the prosties. Fran's energy suddenly drained away, leaving her tired and apathetic. She slumped against the table, hugging herself against the sudden chill. "Never mind," she muttered.

Marty smiled at his customers and draped an arm around Fran's shoulder. "Be right with you," he called. "Got a pastit here who needs some medical attention."

He steered her to her futon, handed her the pill and watched approvingly as she took the tablet and swallowed it.

"Don't worry about it," he told her. "You do what I say, and I'll make sure you've got food, a dry place to sleep, and enough Starlight to keep you from hitting the ground. And I don't have a code to break."

The damp mist that signalled the end of summer had hit Downtown early. A few minutes before time, Fran edged wearily out of Marty's and stood, shivering, next to the entryway. Too nervous to face solid food, she had quickly gulped down some thick protein mixture in order to have something in her stomach for the night's work, but she was still not sure whether it would stay there.

The stores that lined the narrow commercial street were just beginning to close. Directly across the way, the proprietor of a clothing shop that specialized in used uniforms and other oddities had just hit the security shield, producing a vague glow that bounced off the gathering mist. The hard padded walkway muffled all footsteps efficiently, so that the street had a lonely, rather dangerous feel in spite of the occasional passerby.

Fran pushed her hands into her pockets, mentally running over all the old guidelines. Luckily, her clothing was dark and plain enough to provide proper contrast. Her loose sleeves had given her a few uneasy moments until she managed to beg a couple of pins from Michel and fastened the material tightly to her wrists.

Who do you think you're kidding? she finally asked herself. For the past three years, you haven't been within shouting distance of Deaf crew. You haven't conversed in Sign or played with Sign or even thought about Sign . . .

But that was untrue. Even when Starlight sent her soaring, even when the world vibrated and broke apart into scintillating crystals, she sometimes spoke to herself in complete images that had no sound, but whose texture she could feel through her fingers and face. Sign was ingrained into whatever was left of Fran Levi, and she was not yet free of it.

"Fran?"

Startled, Fran squinted out into the darkness at the small figure who had approached while she was lost in her own head. "Raul? Hey, how you doing?"

Raul hunched his shoulders up against the chill and joined her by the wall. "Not bad. Not bad at all. Got a job since you made it into Marty's. A good one too — pays big, little danger."

There was still no sign of her client. Fran slid down until she was seated on the ground; she embraced her knees and stared out into the street. "Nice going. Wish I could do as well."

"You could."

Fran swung her head around. "Don't bull me, Raul. I'm glad you're finally in with the Corp — it is the Corp, right? — but we both know they don't take in pastits. This is as good as I get."

"Agreed." Raul smoothed down his dark, thick hair. "But occasionally my employers — who represent a certain powerful faction of the Corp — need a favor. And they appreciate favors."

"From me? You've got to be kidding."

The man grinned tightly. He put a hand on her shoulder and leaned over until their faces were only inches apart.

"Listen," he whispered. "This Deaf pilot you're interpreting for — don't interrupt, it doesn't matter how I know — do you know what he wants you for?"

Fran shook her head.

"He's intercepted some information, or rather, his hack's intercepted some information, about a politician in whom my employers have a controlling interest. Financial information. Do you understand so far?"

He didn't wait for her to answer. "He is selling this information to an . . . independent operator . . . who has ambitions. And who is, temporarily, out of my employers' reach."

The hand tightened.

"It would be of great help if you were to . . . make a

few mistakes while interpreting for this pilot. So that the information is not transmitted quite accurately."

"Don't be ridiculous," Fran hissed tightly. "His hack is Hearing. She has some Sign — she'll know something's wrong."

"She's going to stay on their ship." A corner of Raul's mouth twitched. "Whoever your client is, he's not an idiot. He's due back at the ship at a certain time. If he doesn't show, if he has an 'accident,' she calls to any outbound craft. And you know what that means."

Fran knew quite well. Interdiction.

Before discovery of the Jump sent Earth's populations streaming toward the stars, its Deaf communities continued to occupy their traditional place in the Hearing world. Isolated within their own culture and language, closed out of the burgeoning technical marketplace by prejudice and lack of training facilities, the few who made it into higher positions pushed desperately for sparse public funding to improve their schools and pay for Interpreters. When space flight started to become viable and the first commercial enterprises pushed past the atmosphere, Deaf technicians fought for their percentage of the new jobs — unsuccessfully. After all, reasoned the corporate personnel managers, what if there were an emergency? They couldn't hear the alarms, couldn't use the radios — obviously, there was no place for the hearing impaired in space.

Until the scientists who perfected the Jump discovered why ships were continually being lost during what should have been clean operations. Although computers handled all of the exacting mathematics involved in entering and emerging from the "fold" that was created in space, although the human mind perceived no time difference from the beginning of the Jump to the end, something about it affected the inner ear. Badly.

Dizzy, disoriented, numb with pain, crewmembers would be suddenly unable to handle the normal functions of their ships for hours at a time. Even when the computers were programmed to handle operations until the crew was once again capable, it was obvious that they could not expect to operate safely with ships full of incapacitated people. Doctors tried drugs, hypnosis, biofeedback. Nothing worked.

Until they crewed the ships with men and women whose

inner ears had already been destroyed. Deaf crews.

The corporations came to the Deaf communities, job lists in hand. We have jobs for you after all, said the personnel managers. Isn't that wonderful?

Very nice, answered the Deaf community politely through its Interpreters. We'll be happy to crew your ships. For a price.

Within a generation, all the intersystem routes were run by a strong Deaf hierarchy that had slowly gained controlling interests in the companies that administered the ships. Interplanetary trade and travel was maintained totally through the Deaf organizations. Military and enforcement authorities, unwilling to concede any power to civilians, originally sought legislation to draft all hearing-impaired eighteen-year-olds for two years of service, but changed their minds when all trade shut down for a month. Now they, along with the corporate community, hired pilots and primary crew on a contract basis. For the first time in human history, the Deaf held power — and they used it carefully and effectively.

The Deaf crews who ran civilization's space lanes were particularly intolerant of any harm coming to members of their culture — even independent operators. If Lee sent word that Stu had been injured or killed, all space travel to Oppenheimer IV would immediately cease — until a standing committee that handled such matters was satisfied either that his death was an accident, or that the offenders were suitably punished. Or until the planet, strangled by short-ages and economic collapse, died.

Fran stared into the evening. "You know this pilot can lipread."

"Who told you that? His hack?" Raul snorted. "If he's so damn good at lipreading, why's he paying a Downtown pastit to do his talking for him?"

She shrugged. "How much would I get for my cooperation?"

"You'd be suitably recompensed. And you would avoid the problems that might occur should you not go along."

"Damn it, Raul . . ."

The man raised his head alertly, revealing a small transmitter attached to the back of his ear. "I think your customer is coming," he said, and stared at her seriously.

"Fran, look. Forget my job. Forget payment. Take my advice — as a friend. Don't make life harder than it has to be. You don't owe anything to this pilot — but the Corp controls your life."

Fran sat still for a moment, thinking. Then she shook her head, grinned and touched his cheek lightly. "Don't worry, Raul," she whispered. "I know who my friends are."

He reached up, and squeezed her hand. Then without another word, he walked quickly down the street.

Fran stood, resigned. Hell with it, she thought. If the Corp wanted her to falsify her interpreting, she'd do it. She'd have to. There wasn't really anything to consider.

She waited.

The man was tall, his details obscured by the gathering darkness. He stopped when he was still several feet away, obviously wishing to verify Fran's identity. His hands moved.

Unexpectedly, something clicked inside Fran's brain. She stepped back so that the lights illuminating the front of the bar would encompass her, and let her hands carve language in the chilly air.

SORRY. LIGHT BAD, YOUR SIGN NOT-SEEN. AGAIN, PLEASE?

He moved closer, into the light. Absently, Fran noted brown eyes set deeply under thick, dour eyebrows and lank brown hair, pulled back at the nape of the neck. He wore a clean, loose-fitting jumpsuit of the sort preferred by working pilots planetside and stared back at her with the direct, unabashed gaze of those whose communication skills were based in sight. Who couldn't afford to cater to Hearings' need to gaze politely off-center.

F-R-A-N L-E-V-I?

She nodded.

INTERPRET BEFORE WHERE YOU?

The question was hostile and Fran's stomach was still rebelling, but she felt more relaxed, more at home, than she had since . . . She felt her body freeing itself from the restraints that verbal speech held on it; her face crinkled into a wry grin.

BEFORE MY BUSINESS. INTERPRET ME CAN, ENOUGH FOR YOU. WANT TEST?

Each word a symbol, a sign, a structure of meaning built from the position and movement of the hands. Each subtle intonation a shift in the set of the body, in the movement of the eyebrows. Language and dance merged into one complete whole.

God, she had missed it.

The man stared at her for a beat, then grinned back. OKAY. TRUST YOU MUST. BUT I TELL YOU, LIPREAD CAN. SEE WRONG SIGN, WRONG SPEECH, TROUBLE-LARGE. UNDERSTAND?

UNDERSTAND.

He nodded. OKAY. S-T-U M-C-D-E-R-M-O-T-T ME, NAME-SIGN STU (the letter "S" tapped lightly on the side of the head indicating knowledge, a common name-sign for a pilot). YOU?

Fran shrugged. NAME-SIGN NONE. LOST LONG-AGO. DOESN'T-MATTER.

DOESN'T-MATTER? His eyelids drooped slightly, deliberately provocative. OKAY, FINE. FRAN. (The letter "F" tapped against the upper arm. The sign for an injected drug.)

Fuck you, Fran thought. You think I don't know what I am? She shrugged again, her face bland and unmoved. HURRY. WILL LATE.

As Fran strode alongside the pilot, she stared at his profile thoughtfully. There had been something wrong with his Sign. No, not wrong — different. At first, she thought that she had simply become unused to the language, had lost some of her familiarity. But that wasn't it. Perhaps an accent? Some new affectation that had come into fashion since she left?

And what the hell was he doing out here anyway? All reasonably competent Deaf crewmembers were assured of well-paying berths the moment they hit the job market, and skilled Deaf pilots could write their own ticket. If this Stu was halfway good at his job, there was no good reason for him to be wandering around a backwater slum hiring decertified Interpreters.

Fran shrugged mentally, and placed the puzzle at the back of her mind. Her client's motives were none of her business. Anyway, right now it was more important to stay alert.

Dusk quickly passed into night. Most of the shops had already closed, and the streets glowed with their security screens. The planet's short night ensured that most of

Downtown's underground economy was conducted in the twilight of the late afternoon; it was only those transactions not privately condoned by the authorities that took place after dark. Fran wondered what she had gotten herself into — and whether it was worth the fee she had agreed to take.

Stu obviously had visited Downtown before; he strode unerringly through the maze of streets and into the square. The marketplace was nearly empty; most of its business had been completed, and the unfortunates who had not managed to sell either their goods or themselves were beginning to drift off, trying to find someplace to spend the night. One couple, their arms twined around each other for companionship or warmth, called out to Fran; she nodded at them but didn't answer. They grinned back, obviously in the belief that she had found herself a well-paying client for the night. They weren't, she thought, that far wrong.

The pilot walked across the square and into a small side street that, Fran knew, held some of the major drug distributors for the City. These were powerful people, most working on behalf of legitimate City politicians and corporations. The storefronts here were deceptively modest, even bedraggled; Fran had heard rumors of the elegant office suites and living quarters that they hid. But she had never dared to even walk down the street — as a bottomline pastit, she knew better.

The back of her neck prickled as they approached a small, unimpressive storefront near the end of the alley. They were certainly being carefully watched. Fran fervently hoped that this Stu knew what he was doing. If anyone got nervous about his presence, they wouldn't stop to ask why she was there with him.

When they reached their destination, they stopped and stood, waiting. No words needed to be exchanged; they wouldn't have been there unless they were invited. The dark, glowing entry suddenly dulled as the security field was turned off. They stepped in.

And squinted. After the dark alley, the well-lit interior was nearly blinding. Suddenly anxious that she would be ready for the first word spoken, and knowing that her addiction had sensitized her to light, Fran fought to clear her vision.

Luckily, she and the pilot were its only occupants. It

was, as she had suspected, expensively and tastefully furnished: well-chosen holographic repros of famous sculptures lined the walls, comfortable chairs were scattered about, surrounding a low table that held a few readers and some small bowls. Fran's breath caught in her throat and she peered at the dishes in a confused welter of hope and fear. She had heard that distributors often offered samples of Starlight to guests the way most hosts offered food. Fran knew that her life was worth very little here if she fouled up, but logic had nothing to do with the craving that suddenly clutched at her stomach. The bowls held only small, hard candies.

There was a sound at the back of the room, and the two turned, Stu moving only slightly slower than his Hearing companion. A carefully coiffed young man barely out of his teens approached through one of the repros and smiled cordially at them. He wore a loose, gaily colored robe that shimmered slightly as he walked; Fran found the effect chillingly reminiscent of flytime dreams.

But that had to be ignored now. Her hand went automatically to the place over her heart where the small badge had once been pinned. An Interpreter's badge displayed the profession's double helix symbol over the ship's colors; when touched, the sensitive metal faded to a dark hue, the darker helix only slightly visible. That change indicated that its bearer was in Interpreter mode and no longer an individual responsible for her own thoughts and words. She had become a conduit through which her clients' conversation passed, to be translated from verbal language to Sign and back again. She was permitted no interruptions (except to ask for a clarification), no opinions, no use of the first person to indicate her own existence. And, according to the Code, no memory of the conversation.

Fran's badge had been removed, with little ceremony, right after her expulsion from the Guild, but old instincts died hard. She quickly pulled her hand back, but not before Stu noted the movement. Now he knew she had been a shipboard Interpreter. A professional.

Well, she thought defiantly, at least he'd find out that she was a damn good one. She composed her face and walked over to the young man, standing slightly at his side, facing Stu. Their host watched her approach calmly, his curiosity evident.

Stu waved out a quick, irritated sentence, pulling the man's attention back from Fran. "Never mind her," Stu told him, "I'm the one you're dealing with."

The young man smiled.

"Of course," he said. Fran's hands worked. "My name is Jerem, and I am the proprietor of this establishment. Thank you for coming."

"Stu McDermott, pilot of the independent tradeship *Beethoven*," Stu answered.

"Interesting name," Jerem commented. He swept a manicured hand toward the group of chairs. "Please, sit."

He dropped comfortably into one corner of a low couch. Stu, after a moment's hesitation, pulled a chair over until it faced Jerem directly. Fran waited until they had both settled themselves, then sat on the couch a few inches from Jerem.

The young man offered one of the dishes to Stu, who shook his head. "I am, of course, aware of the rules of conduct concerning Interpreters," Jerem continued, replacing the bowl. "However, I am a bit surprised that a man as obviously savvy as yourself would hire a pastit who'd sell herself, her friends, and her mother for a two-hour flight. Not exactly the most trustworthy Interpreter you could choose — especially for these delicate matters."

The man's gaze didn't shift from the pilot, but his words were obviously meant for Fran. Stu knew it, too. He smiled politely back.

"I am quite aware of my Interpreter's qualifications," Stu said smoothly through Fran. "I am also aware of the influence that your associates have with many of the businesses on this planet. I decided that I'd be more comfortable with an independent operator."

Jerem nodded politely. "Perhaps. But it is my duty as your host to make you aware that your 'independent' Interpreter was ejected from her Guild in disgrace about three years ago for a rather serious violation of their Code. I believe it had something to do with repeating an interpreted conversation." He raised his eyebrows. "Are you sure you wouldn't like to hire someone a bit more reliable? We have several quite reputable agencies in the City who would be happy to let you verify their standing with the Guild."

Fran interpreted without a pause. Jerem obviously suspected that his enemies had gotten to her, and was trying to replace her with someone he could trust. At the very least, he probably hoped that, by indirectly taunting the Interpreter, he would enrage or embarrass her enough to make her step out of her role — forcing Stu to accept a substitute.

But that would not happen. At this moment in time, Fran didn't care what Jerem said. She had found the center of calm and efficiency that she had been trained in years ago and that formed the base of her persona as a professional Interpreter. It meant that nothing that any of her clients could say, about either herself or anything else, could touch her. In effect, Fran Levi didn't exist. The woman who had tried to submerge her disgrace and failure in a bright narcotic universe had been replaced by an Interpreter. Who spoke and listened with her voice, her hands, her ears, her eyes. Who took into herself a sentence, drew mean- ing and purpose from the words, and then returned it transformed but still whole. Who enabled two cultures to communicate.

Nothing else mattered.

She finished, and waited.

Stu stared at her for a moment. Then, slowly and deliberately, he shifted his gaze to the young man and began to sign.

"I appreciate the advice," Stu said. "But I think we have more important things to discuss than my choice of an Interpreter."

The man shrugged, and carefully smoothed the front of his robe. "Whatever you say. Shall we begin?"

The discussion seemed to race by, as though both men were equally impatient to get the whole thing over with. Fran absorbed the gist of the talk while her mind raced to keep the conversation moving, to replace the words as new ones were said, were signed.

Lee had, explained Stu, in her off hours, intercepted a message in an unfamiliar code. Always open to opportunities, she had spent over a month working on the code, until she had deciphered it. It confirmed that a sizable amount of money had been deposited by the Corp into an account on a neighboring planet. Lee, intrigued, pulled a few strings and determined that the account was in the name of nobody either on that planet or this.

She had persuaded Stu to visit Oppenheimer IV, and had set to work. Luckily, the corruption that pervaded the City had made its way into its computer centers: the hacks that ran the machines were happy to let her play with certain files in return for some vaguely illegal coding.

Lee discovered that the City's Attorney General was overseeing a murder case in which the Corp had some interest. The Attorney General was worried that any interference in the case would make her involvement with the Corp easier to detect and she wanted to hand it over to the Governor's office, under a minor legal point. The Corp, whose hold on the Governor wasn't quite as strong, had established the offplanet account so that the Attorney General could, if any awkward information about her background came to light, comfortably re-establish herself elsewhere.

Jerem was interested. The Attorney General was a powerful figure; it would be a very large feather in Jerem's cap if he could bring the woman down. He would be even more interested if Stu could give him the number of the account. Under what circumstances would that be possible?

The negotiations began. This, Fran knew, was the point at which she should start paying attention to her opportunities. She couldn't fudge on the price Jerem offered for the information; that would be too obvious. Besides, they might still come to some sort of an agreement. But the number of the account would be simple enough to misinterpret. And by the time Jerem discovered the mistake, Stu would be long gone and Jerem would, no doubt, blame the pilot for a bad faith deal. That was it. Of course. And Fran would be back on her futon in Marty's, free and clear. And flying.

Remember, Fran told herself fiercely, you don't owe anything to this pilot and his damn smartmouthed hack. Raul knew what he was talking about — the Corp can cut off your supply, and that means no more flight time, that means watching the world get darker and grayer minute by minute until cutting your throat will seem like a reasonable proposition. You don't have any choice. No choice whatsoever.

She finished interpreting Stu's final offer. Jerem, who had remained as calm throughout the business as if he were discussing the state of the weather, nodded to himself for a moment. "Fine," Jerem finally said. "That seems perfectly agreeable. I assume you wish payment now?"

Stu grinned and seemed to relax slightly. He doesn't like being here, Fran realized. Wonder whose idea this deal was in the first place?

"If that would be convenient," Stu answered easily.

"You realize, of course, that should the information be false, I should be terribly upset."

"That is a chance you are taking." The pilot shrugged. "And the reason that the price is considerably less than the information is worth."

Jerem, without altering a muscle in his face, stood. "I will only be a moment," he said, and disappeared the way he had come.

Stu turned to look at Fran. She touched, this time consciously, the bare place on her shoulder.

THINK YOU WHAT? he asked.

Fran glared at him. The pilot had slumped back comfortably in the padded chair, obviously relieved that the whole affair would soon be over.

NOT MY ROLE she answered irritably. KNOW THAT YOU!

He shrugged. WONDERED. DOESN'T-MATTER.

He glanced around the room restlessly. Fran stared down at the table, mentally rehearsing her role. Jerem would soon be back with payment, and she would have to be ready to change one of the characters of the account identification. One of the middle characters, perhaps. She would increase it one digit — that would be easy to remember . . . .

Oh, hell.

She was an Interpreter. Who, whatever her past was, followed the Code.

No matter what she told herself, Fran would be unable to purposefully misinterpret the conversation. She would, she knew, transmit the correct numbers. And Stu would leave. Jerem would bring down the Attorney General. And Fran would, she had no doubt, die.

Unless, she thought desperately, her failure could be attributed to a lack of opportunity.

She leaned forward and touched his knee lightly.

LISTEN she signed quickly. IMPORTANT.

Stu waited.

DON'T-WANT KNOW ACCOUNT NUMBER she told him, her fingers flying in anxious speed, the gestures small, quick, whispered. MY BUSINESS NONE. WRITE NUMBER.

Stu's eyes narrowed. WHY? he asked. WRONG WHAT?

DOESN'T-MATTER. WRITE NUMBER, GIVE HIM, TELL HIM READ, DESTROY. TELL ME NOTHING. MY BUSINESS NOT. UNDERSTAND?

"Am I interrupting anything?"

Fran jumped and stared up at Jerem, who stood next to her chair, observing her as if she were a child who was suspected of stealing an extra cookie. She swallowed, stood, touched her shoulder, and interpreted his words to Stu.

The pilot seemed unaffected by both Fran's recent demand and Jerem's sudden reappearance. He didn't answer; he simply held out his hand.

Jerem, without pausing, handed him a small safety box. "It's not coded," he said. "You can set the lock yourself."

Stu opened the small drawer and glanced carefully at the contents. Then he closed it, and tapped quickly at the number pad on top of the package. Finished, he glanced up at Jerem.

"Now, about the account number?"

The pilot extended the box in one hand. Jerem looked puzzled for a moment — until he looked down at the small readout. And smiled.

"I see," he said, "you don't trust your Interpreter much more than I do. Wise."

He examined the readout more closely, obviously committing the figures to memory. After about a minute, he nodded. Stu withdrew the box, and, after tapping for a few moments more on the keyboard, slipped it into a pocket.

There was nothing left to be done. Jerem smoothed down his robe with obvious satisfaction. "You know the way out," he said contentedly. "Have a good flight. Both of you," he added, grinning at Fran, who interpreted it without a pause. He turned, and left the room.

Fran watched him leave and then turned back to Stu. The pilot stood, stretched, and in a quick, unexpected gesture, gently touched Fran's shoulder.

FINISHED NOW he told her. COME.

The square was abandoned, except for a few bodies

huddled near the glowing shop doors. Stu headed straight for the fountain and settled himself on the small wall. Fran followed slowly.

Although the fountain had not been used for years, the lights which had been meant to highlight its waters still worked — and probably would until the structure itself fell apart. This did not endear it to most of Downtown's inhabitants, who tended to avoid well-lit areas after dusk. But it obviously made Stu feel a lot more comfortable; he grinned at Fran and patted the stone next to him, offering her a seat.

NOT BAD he told her approvingly. WHEN L-E-E COME, TELL ME SHE HIRE YOU DRUG BAR, I TELL HER SHE CRAZY, FOOL, GO FIND OTHER INTERPRETER. SHE TELL ME, NO TIME, STUCK ME. I THINK SHIT, WHOLE DEAL FAIL, FINISH. THERE, M-A-R-T-Y-S, I MEET YOU, SEE YOU SIGN, THINK MAYBE L-E-E RIGHT. NOW, KNOW. REAL INTERPRETER, YOU. WHY YOU HERE? WHAT HAPPEN WITH GUILD?

None of your business, Fran thought. But she buried her impatience and simply signed YOU HEAR-BEFORE. BREAK RULE.

GOOD REASON YOU?

She shrugged. DOESN'T–MATTER. SECOND CHANCE NONE, FINISHED.

Stu nodded slowly, and his eyes narrowed. UNDER-STAND he answered, his movements sharp, angry. SEE SAME ME LONG-AGO. JOIN ORGANIZATION-LARGE, HAVE POWER-MUCH. IF YOU DIFFERENT, THINK FOR YOUR-SELF, FORGET-IT, SCREW YOU. He glanced at the surrounding trash-strewn square with distaste. BUT WHY HERE?

Fran took a moment to rub her eyes. It was becoming an effort to move, to even think; the world was closing in on her and making too many demands. In the garish light that illuminated the dead fountain, Stu looked like an actor on some small, colorless stage. His hands flickered in complex patterns that were too exhausting to concentrate on.

ENOUGH, she signed wearily, forestalling any further conversation. JOB FINISH. PAY-ME. NOW. She held out her hand.

The pilot peered thoughtfully at her for another moment, his bottom lip caught between his teeth. Then he relaxed, shrugged, and dug a small cashcard out of his pocket.

And paused as her outstretched arm began to tremble. He raised his eyes and stared at her coolly; Fran, annoyed, grabbed the card.

SUGGEST she told him YOU GO SHIP QUICK.

And without another word, she turned and left, running down the darkened streets towards home.

"Hell, Fran, what did you get yourself into the other night? Fran?"

Fran cracked open her eyes and stared up groggily. Marty knelt next to her, one bony finger stabbing at her shoulder. She pushed his hand away impatiently.

"What are you babbling about," she murmured, trying to shake the sleep from her head. She pushed herself up into a sitting position and squinted around the place. The other pastits were still fast asleep; a sliver of orange light had begun to illuminate the bar floor. "Dammit, Marty, I thought I told you . . ."

She stared at the 'tender and a hard, cold knot formed in the pit of her stomach. "Marty, what's wrong?"

He shook his head angrily. "Fran, what is it with you pastits? I can't hold on to one of you long enough to blink. You had it good here. I treated you fairly. Why did you have to blow it?"

"Blow it? Blow what? What did I do?"

"Here." He put a bag into her hand; she held onto it reflexively. "That's breakfast. You'll have to eat it outside; I can't have you here when I open."

They found out. The cold place in her stomach expanded until she began to shiver slightly. "Marty, I tried, I really did, but he didn't let me interpret the number, I didn't get the chance . . . You've got to tell them, it's not my fault . . ."

The man shook his head. "I don't know what you're talking about, and I don't want to," he said intently. "But you've crossed the Corp, and they don't take excuses, you should know that. Especially from pastits. Fran, you've got to leave. Now."

"Okay. Okay." Fran ran a hand through the bristle on her head. "Can I at least use the toilet?"

"Five minutes. Then you've got to be gone. I've got four

groups coming in today; I've got to get ready . . ."

Fran pulled on her boots and stood. She picked up the bag and glanced inside. A sandwich. A drink. That was all.

"Marty?"

He turned.

She simply looked at him. He sighed, and shook his head. "Shit, Fran, I wish I could. But they'd find out. And they've spread the word: you're grounded. Nobody can sell to you. Nobody."

The world turned cold. Starlight's addictive qualities were predominantly neurological: a substance-starved brain would quickly founder in hallucinatory depression until thirst, starvation, or exposure took its toll. She didn't have much time.

"Marty, for god's sake." She dropped the bag and moved toward him, her hands digging frantically in her pockets. "I've got gelt. See, I've got a cashcard worth 35; I'll give you the whole damn thing, just for one day's worth. Oh, for god's *sake*, Marty!"

"Fran, I'm sorry. Really." Marty reached over, and squeezed her arm sympathetically. She pulled away.

"Go use the toilet," he sighed. "Then you've got to get out of here."

Fran went to all her old contacts, including a few whom she wouldn't have spat at in the old days. Everywhere it was the same: the Corp wanted her grounded for what remained of her life — if she got even a single tablet from anyone anywhere, they'd find out who it was and extend the ban. It was that simple. Even Raul seemed to be avoiding her; the prostie who had taken over her old corner said he hadn't been seen for a couple of days.

After hours of wandering desperately through Downtown, Fran finally ended up across the street from the small two-story structure that served as the area's Guild hall. She had come with the vague idea of appealing to the Guild for help, for a job, for something to keep her going. But once there, she lost the will to enter.

She shivered and squinted at the bright double helix above the doorway. Few people came and left; there wasn't much call for interpreting services Downtown. Fran was finding it increasingly hard to concentrate. Instead, she began to wonder what had happened to the thin, anxious man who — was it really three years ago? — begged a Deaf crewmember to help him commit suicide. He was ill, he said, and tired of pain. He wanted the medical technician to "accidentally" overdose him with the drug provided to Hearing passengers during Jump.

Fran leaned against the wall behind her, ignoring the protests of an irritated store owner. She had disliked the man even before she met him, for waking her halfway into her sleep cycle for an emergency job. She began to hate him during the conversation for the way he kept staring at her and talking to her, ignoring the etiquette of interpreting. She hated him even more for sending her out of that room caught between breaking the confidentiality rule or letting a stranger die. But she despised him for his weakness in being unable to take his own life.

"I understand," she whispered to him now. "I couldn't do it either."

Depression pressed down on her like a stone. Perhaps, Fran thought, I should have tried to buy something quick from the last peddler I hit. He might have sold me that. If I had the courage to use it.

Somebody — the storekeeper? — pushed her away from the wall, screaming at her with meaningless intensity. Fran stumbled away, clutching at irritated pedestrians, unable to see through the hideous glare of the afternoon. The light cut into her head, making it impossible to think. All she wanted to do was sit and rest, but every time she stopped, hands would pull her up, force her to move on. It was as if she were being buffeted by a bright, rough sea, and no longer had the strength to swim.

Until she finally found herself curled inside an abandoned doorway, staring listlessly out at a narrow alleyway. Pain became an abstract concept, part of a body she no longer controlled. The street lost whatever color it may have possessed. Reality was a two-dimensional cartoon of blinding white and gray tones in which flat people-like creatures occasionally passed. Time ground to a halt. Everything took on a malign sameness, which would go on forever and ever and ever and ever and ever and ever . . .

There was hot liquid in her mouth. It had no taste,

but it was food, and she was hungry. She swallowed it reflexively. Some sort of cup was placed against her lips, and she swallowed again.

The cup was withdrawn.

Fran blinked, opened her eyes, and tried to focus.

The alley had disappeared. She was propped up on something considerably more comfortable than the doorway in a place that was considerably dryer. There was a ceiling over her head that curved slightly in a familiar fashion; directly ahead, she could see the tiny cubicle that, she knew, held toilet and washup facilities. Crew quarters.

Something moved at the edge of her vision. She turned her head. The pilot.

Fran stared at him with a sort of passive curiosity. He looked washed out, as though she were watching an old historical tape in which the colors had faded until they were barely discernible. It was too much of an effort to wonder where he came from; she lay limply back against the pillow and waited.

Stu signed to her, but it didn't mean anything. Somewhere inside her brain, she knew, the signs were being automatically registered and understood, but at the moment she wasn't capable of making the connection. And didn't much care. She closed her eyes.

"Look at me, damn it!"

A male voice. Too loud, uninflected, but undeniable.

She looked. Stu glared at her, his mild face contorted with anger. "Yes, I can talk," he said clearly. Too clearly for somebody who had learned to speak solely through the feel of the words. Suddenly Fran realized why his Sign had struck her as strange and, at the same time, familiar. He signed like an Interpreter. Like somebody fluent in a foreign language. The *Beethoven*'s Deaf pilot had been neither born, nor raised, Deaf.

This interesting development was enough to push her into a semblance of alertness. She watched as he sat at the foot of her bunk.

"We had a visitor yesterday," he told her in the flattened tones of a man who can no longer hear his own voice. "Called himself Raul. Said you had been ordered to falsify the account number when I gave it to you. Said that the organization that runs this place found out the number passed was correct. Said that you were cut off from your drug supply."

He leaned forward. "Listen. This is a small cargo operation. I own and pilot this ship; Lee hacks. We do enough to get by. I'm a legitimate freelancer — I've got no ties with the main trade associations, but I stay away from anything real illegal. Lee knows enough Sign to get by on ship, but for outside negotiations we need a good Interpreter we can trust. And who will take on gofer duties during flight. What you don't know about ship work, we'll teach you. And you'll get a fair percentage of the cut."

He stood.

"Don't want your answer now; you're obviously in no condition. But if you decide to sign on, you leave your habit planetside. You need medical help to kick, fine, but that's it. And I want a professional. Don't know why you broke the rules, and I don't particularly care. But when you work for me, you follow the Code. You have any problem with what I say, you're free to tell me — when you're off duty.

"That's it. Think about it."

Fran watched as he walked to the narrow exit and wondered how a man who remembered sound had managed to fit into the strong culture of the Deaf crews. Probably, she thought wryly, he hadn't. Functionally Deaf but psychologically Hearing — no wonder he had gone independent.

She swallowed, conscious of the uneasy feeling in her stomach and the gray mist that still clung to the edges of her vision. Although she had passed through the worst of the withdrawal, Fran knew that it would be a long time before the taste of Starlight was out of her system. But her head was clear. And she could feel the Signs twitching at her fingers.

Stu turned, making a final check of the cabin. Fran took a deep breath, concentrated, and managed to move her right hand until it fanned out, thumb side down, from the center of her chest.

FINE.

The pilot nodded at the incomplete gesture, satisfied.

"Fine," he said.

A Token for Celandine

•

Laurell K. Hamilton

The prophet was an old man crazed with his own visions. He crouched against the dark wood of an elm. His fingers dug into the bark as if he would anchor himself to it. He gasped and wheezed as he drew in the morning air.

We had been chasing him through these woods for three days. And I was tired of it. If he ran this time, I was going to put an arrow in his leg. Celandine could heal him of the wound, and she could finally ask her question. I had not mentioned my plan to the healer. I thought she might object.

The old man looked into a bar of dazzling sunlight. The glow showed his eyes milky with the creeping blindness of the very old and the very poor.

He was sick, blind, and crazy, and he had eluded me for days.

His prophecy protected him or perhaps the voices he called out to told him I was near.

He turned his head to one side as if he were listening. I heard nothing but the wind and a small animal scuttling in the brush.

He turned his blind eyes and looked directly at me. The flesh along my back crawled. He could not see me, but I knew he did.

His voice was an abused cackle that never seemed to finish a thought completely. I had listened to him rant, but now he spoke low and well. "Ask," he said.

It was Celandine's question, but while he was in the mood to answer, I asked. Not all prophets are able to answer direct questions. Those that do tend to answer only one question for each person.

"How do I find the token which Celandine the Healer seeks?"

"The black road must take. Demons help you. Fight

in darkness you will."

I heard the whisper of cloth that announced the healer. She came up beside me, white cloak huddled round her body.

Without taking my eyes from the old man I asked, "Did you hear what he said?"

"Yes."

"Ask him something."

"Where is the token I seek?"

"Demon, demon inside." He coughed, his body nearly doubled over with the violence of it. Bloody foam flecked his chin. Celandine stepped forward. "Let me heal you."

His eyes went wide. "Death want, death seek, no heal." And he was gone vanishing into the underbrush noiseless as a rabbit.

Celandine stood there, tears glistening in her eyes. "He'll die."

"He wants to die."

She shook her head, and one tear drop slid from crystalline blue eyes down flawless white cheek. "He doesn't know what he's saying."

I touched her arm. "Celandine, no healer can cure the madness of prophecy."

She nodded and pulled the cloak's hood to hide her face. A strand of black hair trailed across the white cloth like a stain.

I said, "This is the seventh prophet, Celandine. We must trust the information and act upon it."

She spoke in a low voice that I had to strain to hear. "Aren't you afraid, Bevhinn?"

I debated with myself whether she wanted truth or for me to be strong for her. I decided on truth. "I fear the black healers of Lolth. I fear being a female trapped behind their dark border."

"And yet you will go?"

"It is where our quest takes us. We must go."

She turned to me, face framed in shadowed hood. "It is death by torture for me if I am caught."

I had heard the stories of what Loltuns did to white healers. They were tales to curdle the blood round winter fires.

"I will die before I let them take you. You have my word."

She spun round as if she would find an answer in the

spring morning.

"I have your word." She turned back to me, blue eyes hard. "What good is your word? You aren't human. You don't worship the Goddess that I serve. Why should I trust you to give your life for me?"

I clamped a six-fingered hand 'round sword hilt. Five months I'd traveled with her. Five months of living off the land, killing that we both could eat. I had slain winter-starved wolves and fought bandits. I had guarded her back while she healed the sick. I had been wounded twice, and twice she had healed me.

And now this.

I let the anger flow into my face. I stared at her with my alien purple eyes, but I kept my voice low with menace. I had no desire to shout and bring men or a wild beast upon us. "Your fear makes you foolish, Celandine. But do not fear. Your father paid me well to guard you on this exile's quest."

"You sell yourself for money like some harlot."

I slapped her hard, and she fell to the ground. She looked startled. I had never offered her violence before. "Your father bought my sword, my magic, and my loyalty. I will lay down my life to protect you, but I will not be insulted."

"How dare you. I am a white healer . . ."

I finished for her, "And bastard daughter of the King of Celosia. I know all that. He hired me, remember."

"You are my bodyguard, my servant."

"I'm not the reason we're out here in this godforsaken wilderness. You killed a man. You took that pure white gift of yours and twisted it. You used black healing and took a life."

She was crying now, softly.

"The only way to end this exile is to follow the prophet's advice and go to Lolth."

"I'm afraid."

I grabbed her upper arms, pulling her to her feet. "I'm afraid, too, but I want this over with. I want to go back to Meltaan. I want a bed and a bath and decent food. I want someone to guard my back for a change." I let her go, and she stumbled back, sobbing.

"I will not let your fear keep me out here forever. Your father didn't pay me that much."

"You can't leave me."

"I could, but I won't. But tomorrow we travel the dark road."

Morning found us on the bank of Lake Muldor. A blue cloak to match her eyes replaced the healer's cloak Celandine usually wore. She kept it pulled close around her though it was very warm for spring.

The sun was warm on my face. The light shattered diamond bursts off the lake water and the silver of my armor. I had bound my breasts tight under the scale mail. I was counting on the fact that most humans think male Varellians look effeminate. And that they would look at sword and armor and think me male.

Celandine would simply go as my wife. It was rare, but it was done. That would explain my exile. The problem was that we both stood out. We could not simply blend with what few travelers there were.

Celandine was too aware of her royal heritage to play the common wife. She had no talent for lying or being false. I could have wasted magic to disguise myself as human, but it wouldn't have been safe. I was earth-witch, not illusionist, and disguise was not one of my better spells.

So I rode as a Varellian. My hair was spun snow with a purity of color that few humans achieved. The hair could have been dyed, the odd-shaped ears hidden, but a sixth finger was something else. It was considered a mark of good fortune in Varell but not among the humans. And of course my eyes gave me away. Purple as a violet, the color of a grape.

We were not your usual traveling couple. I rode a unicorn, which was very hard to hide. The unicorns of Varell are as big as a war horse. They were the mounts of royalty and of the royal guard. Once a unicorn and a rider were bound, it is a life-long binding. So through no fault of his own, Ulliam shared my exile among the humans and the horses.

But he also shared my magic, though he can only feel it and not perform it. His great split hooves danced on the damp meadow grass. The earth-magic of spring was calling. My power was tied to the ground and that which sprang from it. Every meadow flower, every blade of grass, was hidden power for my magic. My power called to other things. I shared the joy of the swallow as it turned and twisted over the lake. I froze in the long grass with the rabbit waiting for our horses to pass. Spring was one of the most powerful times for an earth-witch, as winter was one of the worst.

And Ulliam danced with me on his back, feeling the power. I hoped I would not need it.

Celandine rode silently, blue cloak pulled over a plain brown dress. Visions of torture still danced behind her eyes. Her fear was an almost palpable thing.

She rode one horse and carried the lead for a second. She would need a fresh mount if we were to make good time. I would have liked to rest Ulliam, but war horses were not easily found in the wild lands. I would not ride less. You could not fight off the back of a normal riding horse.

The clang of metal, the swinging shield, even drawing bow and arrow, could send a horse racing in fright. And you couldn't afford that in battle. A war steed had to be trained to it from birth; there was just no other way. Ulliam and I had been trained together. No other mount could have known my mind as he did.

I had used magic to make him less noticeable. Most would see a great white horse and nothing more. If a wizard concentrated, then perhaps he would see past the glamour, but it was the best I could do. In Lolth they sacrificed unicorns to Verm and Ivel.

I asked Celandine, "Have you ever worshipped Ivel?"

She made the sign against evil, thumb and little finger extended near her face. "Don't use her full name."

"As you like. Have you ever worshipped Mother Bane?"

"Of course, you must not ignore any of the three faces of the Great Mother."

I didn't argue theology with her. We had found we did not agree on matters of worship. "You've never spoken of Mother Bane as one of your Gods."

"Because it is not wise to do so."

"Why do the Loltuns sacrifice women to Her altar?"

"It is a matter of theological interpretation."

"Interpretation?"

"Yes." She seemed reluctant to speak further so I let the subject drop. Celandine was not happy that I could argue her into a corner using her own sacred tomes. The black road erupted from the damp meadow grass without marker or warning. It seemed to be made of solid rock, black as if the earth had bled. Legend said that Pelrith of the Red Eye forged the road. And seeing it lying there on the shore of the lake, I believed in demigods calling things forth from the earth.

I urged Ulliam forward.

The moment his hooves hit the road, I felt it. The road was dead; no earth-magic sang through it. The horse Celandine was leading shied at the black surface. I moved Ulliam to calm it before the horse she was riding could bolt as well. We rode into Lolth three abreast with the skittish horse in the middle.

I noticed bumps in the smooth surface of the road, but there was no pattern to them. I dismounted and walked Ulliam until I came to a bump that seemed higher than the others. I knelt and ran a mailed hand over the blackened lump. My eyes could not puzzle it out at first, then suddenly, it was clear. A human skull gaped from the road, barely covered in the black rock-like stuff. And I could not force the image from my mind.

Celandine called, "What is it?"

"Bones. Human bones."

She made the sign against evil again.

I mounted Ulliam, and we rode on. My eyes were drawn with a horrible fascination to each half hidden shape as we rode. We traveled on the burial mound of hundreds.

We came to the border guard then. There were only four of them, but two shone magic to my eyes. And I knew that I shined as well. But there was nothing illegal about being a wizard; at least I didn't think there was. A female wizard might have been stopped, but healers do not shine like wizards. Celandine would seem merely a woman until she healed someone. When she laid hands, she glowed like the full moon.

One man came from behind the wooden gate. He stood in front of me. "Well, you must be an ice elf."

It was a rather rude way to begin, but I had been prepared for that. It was a killing insult in Varell, but I had been five years from there. It wasn't the first time someone had called me 'elf' to my face. It would not be the last. "I am Bevhinn Ailir, and this is my wife Celandine."

His eyes turned to the healer, and he said, "Oh, she's a beauty." He walked over to her and put a hand on her knee, massaging it. Celandine glared at him.

The hand began to creep up her thigh, and she yanked her horse backwards. It bumped the man, and he backed away smiling. He said, "You could make money off of this one. She would bring a fair price every night you stay in our country."

"She is a wife, not a whore."

He shrugged.

"There isn't that much difference, now, is there?"

"There is where I come from."

"Yes, the Varellians and their reverence for females. You and your queen."

I had had about enough of this. "Can we pass, or must we stand here and be insulted?"

He frowned at that and said, "I'd keep that fancy armor hidden. There are those who would take it from you."

I smiled at him, forcing him to stare into my alien eyes. "It is good armor, but surely men aren't eager to die for a suit of armor they would never fit into."

He returned the smile and said, "I would love to see one of your Varellian women. You're pretty enough to eat yourself."

I said, voice low, "Your two friends over there can tell you I'm a wizard. And this wizard has grown very tired of you." I flexed a hand for dramatic emphasis, and he backed away. Truth was an earth-witch wasn't big on instant magic, but they didn't know that. With my power tied to the spring, I sparkled like a sorcerer. It was a good time of year to bluff.

The gate opened, and he called after us, "May you run afoul of a black healer."

I answered back over my shoulder, "And may the next wizard you torment blow your head off."

Forest stretched on either side of the road. The birds and beasts didn't know they had crossed a border. In truth it looked much like the wild lands where we had spent the winter, except for the road.

Farm land opened on either side of the road, fighting back the trees. the smell of fresh plowed earth was strong and good. The soil was a rich black. I felt an urge to crumble the dirt in my hands and feel its growing power, but I resisted. Ulliam danced nervously under me.

Forest returned, hugging each side of the road. But no

blade of grass, no wild flower, dared to encroach upon the black road. It was late in the day when we heard a loud cracking noise, like a cannon ball striking wood. The horses pranced in fright, and even Ulliam shivered under me. There was a tearing sound, as if the earth itself was being pulled apart. We rode cautiously towards the sounds.

A wide path had been freshly cleared from the forest. Trees with jagged trunks lay in heaps on their side. Stumps lay in a second heap, earth-covered roots bare to the sky.

Stooping to pull another great stump from the ground was a demon. His skin was night black. Muscles bulged along his back and arms. His ribbed bat ears curled tight with his effort as he strained upwards. The roots ripped free of the earth. He put the stump in the pile with the rest. He caught sight of us on the road, and we all stared at each other. A silver necklace glittered round his neck. The cold eye of a diamond the size of a hen's egg winked out from it. From here it glowed with magic.

Celandine looked at me. Was this our demon's help, or was the token inside the demon? I hoped it wasn't the latter. I didn't see myself slitting the gullet of a greater demon. A man stepped out of the trees. He was thin, and a scraggly beard edged his pointed chin. He said, "Be on your way. You're distracting him."

"I am sorry, good farmer, but I have never seen a greater demon before."

A look of incredulity passed over his face. "You swear by Loth's bloody talons that you've never seen a greater demon?"

"I swear."

He smiled then, friendly. "Well, you have started out with a higher demon named Krakus. He's been ensorcelled to the farmers here about for over fifty years. He's cleared most of the fields along this road."

I stared at the demon and there was something in his smooth yellow eyes that said *hatred*. A hatred deeper than anything I could feel.

"Good farmer, are you never afraid of him breaking free?"

"No, the enchantment on him is strong enough."

"What would happen if he ever was freed?"

The farmer looked back at the demon, the smile gone.

"Why, he'd kill me and everyone else he'd worked for."

"Where do you keep the demon when he's not working? Does he go back to the pits from which he came?"

The man found the question very funny. "Why, you don't know anything about demons. An ensorcelled demon can't leave the place he's been put, just can't leave. We keep him chained at night near where he's working."

I shivered under the gaze of those sullen yellow eyes. "I hope you keep a guard on him at night, farmer."

"Oh, we do, but nothing to worry about. He'll still be pulling stumps fifty years from now." The farmer walked back into the cleared area and slapped the demon lightly on the arm. "No, we couldn't lose such a good worker. Get back to work, Krakus." The demon turned without a word, or a snarl, and stood before a full grown tree. With one gesture and a flash of sorcery he felled the tree, blasting it off a few feet above the ground.

The farmer went to sit in the sunshine. Our interview was over.

Celandine and I rode in silence for a short time, then she asked, "Do you think that is the demon who will help us?"

"I don't know."

"You don't know. Then what are we doing here? What good is prophecy if you don't know what it means?"

"None, I suppose."

"Then what are we risking ourselves for?"

I grabbed the reins of her horse and said, "The only way to understand prophecy is to do what it says. Now stop sniveling."

She glared at me but kept her peace. Her fear kept her silent more than I did.

Twilight had fallen, spreading a blue haze across the trees. An inn sat in a small clearing. In the dim light I made out a sign. It had a crude drawing of the demon we had just seen and words proclaimed it the Black Demon Inn. Krakus had been here a long time.

I tied the horses up outside, and we entered. The place smelled stale. The windows were open, and the spring wind blew through the place, but it would take weeks for the sourness of winter to be blown away.

When my eyes adjusted to the dim lighting, I saw the

place was almost empty.

Only three of the small scarred tables were in use. A group of five farmers sat drinking and laughing. Two men in chain mail sat eating at another table. Their swords were out on the table beside them, sheathed.

And a young man dressed all in black sat at the last table near the stairs. A young girl no more than twelve sat with him. Her eyes were downcast, and she was obviously afraid.

Celandine stiffened beside me. She had recognized the robes of a healer, a black healer. The host came over to us, smiling, "And how may I help you this night, travelers?"

"Food, stabling for the horses, and a room for the night."

"One gold ducet will get you all you desire." His leer was obvious. I looked blankly at him. He explained patiently, "All our guests have the choice of three fair ladies to keep them company for a time."

"No, thank you. My wife and I are quite fine, alone."

He shrugged. "As you wish, but if I were you I'd have my wife pull up her hood. And have her lower her eyes."

"She is fine as she is."

He shrugged again. "Just trying to help. The stables are to the left. My boy will see to them. When you return, I will have your dinners waiting."

We went out and led the horses and Ulliam to the stables. They were cramped, and a dirty boy of about ten scuttled up to take the horses. He did not try to take Ulliam, and I did not offer. While he brushed down the horses, I tended the unicorn. The boy was dirty and perhaps not quite bright, but he brushed the horses well, and the feed he gave them was good quality.

We took a small table near the wall so I could watch the room. It was then that I noticed a small demon, barely three feet high, cleaning tables. He balanced the dirty dishes above his head with impossibly long arms. He was a bright green in color and scaled rather than skin-covered. Celandine and I stared after him as he disappeared into the back.

She stared at me, and I shrugged. In the end it would be Celandine who said what the token was and where it was. My job was just to help her get it.

The little demon also brought our food. Neither of us spoke as it put down bowls of stew, thick slices of brown bread, and tankards of some liquid. He seemed accustomed to silence and raced back through the tables with his empty tray.

The stew was hot, the meat and vegetables a little stringy, but it had been a hard winter. Stores were running low everywhere, but the bread was fresh and good.

One of the farmers I had noticed earlier came to stand beside us. He bumped into our table unsteady on his feet. He smelled of beer. "Is this pretty thing your wife, Varellian?"

"Yes."

"How much for a night with her?"

I stared at him a moment, not sure I had understood. "I said she is my wife."

"I heard you. How much for the night?"

"We are new to Lolth and do not understand all the customs. Are you saying that Loltuns sell their wives for money, like whores?"

"You brought her in here, with her face showing. She looked at every man in the place, bold as a basilisk. What else would you be doing but selling?"

I understood the host's warning now, but it was too late. "We are not Loltun, and I am not selling my wife."

He scowled at that. "The other three women are busy, and I don't go near a black healer. I have need of a woman, and she is the only one available."

"You'll have to wait then."

"Loltun men do not wait for women." He grabbed at Celandine surprisingly fast and jerked her to her feet.

My sword was out before I had time to think. "Let her go, or die."

The sight of naked steel seemed to catch his attention. He let go of her, and she sank back into her seat. The man stared at the end of my sword, and finally said, "Well, if you don't want to sell, then have her keep her eyes to herself. You could get a man killed over a misunderstanding like this."

I said nothing as he shuffled back to his companions.

Celandine pulled up her hood without being asked. I resheathed my sword, and we ate in silence. But there was another scene taking place.

The black healer and his girl were having a fight of sorts. He would touch her, and then laugh, and she would scream.

142

And then he would touch her again and laugh. I asked Celandine, "What is he doing?"

She swallowed. "I think he is hurting the girl and then healing her."

"To what purpose?"

"Many black healers are insane. They pervert their healing power into harm, and it contaminates them."

The girl was pretty. She had long yellow hair and light eyes that I guessed were blue, but couldn't be sure at this distance. Her body had just begun to swell to womanhood, but she was still more child than woman.

A bleeding scratch appeared on her cheek. He touched it, and the cut vanished.

"How did that cut appear? He didn't touch her."

"He is a very powerful black healer. He has a gift similar to sorcery."

"As you have."

She nodded. "As I have, but I must not use it again on peril of my soul."

That was what the quest was all about. The token, whatever it was, would cleanse the healer's soul of the stain of black healing.

The girl screamed, a full-blown shriek. She stood, knocking her chair backwards. Even in the dim light I could see the open sores on her arm.

Celandine started to rise, and I gripped her arm. It was automatic for her to help the sick, but not here. My grip seemed to remind her of her fear, and she sat down.

I had seen this sudden bravery many times. It came from her healing. She was afraid of so many things. But her healing made her different. I had seen her risk death to save a drowning child. Many times she had walked among bandits to heal their sick. It was as if all her strength, all her bravery, went to healing, and there was none left for Celandine, herself.

The black healer caught the girl-child. She struggled as he clutched the diseased arm. She broke away from him and stared at the now–healed arm. He laughed.

The host went up to him, and his voice carried in the sudden silence. "Sir, we are honored at your business, but your lady friend is upsetting the other guests. Would it please the most honorable healer if he would take her up to his room?" The man had bowed low but never took his eyes off the healer.

What would the host do if the healer moved to touch him?

The healer laughed again. "You should be honored that I come to this piss hole of an inn. I am of the highest rank of healer. I talk to your Gods for you. I face them when you cower in fear." He was addressing the entire room now. "I hold the power that pacifies the Gods themselves. I consort with the demons of the pit. I do things that would crack your minds like brittle kindling." And he walked over to the now quiet farmers. "But you turn away from me when I show power. Oh, heal me, please, heal me. But then leave us alone. That's how it is."

He went back to the girl, and she backed away crying. She begged him, "Please, let me go, please."

"Come, girl, it is time someone here learned what it is to embrace a black healer." She screamed as he grabbed her. He pulled her towards the stairs. Her hand gripped the banister, and he tugged her. Her fingers slipped, and he grabbed her close to his body. He carried her like that up the stairs and paused at the very top. He yelled at the host, "Which room is mine?"

The host made a half bow and said, "Turn to your right. It is the last door on that side. It is the nicest room in the inn."

"And it will be poor," he said and walked from sight with the struggling girl in his arms.

My fingers bit deeply into Celandine's arm. Her blue eyes glowed with anger. But I thought some of it was directed inward at her own fear. There were white healers I knew who would have challenged him regardless of the cost. They would not let such evil go unquestioned. For once I was glad that Celandine was not so zealous. She would be killed for being a white healer, and I would be killed defending her. It was not the way I wanted to die.

The first shriek sounded from upstairs. It cut through the fresh conversation and killed it. Everyone downstairs sat, waiting. A second scream came, piteous, all hope gone; choking sobs followed it.

The farmers got up and paid their bill. Only the two fighters were left. And they, like us, were travelers with no other place to go.

Celandine nodded. I motioned to the host, and he came over. There was a light dew of sweat on his face.

"Good sir, we are ready for our room."

"Was the stew to your liking?"

"The food was good, but we seem to have lost our appetites."

"He is a high priest of our people. But to strangers, who do not understand, well . . . he may seem extreme."

"On the contrary, mine host, I do understand. Even in other lands some magics drive the sense from a man."

The host looked nervously about as if someone might overhear. He said, "As you wish. Your room is to the right, the first door. It is as far away from the noise as I can put you."

"We appreciate that."

He nodded, and we stood. Celandine followed me, hooded, eyes down, more to hide her anger than to hide her face.

We mounted the stairs to the sounds of screams. The screams became words, a prayer. I didn't need to look behind me to know Celandine was stiffening. The girl was praying to Mother Blessen. She was praying to Celandine's God.

The prayer was cut short as if she had been cuffed.

We stepped into the dark hallway, and both of us simply stood as if waiting. The child's voice rose again in prayer. He was beating her. But she had decided that she would probably never see daylight. So she prayed, and he hit her. Celandine let her hood slip back. She turned to me word-lessly, and I met her eyes.

I whispered, "The token?"

She nodded.

There was logic to it. The girl was inside the Black Demon Inn. The token was inside a demon just as the prophets had told us it would be.

My sword sighed from its sheath, and I hefted my shield, balancing it on my arm. She smiled at me then. Fear danced in her eyes, but that curious strength that she had when healing, it was there, too.

She whispered to me, "You must cut off his head, or take out his heart. He will simply heal himself otherwise. And you must kill him as quickly as possible for he can do us all great harm."

"Surely he has used most of his power already tonight."

"He is high in the favor of the dark gods. He may have more than his own power to draw from."

I prayed silently, "Balinorelle, let it not be so. Guide my hand and allow me to slay this demonmonger."

Celandine waited for me, and we walked to the room. She opened the door quietly, for we didn't want to alert the men down below. I went in ahead of her, shield held close, wondering if it would help.

The girl lay on the bed partially nude. Her small breasts and entire upper body were covered with the green spreading sickness. It was something that killed thoroughly and quickly. The black healer lay next to her fondling her diseased body.

Celandine closed the door behind us.

The man said, "What do you want?"

He spied Celandine behind me and leered, "Have you come to offer a gift? For a gift as fair as she, you could have much."

"I have come to ask if you will sell the girl to me."

He stared down at the dying girl and laughed. With a careless hand he healed her. The disease absorbing into his skin, where the green sickness faded away. She was pure and unblemished once more.

"I don't think I'll sell her to you, elf. But I might trade."

I shook my head. "No, black healer, no trade."

He knelt on the bed and said, "Then you can fight me for her." A thin smile curled his lips. He gestured, and I felt claws sink into my cheek. Blood trickled down my face, from under my helmet.

He laughed, "How badly do you want her?"

I wiped the dripping blood with the back of my hand and said, "Badly enough."

I advanced, holding shield and weapon up, but another claw raked me across the ribs as if my armor were not there. Stealth gained me nothing, so I rushed him. He motioned, and my sword hand was cut and bleeding.

A sorcerous claw raked over my eyes. I shrieked and fell to my knees. I gripped shield and sword in the crimson dark. Blind. I fought the pain and the panic. I had been trained to fight blindfolded: darkness was darkness. The pain was overwhelming and I crouched and tried to think past

146

it, tried to hear past it.

A sound, footsteps. The girl's scream. A rush of cloth which was Celandine's dress. The heavier sloppy footfalls of the black healer.

"It seems I will enjoy two beauties tonight."

Celandine backed away from him but kept close to the bed and the girl. She called out to me, "Bevhinn!"

He moved round to the foot of the bed to come at Celandine. I had to make my first strike deadly or all was lost. I listened to his breathing and his movements. I would go for stomach and chest, not knowing if he was facing me or not. Then he spoke again, "Such a pretty pair." He was facing away from me.

I rose and struck. The blade sank into flesh. I pulled it free and struck point first through his neck. The blade grated on bone and was through to open air. I knew where everything was now. I took five strikes to cut off his head.

The smell of blood was thick and violent.

Celandine said, "Bevhinn, you've killed him."

She was beside me lifting off my helmet. I felt her finger tips touch my eyes. I felt the pain again like a lance through my brain, and it was gone. I blinked.

The black healer lay sprawled on the bed. His head was a short distance from his body. Blood soaked the bed clothes to drip on the floor. The girl looked up and smiled her gratitude at me. She paled only a little at the sight of the headless body. She had probably seen worse things in her stay in Lolth. Celandine retrieved the girl's cloak and spread it over her torn dress.

I cleaned my sword on the edge of the sheets and sheathed it. I forced open the wooden shutters on the window.

I strapped my shield to my back, and scrambled out to kneel on the sloping roof. The girl crawled out to me, and Celandine followed.

We slipped unseen and, hopefully, unheard to the ground. I led the way to the stables. We entered, and the boy scrambled down from the loft where he probably slept. I said, "Come here, boy."

He came, but he was afraid. I gripped him quickly and put a hand over his mouth. "Find some rope and cloth for a gag."

Celandine and the girl moved to obey. The boy's eyes were huge with fear, showing the whites of his eyes. "Boy, we will not harm you." He wasn't convinced, and I didn't blame him.

When he was tied with some good quality rope and gagged with a questionably dirty rag, I shoved him up in his loft. Hopefully, no one would find him before morning.

We saddled the horses while the girl kept watch. So far no alarm had been raised. But sooner or later the host would raise courage enough to check the strange noises in the healer's room. We had to be away before that.

We led Ulliam and the horses out onto the road, but I motioned for them to follow me back the way we had come that day. When we felt it safe to talk, Celandine asked, "Why are we going back?"

"We cannot go on to the next inn. You and the girl might be able to disguise yourself, but Ulliam and I are not so easily changed. We could run back to the wild lands but the Loltuns would chase us down. We are at least five days from the Meltaanian border. Every hand will be against us by morning. We must leave Lolth tonight."

"But how?"

"We're going back to the demon, Krakus."

"The help of demons?"

"Let us hope so."

The girl rode our spare horse, and she rode well enough. We raced through the night, riding the horses hard because we wouldn't be needing them much longer.

We came at last to an area of newly cleared land. The demon's shattered stumps and trees were piled high on either side of the road.

I left Celandine and the girl-child with Ulliam and the horses. And I crept through the woods towards the two men who were guarding the demon. One was simple, a dagger thrust in the throat when he went to relieve himself. But the other stayed near the fire and kept his sword naked and near at hand. Guarding a demon seemed to make him nervous. Every time Krakus rattled his chains, the man jumped.

He kept staring back at the demon. I stepped up behind him and put my sword through his throat. I cleaned the blade in the tall grass and sheathed it. The demon was watching me with eyes that caught and reflected the fire.

Heavy chains bound Krakus, but the keys to those chains glinted at the dead man's belt. Celandine and the girl entered the clearing with the horses and Ulliam. The demon's eyes flicked to them and then settled back on me.

I said, "I would bargain with you, Krakus."

His voice was deep and seemed to come from a long way off, as if from the bottom of a well. "What manner of bargain?"

"You teleport the three of us and the unicorn just across the Meltaan border at the city gates of Terl, and I will free you from your enslavement."

"I like this bargain, elf. Free me, and I will do as you ask."

"Not yet, demon. First we take blood oath so I know you will not desert us, or teleport us to a harmful place."

"Why would I do that to the ones who free me?"

"Because you are a demon."

It laughed, baring white fangs. "I like you. You understand the way of things."

His voice sank even deeper until it was almost painful to hear. "But what blood oath could bind a demon?"

"One to the hounds of Verm and the birds of Loth."

The smile vanished from his face, and he said, "Have you ever made blood oath with a demon?"

"No."

He laughed again. "Then let us proceed."

I cut my right hand in a diagonal slash. The blood was bright red and poured in a sheet down my palm. It stung with the sharp pain of all shallow cuts. The demon extended his left hand, and I sliced it. The blood was black and slow to ooze.

We clasped hands and suddenly I felt dizzy. I stared up into those intent yellow eyes and said, "What is happening, Krakus?"

"What always happens when you bargain with demons, warrior. I am taking blood price. But because this oath holds us both, you are getting my blood in return." He hissed, "You are demon kin now, elf. Those who have the power will see the taint and act accordingly."

It felt as if someone had thrust a red hot poker into my hand. Fire filled my veins. I fell to my knees, gasping in the cool night air. I could not afford to scream. If we were being chased, screams would bring them. That was the last thought I had before blackness engulfed me.

I heard Celandine from a distance. "What if she dies? Then you will still be a prisoner because only she can free you."

The demon's voice came, "It is the way of demon bargains, healer. The mortal must risk more than the demon. I cannot change my nature not even to save myself."

I woke with the sky clearing towards dawn. The cut on my hand had been burned shut and formed a scar across my palm. It had not been Celandine's magic that had closed the wound.

She was there beside me. "How do you feel?"

"Good enough." I sat in the morning damp grass, waiting to feel whole again. I got tired of waiting and called to my magic.

It answered but with a difference. It seemed sluggish as if it moved through thick air to reach me. My magic felt tainted, but there was no time to worry about it. I had to free the demon.

The spring dawn was close, and the spring night still here. The world was poised between the two, so I called upon both. I drew the cool spring darkness and the soft call of an owl. I breathed in the first hint of dawn on the wind. A rabbit stirred in its sleep, and I took its dreams and wove them into my spell. The bark of a fox and the fleeting shadow of a night hawk mingled with the aroma of fresh-turned earth. The power stretched like a second moon, swollen with spring's bounty. I stood and cupped my hands, letting the magic fall into my palms like moonshine. I engulfed the diamond of the demon's necklace in white magic. I felt the enchantment snap. Krakus bowed his head, and I slipped the necklace free of him. The diamond still glittered like warm ice, but it would take an enchanter to reactivate the necklace. For now it was only a piece of jewelry.

He rose to his full seven feet and stretched. The chains fell away without benefit of keys. He leered down at us. "Let us go and fulfill my part of the bargain." He offered me his left hand, and I saw the matching burn scar across his great palm. I took his hand, and Ulliam shied but came to stand on the other side of me. Celandine touched his white flank, and the girl clung to her. We were an unbroken chain. The world shifted, and we were before the gates of Terl. It was already dawn there, and a farmer with his load of chickens fought his mule to keep it from running away. It did not like the smell of demons.

Krakus let go of my hand and said, "I am sure I will not be the last demon you see, earth-witch; blood calls to blood."

He vanished.

Later that day we stood before the High Priestess, and she welcomed Celandine back into the fold of the white healers. The girl-child had some healing magic and was being sponsored as an apprentice healer. She was a worthy token for such a quest.

Celandine's father held a great feast, and I was invited.

I had the gratitude of the most powerful petty king in Meltaan, and I had a diamond only slightly smaller than my fist. It would be a long time before I was forced to guard someone else's treasures again.

Celandine was in her element, bejeweled and dressed in white silk. She did not look my way. She was cleansed, and her soul was her own again. And I was a reminder of less pleasant times.

I watched the girl we had saved, laughing with the other young healers. I felt good at having saved her, but my eyes were drawn back again and again to the burn scar on my palm. Celandine had done nothing on this quest. Yet she was cleansed, and I was tainted.

I wondered, was there a cleansing ceremony for the demon-touched?

The Harmonic Conception

•

Nona M. Caspers

I was standing at this bus stop on Chicago and Lake in Minneapolis, waiting for the 21A to carry me to my "Women and Power" class, when a man with an unusually long rubbery neck walked up to me, reached out one finger, pressed it over my left breast, and said, "Ma'am, you've been chosen."

Since I had not entered any sweepstakes or applied for any grants, I replied, loudly, "You get your finger off my body, sir, or I'll twist it off along with some other parts."

He quickly and with some grace removed it. That's when I noticed the tip was glowing. I followed his neck, which seemed to sway like one of those rubber Bozo or Gumby dolls, up to a peculiar face. It was the face of a little boy, or a little girl, enlarged to fit the body — the eyes were beyond innocence or age. They were eyes that had never witnessed dogs mating or the six o'clock news, never filtered clippings of Nagasaki-Hiroshima or reruns of "Dallas."

Yet there had been something slightly southern, slightly Eastern European in his voice, and I wondered where this fellow, if it was a fellow, was from — Texas or Czechoslovakia?

"I am not trying to bother you, madam, but I have been sent to . . ."

"Go away." I barked, sweet face or not. That morning, at 5:30 a.m., my three housemates and I had all dragged our bodies over to Lake Harriet to bask in the Harmonic Convergence — so I was tired and crabby.

"I will go soon. I just came to confirm it. That you HAVE BEEN CHOSEN."

"For what?

"To carry the holy child, the messenger . . . uh, the next Buddha or Moses or Christ or Baha'u'llah or whatever your people name it."

"Oh god, you are nuts." I moved to stand next to the bus sign. Long Neck followed me, looking perplexed. He or she was obviously not getting the expected reaction.

"Please prepare," he said gently, rubbery hand on my arm. "As we speak, the first cell is dividing and soon will be implanted."

I jerked my arm away, and noticed a tear dwelling in this mad person's eye. The 21A rolled up like a great old whale sputtering. Alright 21A, on time again, I silently cheered. As I jumped on to the bus, I heard the soft voice behind me say, "Good luck. Bless you and the child." And I swear his finger was glowing — it reminded me of one of those flashlight pens.

I threw myself into a back seat, wiping the grime off the window to see, but Long Neck and finger were gone. The bus bumped on. I felt a tiny twinge inside — like a tremor before an earthquake. It reminded me that I was heading into the premenstrual-creative phase of my cycle and was prone to imagination and drama.

I didn't think seriously of Long Neck again until three months later as I crouched on the bathroom floor heaving my breakfast of apple, tahini, and raspberry tea into the toilet, while my three busy yet loving housemates lined up and pounded on the door.

"What are you doing in there?!"

I was slouched over the toilet, waiting for the last wave of electric nausea to sweep up and out of me.

"I'm sick." I choked out with stinky breath.

"Again?" Their sympathy was contaminated by the ticking of the clock. I finally opened the door.

"I mean it, girls, I feel strange."

Six arms came around me — "Oh, you poor thing, you look horrible."

It was like being held by a motherly octopus.

"You come with me to the clinic and get a check-up. No common flu virus goes on for three months." Le-ling was doing a community health internship at the Southside Clinic.

I crawled to my room and studied my body in the mirror. All the heaving had trimmed the fat off — except one place which had thickened and I stared at this place until it was the size of an MX missile.

"Knock, knock." Le-ling smiled at me in the mirror. "Going to get dressed?"

With a sudden motion, as if unveiling a second head, I lifted my pajama shirt and grabbed her hand — "Feel this!" I rubbed her palm over my tightened ball of abdomen. Our eyes met in the mirror, Le- ling's widening, then pulling back skeptically.

"What is it?"

"I don't know, but not a drop of sacred womanhood *in three months*."

"You mean?" She shrunk in disbelief.

"Oh don't be silly — but there is something in there."

Now both of us stared at the shiny protrusion — we had seen "Aliens" twice that winter . . .

"A cyst? Or tumor?" Le-ling offered sanely. "A lot of young women are getting them. There is a good doctor at the clinic who I think is lesbian. Ask for Dr. Randez."

"Shit, Le, I don't have the time or the money for a tumor."

Dr. Randez pressed and poked my tumor, asked me questions, and ran some tests. I waited for the results. After I had read "People" magazine forwards and back, she called me into her office. I leaned forward in the chair across from her. The fluorescent light buzzed over our heads.

"So what is it, Doc, a tumor?"

"No. It's a fetus."

"A what?" Dr. Randez was looking at me like I was a silly cow.

"You are pregnant," she said clearly, tilting her head and squinting.

I blinked and swallowed and swallowed and blinked — like a cow. There was a long patch of silence between that doctor and I. Because somewhere inside me, guess where, I knew it was true — had known for weeks.

"Dr. Randez," I whispered, "I'm a lesbian."

She was near laughter and whispered back, "Lesbians get pregnant too."

"But Dr. Randez," I started to whine, "I haven't been near semen for seven years."

"Oh." A nugget of truth. Dr. Randez straightened.

We repeated the tests until our stomachs growled, the

light dimmed, and the tumor began to kick. Dr. Randez said tumors don't kick.

I left the clinic and wandered the streets like a bag lady without a bag. My feet slushed through burnt orange and burgundy leaves as the sun tried to warm the back of my neck and failed. Every time I saw a bus I relived that day, Long Neck's words, and the glowing finger... I was so dazed that I didn't recognize Carry, an ex-lover, crossing the street and waving. She ran up and gave me a hard hug, tossing our pelvises together. Mine must have felt immediately distorted to her because she pulled back and frowned down in shocked surprise: "Sperm bank or private donor?"

"Neither." I answered like a robot.

"God, don't tell me you're doing it with a boy?" Her body seemed to shrivel and recoil, as if my halitosis breath bore strong winds from Chernobyl.

"What an absurd thought," I replied numbly. "I haven't been doing it with a boy. I've been doing it with an angel."

So the news was out. Soon all sorts of inquiring minds would want to know. Stories and opinions would be colliding like ions through the lesbian airwaves. I already felt like an outcast. I envisioned my face and mysterious bulge propped up in check-out lines across America. I would look as if no one had ever loved me, like a lonely freak of society drowning in fuzzy green print: "LESBIAN BETRAYS CULTURE, HAS SEX WITH MALE GOD" or "DYKE'S WATER BREAKS — CHRIST CHILD EMERGES."

To the straight world I would be the same — crazy and ill. But to my people? A Traitor. A Leper.

As you can see, my faith was not as high as my estrogen level. I decided that I was miserable and that my entire life was ruined. Though I was penniless and depressed, I managed to find an abortion clinic; it looked like the home of a wealthy dentist. There were heavy-footed picketers marching up and down the walk in front of the entrance, holding signs like baseball bats that read THANK GOD MARY DIDN'T THROW JESUS IN A GARBAGE CAN. I had neither the guts nor the money to pass.

My weary feet finally brought me back to the fateful 21A bus stop, and with many tears I pleaded, "You with the finger . . . angel or alien or whatever, please help me . . . PLEASE!" A few disembodied murmurs hesitated, then passed. I slumped onto the bench. Suddenly, Long Neck appeared next to me, placing a comforting rubbery hand on my back as the face, which was looking more and more like a woman's, swayed before mine.

"You came!" I cried.

Long Neck smiled. "How are you and the Blessed-To-Be?" This time the voice sounded like my mother's. I did not waste time.

"This fetus has got to go, Blessed-Be or not. Now you put it in there, so I expect you to get it out."

The clear soft eyes seemed to float as the neck swayed in the slight fall breeze and they searched my body. "We thought you were willing to help this world reach its harmony phase. If we undo this now, we'll have to wait a long time for just the right alignments of planets and energy."

A guilt trip, I thought; this must be my mother. "But I don't want a baby!" I shouted. "I'm a dyke with no money, no charge cards, no insurance, no partner, no college degree . . . DON'T YOU GET IT? A child needs good care — holy or not — and I can't give it. Who's going to pay the bills? You? For god's sake, I'm a check-out girl at Target and I DON'T WANT TO BE THE SECOND VIRGIN MARY!"

"Oh, there's been more than one."

"Whatever. You really should have asked."

"We thought we did," Long Neck said quietly. Suddenly I had a clear memory of what had happened in that crowded pavilion, during that early morning drizzle while my house-mates and I meditated for world peace. There had been a question, a feeling; something specific was being asked of me . . . a commitment that would give birth to global change. I, of course, had taken this question metaphorically and without thinking — answered "yes."

"Oh that . . . " I mumbled. "Well, I'm never quite awake till noon and my third cup of tea."

Long Neck rose like flowing neon. "We'll have to process these new feelings and information and decide what's best for all. I'll get back to you, ma'am."

"Don't take too long." I pointed to the kicking intrusion.

I waited three weeks, wearing baggy clothes and avoiding questions. The heaving stopped. I quit caffeine and nu-trasweet and "Dallas" — just in case I was stuck with this savior. I felt healthier and saner than I had since I was three and discovered a third hole that I really didn't think was necessary and so tried to plug it with a Lego block. Finally, one night after we'd all come home from a seminar on acid rain, I called a house meeting. We gathered on the living room rug and lit a candle.

"Well, girls, let me tell you a story . . ." And I did, and they listened — all six eyes on my hidden bulge.

"It's too weird. It just can't be, are you sure you haven't been fooling around with some guy? You can tell us," Tally, the carpenter, assured me. "I am telling you — it's an immaculate conception."

"Yeah, right, you're hardly immaculate — three lovers in two years . . ."

"But I haven't been in spitting distance of a boy."

"Turkey baster?" Le-ling asked.

"No."

"Then you just can't be pregnant, it's a mistake." Again I lifted my shirt, showing a belly as puffed as the fatal mushroom cloud. There was a long, candlelit silence.

"Parthenogenesis," Lucia said firmly. She was a major at the university and had just finished a biology class taught by a separatist.

"What exactly do you mean?"

"It's obvious. The convergence stimulated two of your eggs to release at the same time and one penetrated the outer membrane of the other, which triggered the process of chromosomal coupling and cellular reproduction which produced a zygote that continued along its way, cleavaging into the morula which then implanted in your endometrium lining and grew into a fetus."

"Thank you," I said and dropped onto my back. Then I felt a tiny hard toe jab at my belly button.

"Oh, girls, the holy fetus is kicking! Come feel!" They took turns with gentle hands and ears at my belly.

"It's a miracle." Tally and Le-ling breathed over my skin.

"No. It's simply a rare but natural occurrence," Lucia corrected.

I laughed, bouncing against her ear. "Talk about inbreeding."

"So you're gonna have it?" It was everyone's question, including my own.

"I don't know. I mean . . . I can't afford a kid, and I'm not that great with them and . . . why me?"

We all meditated on this long enough to let wax drip on the rug, and that must have been a sign because Lucia said stridently, "I have an idea. You have it and we'll all be co-parents. It was meant to be."

Tally and Le-ling squealed like expectant girlfriends.

"I don't know. Raising a kid is a big responsibility . . ."

"Not as big for four women," they argued.

I searched each face for unspoken doubts, remembering what I'd read about Kennedy and the Bay of Pigs. Tally looked troubled.

"What is it?"

"One thing . . ." she spoke hesitantly. "What if it's a boy?"

"Oh god, I hadn't even thought of that," I moaned, "Those holy children are always boys, aren't they?"

"The ones that get famous anyway."

"Can't be a boy," Lucia declared. "The Y chromosome has to be provided by the sperm — and there was none."

I was still skeptical — hard enough to raise a kid, but a boy?

"You know," Le-ling began thoughtfully. "I think God or Goddess or whatever planted a girl this time. That is why it's in a dyke's body, in a dyke's household. To give her a chance to take herself and her mission as seriously as the guys did."

"Raising a Savior is a big responsibility," I reminded again. "I am not giving up sex."

We processed the idea for another candle, airing all sorts of hypothetical difficulties and feelings, and still in the end, after letting the fetus kick them in the face a few more times, the decision and commitment were made — we drew up a contract and signed. The Twentieth Century Savior would be raised by a household of lesbians.

During the next five months, the holy fetus swelled my belly so that the girls had to levitate to hug me. We bought red jumpsuits and purple jammies at thrift shops; painted fluorescent galaxies on the ceiling of my bedroom, where the kid would sleep until old enough to go the night without nursing; attended birth classes and hired a compatible midwife. For my birthday I got a breast pump. By the time I'd begun to dilate, we were prepared to welcome the strong legged little Savior into our lives.

I chose to deliver in the bathtub, squatting in warm water which lapped between my legs, soothed my aching back and thighs and provided a familiar gentle welcome for the kid. Le-ling, Tally, and Lucia took turns holding my hand, panting me through contractions, massaging my perineum, and feeding me cherry juice with crackers. The midwife came at seven fingers.

"Ok, you're doing great," her soothing voice encouraged. "Do you feel like pushing?"

I nodded. "This kid has a big head, I can feel it."

"Relax now, and whenever you are ready, push."

A short while later, I yelped. "Holy shit!" I felt like a huge bowel movement was coming out the wrong hole and I wondered if that Lego block had grown into a house. I began to push and push. Fire leaped through my crotch up my thighs to my knees . . . and then, in the middle of a long hard flaming grunt, I saw Long Neck's eyes wavering above me.

"Ma'am?" she whispered, for I had decided it was female. No one else in the room seemed to notice.

"What do you want?" Pant, pant . . . "You could have told us you were coming to the birth. Ugh . . . God, I'd better get a great afterlife for this . . ."

"I am sorry that it has taken us so long to get back to you. It's been a painful emotional process, but we have finally reached a consensus and we now believe that our earlier decision might have been a bit hasty. Some of the gir . . ., I mean, spiritual beings, have shared some strong feelings . . ."

Pant, pant . . .

"Anyway. We've decided to postpone this particular messenger's entrance into this world. This world just isn't ready."

I glared up at her incredulously, hoping the flames might scorch her long neck.

"Well, this world had better damn well get ready," I shouted, "BECAUSE HERE SHE COMES."

And with one more long noisy push that sounded like

the launching of a nuclear warhead and felt like it too, a baby with compact genitalia and brown glowing skin, just a shade darker than my own, came flowing and rolling out.

Long Neck vanished.

Epilogue

After the birth we put a notice in the local lesbian and gay paper: CHILD BORN ON THE 16th OF APRIL TO THE JACKSON, WONG, SANCHEZ, AND GOLDBERG FAMILY." We have not been contacted by the larger media — though I expect it will happen soon.

Lucia tells everyone it was parthenogenesis — people think what they want — we hear some buzzing. I was afraid the kid would look like Long Neck, but the truth is she looks like the four of us mixed together. It's amazing.

So now I am one of four mothers and the child grows wiser each day. We chipped in and bought her a computer, which she has programmed to give planetary layouts and to process her revelations during meditation and prayer. I went back to caffeine and "Dallas." It's not an easy job, being a mother, and this kid is getting harder and harder to keep up with, even for four lesbians. The other day she disappeared out of the herb garden where she was planting garlic and after we searched for seven hours, we finally found her in a suburban shopping mall. She was perched on a stack of designer jeans speaking to the crowds in parables and chanting, "TO SHOP IS EVERYTHING ... TO SHOP IS NOTHING ..."

Children of Divers Kind

•

Mary Ellen Mathews

My lover Lillian gained so much weight that she could no longer wear our clothes. I didn't notice it when it was happening; she ate a little more, but I assumed it was because of her harder and more physical work as an agricultural laborer. Then one day she couldn't button the waistband on her work pants. She pinned them as high up the zipper as she could and let her shirttail flap down over the pin. "Pre-period bloat," she told me. I frowned, and I made dinner that night: steamed fresh vegetables and apples for dessert.

I don't know if she ate even more after that, or if I just noticed it. On her turns she cooked enormous dinners — whole roasted chickens, tubs of sweet potatoes, cornbread, black-eyed peas, and always dessert. Our flour and sugar rations were used up early every month; Lillian contrived to share our friends' supplies. "Let's go over to Hannah and Nicole's and see if they want to bake cookies!" she'd suggest, eyes alight, and we'd go. And we'd have a wonderful time, as though we were all young girls with our first kitchens, and Lillian would eat most of the cookies.

"Lillian!" even quiet Hannah would scold. "You're going to get as big and ugly as a ThelmaWilliams if you don't watch out!"

Finally the day came when she couldn't get into her work pants at all. We had a pair of baggy exercise pants; she wore those to work. Of course her supervisor noticed it and sent her to a doctor for a checkup.

"Alice," she told me later. "Alice — I've got her number written down somewhere; has a small scar on her chin."

"I know her," I answered. "She was in medical school with me. She fell and cut her chin in the lab one day. What did she say?"

"She said I'm too fat."

"And?"

"And? And I have to lose weight. She had all these charts. It was discouraging. 'Standard Height Variance Among KaySearles'. 'Optimal Maximum and Minimum Weight Differentials for KaySearles'. Stuff like 'desired bicep measurement (flexed)'. They've got it down to the fucking dot on the i."

We were sitting at our eating table, waiting for water to boil for tea. Lillian pulled at the skin on her fingers.

"Of course we have all the facts," I told her, aligning myself with the rest of my medical profession and with "them." "We've had over a century to study and unchanging type, so by now we *should* know what's best. So what do you have to do?"

"Get new clothes." She grinned. "I *could* wear a ThelmaWilliams' clothes right now, I'm the right size; but they think it might be 'disruptive' or something — all those pinks and bright yellows — so they ordered some from Sudamerica."

"What about the weight?" I asked.

"You know, I used to think Sudamerica was another C-group. 'Sue Damerica'." Lillian traced patterns on the table with her finger.

"The weight," I persisted.

"Close rationing." She looked up at me. Her eyes were wide, a little guilty. I thought it was only because the close rationing would affect me, too. "I'm sorry, Grit," she said.

"No problem," I answered. It really wouldn't hurt me to eat properly for a few weeks. "It will be healthier for you, you know, Lil."

"Yeah, that's what Alice said," she answered mildly.

The close rationing was trial. Most of the staff at the pediatrics center brought lunch, since a commissary lunch was so bland and unappetizing. But with close rationing imposed on my home, I was forced to apply at the commissary counter. "Margaret 4117," I said. The commissar checked her console. "Close rationing, but normal lunch," she read out.

"Strange. Oh, I see. Close rationing imposed on housemate. Lillian 345. I think I know who she is. Farm worker, right? Heavy?"

"Right," I said. Funny, I mused, that someone could identify Lillian other than by her name and job.

"Here go, Doctor." She pushed a tray at me. "Hope the diet works."

It didn't. Lillian got fatter. "Are you going to eat those peas?" she would say to me when she saw I was just pushing them around on my plate. The close rationing food was so boring that I only picked at it.

"No, and you shouldn't either."

"Come on. They're peas. Vegetables. Healthy, good for you, green vegetables. How could they be fattening?"

So she ate the peas, and anything else I left on my plate. And then she ate food I wasn't intending to leave, flirting and cajoling until I gave it to her. I worried about her, unable to think of a condition that would leave her hungry all the time like that. "Really, Grit, I'm *starving*," she'd say. So she grew.

She probably talked co-workers out of some of their lunches, or she took some of the food she was laboring to grow — soft young milky corn, tender beans. But she outgrew the special-order clothes and was sent into the hospital for tests. The tests came to nothing. Doctor Alice was baffled, as I was. I was also upset.

"Why, Lil?" I pleaded. We were at home; Lillian was leafing through a catalog they'd given her at the quarter-master's. "I know there's nothing wrong with you. Why are you eating that much? Are you *really* that hungry?"

She looked up at me, with big, solemn eyes. "Sometimes it's pure hell getting all that food down."

"Then why? Why do it?"

She looked back to her catalog. "Do people ever say to you, 'Lillian, the fat one'?" she asked.

"Yes, they do," I said sternly. "They certainly do." I thought this was the sort of thing to make her stop, to make her realize how people saw her, what they thought. But she was pleased with my answer.

"Isn't that great?" she said. "Now, when people are talking about me, they won't have any trouble differentiating me from the hundreds of other Lillian KaySearles, because I'm the *fat* Lillian."

"What does *that* mean?" I sneered. "What difference

does that make?"

"Grit," she said softly. "I love you."

I was tired, hungry, and concerned. I didn't realize how worried I was until she said that. Tears came.

"And I love *you*," I said. "I love you, Lil, but what are you doing? What's happening to you?"

"Why do you love *me*?"

"Well," I gulped. "You're my lover. I feel close to you. I —"

"Yes," said Lillian. "But why *me*? Why did you pick me, instead of Hannah or Nicole or Daisy or Susan or Doctor Alice?"

Was she feeling insecure? Was that what this weight thing was about? I thought about her question for a moment. Lillian was a bulldog for facts; she'd never be satisfied by an easy answer.

"Well, you're a stickler for the truth," I said, and grinned weakly. "And I like that because I have a touch of that condition myself. And you have a better sense of humor than anyone I know. And you're practical and down-to-earth."

Lillian smiled ruefully. "Not a lot of differences to choose from, are there? Since we're all each other's twin sisters?"

I frowned. "We aren't really," I said.

"Sure are! That's all what they used to call 'identical twins' are, is clones. Now I love *you*, Grit, because you're so literal. And because you have the prettiest eyes I've ever seen."

"My eyes are just like everyone else's!"

"No, they aren't. You have this way of holding them, wide open and innocent. I love it."

She was serious. I almost blushed. "What's the catalog for?" I asked to change the subject.

"New special-order clothes again." She sighed. "I've gotten beyond the 'standard' special order. I have to take measurements of everything down to my toenails and fill out this form for the Sudamerican garment industry. I also have to 'estimate how many articles of work clothing and social clothing' I'm going to need for the next six months, and which ones, remembering to 'allow for change of seasons'. They'll all be in our lovely KaySearle colors, of course."

The KaySearle colors were the ones I would have picked myself, so I can be proud of having good taste. It was decades ago that someone decided that with our chestnut hair and light-brown eyes, we looked best in browns and brick reds, golden ochres and moss greens, rich indigos and silvery grays. A busy KaySearle street looks like an autumn hillside against a twilight sky. Why Lillian would want any other colors, I couldn't understand. And I shuddered at the thought of a KaySearle in any other color.

I glanced over her shoulder as she scanned the catalog. "There's more than clothes in that," I observed.

"Very commercially oriented, these Sudamericans," answered Lillian. "Whatever someone will pay for, they'll sell. No wonder. While our people were making lofty scientific plans for the survival of the human race back there after the war, the Sudamericans were scrabbling around in the mountains, making immediate practical plans for the survival of *them*. They learned a few things." She filled out the order form and dropped it at the quartermaster's.

It took a week for Lillian's new special order to arrive by roboplane. I stopped off at the quartermaster's and picked up the parcel for her. It was huge; I had to request a taxi, which our energy allowance could barely pay for. At home it almost covered the bed. When Lillian came in from work, she opened it and laid out the large garments.

There were some brown bottles in a small parcel inside. "What's that?" I asked. "Must be a mistake."

"No mistake," she answered. She scooped up the bottles and went into the bathroom, where she stayed for over an hour. When she came out her hair was wet and hanging in dripping strands over her shoulders.

And it was blonde. Golden, almost yellow, blonde.

"Lillian!" I shouted. "What did you do?"

"I dyed my hair. The Sudamericans do it all the time."

"But — *we* don't!"

"We?" she said, almost coldly. "No. *You* don't. *I* do."

I was distraught about her hair. Pressed, Lillian would only say that she liked the idea of being the only fat blonde in a town full of thin brunettes. She dried her hair and dressed in one of her new outfits, a shapeless smock that was only like what the rest of us wore in its indigo hue. "Let's go visit Hannah and Nicole," she insisted.

Walking over, enduring stares from neighbors, she asked, "Do you like Hannah and Nicole?"

"Of course I like Hannah and Nicole," I said.

"Which one do you like more?"

"That's silly."

"No, it isn't. Which one?"

"I like them both the same."

"Sure you do," she answered, "because they *are* both the same. Now, us, we're different. You're like Hannah and Nicole — and every other KaySearle — and I'm big and blonde and — nonconformist."

"I'm not like every other KaySearle," I countered.

Lillian roared with laughter.

Hannah and Nicole were not happy to see Lillian the way she was. They were polite, of course, but they didn't like how she looked, and it was obvious. In one unguarded moment I caught Nicole with her teeth bared, almost snarling at Lillian's back. I had never seen that much hatred on anyone's face before. After a very strained, very short visit, we left.

"What's the matter with them?" muttered Lillian.

"Lillian, it's — a little disconcerting to be around someone who's — not like us. You're making life pretty difficult."

"I'm not even as different as, say, a HollyAppleby. Or, better, a GeorgeKernan. Or —"

"Well, it's a moot point, because we don't have to be around any of those. We do have to be around you. I wish you'd —"

"'Have to'? Don't you feel in the slightest, doesn't it occur to you, that it's a little strange that you only know people who are identical to you? Wouldn't you at least like to meet a HollyAppleby sometime?"

"No, I don't and I wouldn't," I answered stubbornly. "I like things the way they are."

"It's pretty damned unnatural," Lillian persisted. "The Scandinavians don't live like that. The Sudamericans don't. The Africans don't. It's only us Usans, and I think it's perverted."

I didn't say anything. I wasn't going to argue with her. There were one hundred different C-types in Usa, and we hadn't intermixed for a century, and she could do all the crazy things she could think of, but it wasn't going to change overnight. I personally was glad of that. The thought of coming face to face with a HollyAppleby — I could truly imagine it from their pictures; they were tall, almost giant-esses, and pale — gave me a queasy feeling in the pit of my stomach.

A few days later Lillian was released from work for a few days until a new job could be found for her. The other farm laborers had complained about her strange appear-ance; no one wanted to work with her. They would find her something, they told her, where she could work alone. Angry, she stomped and slammed around the house; then she began a project. She picked one of her smock dresses apart, laid the pieces out on one of our tablecloths to cut duplicates, and began to sew herself another garment. The tablecloth was pink. I felt my jaw tense, but I didn't start the argument.

"Do you know," she said, "I used to want to live in Scandinavia?"

"But you don't any more?" I asked hopefully. Her changes by now made me feel ill whenever I thought of them. Wanting to live somewhere else was insanity, pure insanity. I knew what I was terribly afraid to know: Lillian was sick.

"No. I'd much rather live in Sudamerica," she told me gleefully. "The Scandinavians are so hoity-toity, they openly disapprove of us, and they're snobs; basically they're just snobs. But the Sudamericans are open-minded, colorful, energetic. And it's warm there, and there are jobs, especially for agricultural workers." She didn't look up from her sewing; she thrust a needle enthusiastically through the fabric. "No KaySearle has ever emigrated, but then none has ever asked for permission. I've been thinking about asking one of our Government reps at the next session break."

And they'd let her go, I thought. The Government reps were used to different kinds of people, living like they did; and they wouldn't be horrified. And anyway they'd see her as a problem offering its own solution: let her leave Kay-Searle, let her leave Usa altogether, and the Sudamericans would be glad of the productive power of another worker. And I didn't want her to go.

Oh, for one horrible, mean-spirited little moment I did want her to leave; she was making my life miserable and she was sick; she was an embarrassment at best. But I loved her very much. My eyes filled with tears and overflowed. "Don't," I whispered.

Lillian looked up, surprised. "Oh, Grit," she said. I

wouldn't think of going without you. Both of us, I meant. I wouldn't leave you."

I was sobbing. She put her sewing down and held me. "The Sudamericans would be glad to get a pediatrician, too," she murmured in my ear. "Taking care of all those Sudamerican babies, those little products of sexual reproduction, could you stand it?" She was teasing me. I was at such a low point I just let it all come out.

"I don't know if I could stand it," I choked out. "I want to be with you, and I want to live here, in my home, and I want you to get back to normal and have brown hair and be thin and wear KaySearle colors and be like me, like everyone else."

"No, you don't."

Her voice was so hard I was startled. I expected more gentle treatment in my desolation.

"I've always been a little different from everyone else, always, Grit. I laugh louder and I play faster and harder and I always win, don't I?" I nodded. "And a lot of other things. Everyone else put in for the job lottery so they had a chance to be musicians or" — she cocked her head at me — "doctors, but I didn't. I asked to be a farmer. They let me, because that's not a high-preference job. Why did I want it? Just because by wanting it I could control something in my life. I want — if I'm like everybody else, and have to stay like everybody else, then I don't control —" She stopped and shook her head. She was almost crying herself now.

"And you always knew it," she continued. "You knew exactly what I was like when you met me, and you chose me."

"You weren't like this," I contended. "You were the same size as everyone else and you had brown hair."

"Trappings and suits, madam! But I have that within which passeth show."

She stuck her lower lip out and raised her eyebrows in such perfect imitation of the actress we'd recently seen playing Hamlet in the repertory theater that I had to relax and laugh a little. "Fancy yourself a melancholy Dane, do you?" I joked weakly.

"Any kind of Dane would do," she returned.

"Please don't ask the Government rep."

"In Sudamerica my name would be just Searle, Lillian

Searle, like Kay Searle herself. Sounds nice, doesn't it?"

"Please don't."

"We'll talk about it later," she said. She picked up her sewing again, and there was no discussing it further.

When she finally finished the pink dress, nothing would do but that she wear it immediately. It was a free day; neither of us was working. I had some errands to run in town center and Lillian insisted on accompanying me, wearing her creation. The people who lived in our neighborhood no longer stared at Lillian. Even with the addition of the strange pink garment, they pointedly did not look at us, did not greet us or say hello. My cheeks were brighter than her dress by the time we left our quarter.

"Hey!" someone shouted. We both turned. The part of town we were in was only slightly familiar to us; we didn't know anyone here. It was strange to be hailed.

Up the street came a group of teenagers, the oldest about sixteen. They all wore identical brown slacks and ochre shirts — gangs commonly dressed alike — and identical frowns. "Hey. What are you and what are you doing in KaySearle?" the one in front demanded nastily.

"She's a KaySearle," I put in hurriedly. There were too many of these girls and they were too angry; I was nervous. "She's had some medical problems so she looks different —"

"Yeah?" said the girl. "If she's a KaySearle I'm a HollyAppleby. She's not supposed to be here."

"No, really." I stepped forward to confront the girl; I wasn't prepared for her to grab my shoulders and fling me aside. Two of her friends caught me and pinned my arms behind my back.

"Leave her alone!" Lillian started toward my captors. But the first girl moved in front of her and hit her; and then the street was a mass of flailing arms and legs and fists. I was screaming. I fought free of the two girls and struggled to get to Lillian. They clutched at me again and I struck out. I couldn't see Lillian; she was at the bottom of a squirming pile of vicious teenagers. "Shoulda stayed where you belong, fucking foreigner!" one shouted.

Desperately I hauled at the back of one of the girls on the pile. Several other girls were now pulling and hitting at me. My lip was split and blood poured down my chin.

Fingernails raked my arm. "Lillian!" I wailed.

We heard sirens. Someone had called the security force. Suddenly the girls all disengaged themselves and ran away in different directions. I was left weeping over Lillian, who lay unmoving in the street, her neck at a sickening angle.

I had contusions and shock from blood loss. I had to spend two days in the hospital. Hannah and Nicole came to visit, sorrowfully, kindly. They talked a little about Lillian — about how she had been before she started making the changes, as though that were the only Lillian we would remember. Other people we both knew came and expressed their condolences. The security force arrested some girls on suspicion, but I couldn't honestly identify them, so nothing came of it. I went home from the hospital and tried for a few months to pick up my life and get used to living alone.

Being alone was not the worst of it. After a while my friends began to invite me to gatherings, where I always found another single person they thought I'd like to meet. I dated some of them, but they all seemed interchangeable and it was basically boring. I fell into a pattern of working and coming home and then spending the evening thinking — that painful thinking. The next year, when Government took a break and our reps were in town, I made an appointment with one.

"Hello —" she glanced at her notebook "— Margaret. Margaret 4117, right?" She smiled and held out her hand. "I'm Katherine 563. I'm very glad of a chance to meet you — not just because you're a constituent, but because of the unfortunate death of your housemate."

I hadn't meant to talk about Lillian, and I wished she hadn't started our meeting that way. "Yes, well," I said. "I've come about another matter."

She was in her sixties, a classic KaySearle. As might be expected, her indigo suit became her. "What can I do for you, Margaret?"

I took a breath and plunged in. "I want to emigrate. I want to live in Sudamerica." I said it as fast as I could so it would all be out before I had a chance to think.

Katherine was surprised. "Why?"

"Well," I said. How could I explain all this? "I just don't — fit in any more. I don't know. Lillian — my housemate who —"

"Lillian 345," she said. She didn't have to consult any notes for Lillian's name. "That was a tragedy, Margaret, and one which deeply concerns Government."

"Yes, well, she was *different.*" Katherine nodded grimly. "Now, everyone's the same, and — something's *missing.* I've tried, but I've changed. I didn't mean to," I hastened to add, "but I have."

"But why Sudamerica?"

I didn't have a good reason to give her. I didn't really want to go to Sudamerica; I wanted more than anything to stay safe in my home. But where I lived didn't seem like home now. "Oh, the people are energetic, colorful. It's warm. They could use a pediatrician," I recited Lillian's words.

Katherine leaned back in her chair. "Would you consider going to a mixed city here in Usa?" she asked.

"Government? Oh, but don't you have to be brought up from childhood for that, so you're used to the other C-groups? I don't think I could —"

"But you could manage Sudamerica, huh?" Her eyes twinkled for a moment, then became grave. "You say Lillian changed. We're seeing that kind of changing cropping out everywhere, actually, and often with the same tragic results. When our — progenitors, I guess you'd say, Margaret, when Kay Searle and Holly Appleby and Robert Ellis and all the rest of them began the C-groups, they never meant for it to go on forever."

"No, I know. It was to preserve every bit of what they thought was a very small gene pool. They had no way of knowing that places like Sudamerica and Africa and even Scandinavia survived the war so well. That wasn't *their* intent, I know, but we've found that with a stable body type and personality type we can better combat disease and preserve the quality of life —"

"I've heard all the arguments, Margaret, at least as often as you have," she said. "But people have started dyeing their hair and losing and gaining weight and shaving their heads and scarring themselves deliberately and even cutting off fingers and ears. And then finding out that most of our population are neurotically frightened of differences. But they keep making the differences. It's time, Margaret, to follow up on what our progenitors intended."

"You want me to . . . reproduce sexually?" I could barely

get out the words.

Katherine laughed. "No, certainly not. But we do need a doctor for the babies."

A small town was begun, she told me. People were brought in one at a time and acclimated to the different people there. They already had a large number of babies, the products of sexual reproduction but of in vitro fertilization and of an artificial womb just like the cloned babies. And there were even some cloned babies. It was a small start, but a necessary one; it would take a generation, Government thought, before the changes would spread throughout Usa. "Eventually, we hope, people will be able to take control of their own lives."

And I agreed to go.

The robocopter left me off on a concrete platform. The place was flat, empty-looking. Windblown dust stung my legs. There were some buildings nearby, but they were long gray caterpillars of cinderblock roofed with corrugated aluminum. The red dirt paths between the buildings served as streets. It was ugly and completely cheerless.

Then I saw a person standing nearby. I jumped, partly because I was startled and partly because I was afraid. This person was a *man*; he was *black*. I had never been in the actual presence of someone even slightly different from myself, let alone *so* different. He was a RobertEllis, I knew from pictures in books.

He smiled at me. His smile was a thin, pale ghost — not the warm, toothy smile I had seen in the pictures. Those picture faces of RobertEllises had practically sprung, I remembered, from the glossy pages, swimming straight at me with exuberant joy, passion, *maleness*. I had been a little uneasy at seeing them. (I later learned that new arrivals were given the gentlest of treatment, no touching or other intense contact. The full wattage of a RobertEllis smile would have driven me right back into the robocopter.)

"Margaret? Margaret KaySearle? Well, I'm sure about the KaySearle part, at least." The RobertEllis picture grin threatened to shine forth. I nodded.

"I'm Jack." He didn't offer to shake my hand, nor did I hold my hand out. "I guess the place looks pretty depressing, huh?" He almost laughed at my look. "But we've only been here a short time. The buildings are temporary; some of the new people coming in are architects and construction workers, though. Give us a couple of years and it'll be beautiful."

I managed to smile a bit myself. I squinted against the wind and looked around. A hillside rose behind the town, pretty in autumn colors.

"That's your building right over there. Your apartment is number twenty-three. Need any help with your bag?"

Thanking him, I walked to the building he indicated and entered a dark, cool hallway. The numbers were painted in large numerals on each door. Mine was halfway along.

It was a large, light room painted yellow. Two windows looked out on the tree-covered hillside. There were a closet and a bathroom at one end, and a small kitchen area tucked into the back. I set my bag down.

I was more scared than I'd ever been in my life, more even than during the fight that killed Lillian. That had been dreamlike and unreal. This was completely real and I was aware of it every minute: I was surrounded by people who were not at all like me, who didn't think like me or behave like me, who might be smarter or less smart or stronger or weaker or more or less even-tempered, who were *unknown*. My heart was pounding. I took deep breaths to calm myself.

"Hello?" someone said. "Mind if I come in?"

I could tell by her voice she wasn't a KaySearle. There was a more metallic quality to it. "Please, come in," I said, gasping for air.

She was a HollyAppleby. She was big — tall, athletic. Muscular arms hung from the sleeves of her blue shirt. And she was so *blonde*. Her hair was almost white and her eyes were light icy blue.

"I'm your neighbor," she said, "and I heard you come in and thought you might like a cup of tea to restore you from your journey." She carried two steaming mugs.

"Yes, thanks," I answered. The tea was sweet and scalding. I sipped it and began to feel better.

Here was I, drinking tea with a HollyAppleby, when I had told Lillian I would never want to meet one! Here was I, getting to do things Lillian always longed to do.

"I'm Jennifer, by the way," said my neighbor. Her hand fluttered at her side, as though she meant to offer it to me but stopped herself.

I never have to touch these people, I thought. I can live here forever and keep to myself, know no one but myself. That *is* possible, I thought.

I planted both feet on the ground, looked at my new neighbor, and smiled. "I'm glad to meet you, Jennifer," I said. I held out my hand for her to take. When she did, her hand was warmer, moister than mine. But it wasn't unpleasant. "I'm Margaret Searle," I said.

Meaningful Dialog

•

Kiel Stuart

The Darwin Memorial Institute For Primate Research opened its hatchway.

Kitry Newcomb zipped into the corridor, hoping to avoid Shuster and company. Maybe he wouldn't even know she was late. And she imagined Sambal was getting pretty impatient.

Sambal Goreng was inclined to moodiness. Even more so now, as he struggled to finish his second novel, "Golden Fruits."

Kitry had seen drafts of this. A metaphorical journey through the tormented soul of a self-aware being, disconnected from nature, it was going to set the linguistics world on its ear.

She hoped.

She heard muffled thuds and stopped outside Sambal's cubicle. She entered carefully. He was bashing Thomas Wolfe's portrait with a plastic chair.

Cubicles always obliterated the familiar, pungent chimpanzee smell. It never seemed quite right to Kitry.

"What's up, Sambal?"

The big chimp slowly lowered his chair, grunting. "Damned Thomas Wolfe," he signed.

"Last week it was damned Kurt Vonnegut and the week before, damned Kookie McDaniel. What's going on this week?"

Sambal waddled to his terminal. The screen flashed. "I'm struggling with the transition from the death scene to the protagonist's realization of transcendence."

Kitry pushed aside a copy of "Writer's Market" to sit on another plastic chair. "Aw, c'mon," she said. "You'll do it, don't worry." Shuster hated for her to speak English to

175

any of her charges. He wanted all transaction to take place in sign language or through the computer. Kitry always ignored his wish.

Sambal sulked. Collette flopped down from the databank and lumbered onto Kitry's lap. In the course of his extensive readings, Sambal latched onto the idea that authors need cats and had kicked up a fuss until he got one. Collette, taken in as a tiny kitten, was now the size of a small cougar with grappling-hook claws and a mean right cross. Shuster and Marshall were terrified of her; Kitry loved her whisky-bar growl.

"Magnum House has already granted me two extensions," signed Sambal. "This is it. I'm finished. The end of all our hopes and dreams. The end of a bright new tomorrow for chimpanzees everywhere . . ."

"I think you're suffering from plain old writer's block," said Kitry. "I'll ask Shuster for a pass. Maybe he'll let us out this time, and we can go down to the Cimarron River Park. Who knows, the Muse might visit you there." She saluted and left.

Kitry edged smartly towards Shuster's offices, took a breath, popped in, and said, "I'll like a pass for me and Sambal."

"That's not language," he said.

"I'll try to do better next time," she said.

Jin shook his curly young head. "Gee, Dr. Newcomb, Henry Fuzzyface asked me for a *light*." He swallowed. "I mean, really. So I was asking, doesn't that constitute language?"

Both Dr. Jacob Shuster and Professor Lana Tillman Marshall wore very smug expressions. Jin tried to squeeze into a corner.

"Newcomb," said Shuster, voice an equal mix of contempt and noblesse oblige, "late again, weren't you?"

"Flying Dutchman," explained Kitry.

"Stupid ghost trains," said Shuster. "Can't the MagTube computers get rid of them?"

Kitry shrugged, settling on Marshall's desk. Marshall recoiled and snatched some papers away from possible human contact.

"I still maintain that most of what you call language is mere parroting on the chimp's part," said Shuster. "And that has been the definitive linguistic statement for over 35

176

years. Besides, their grammar is atrocious."

"Was," said Kitry. "You have to admit their grammar ain't half bad these days. Can we have a pass?"

"Ah," Shuster lifted his chin. "You leave out intent of meaning."

Jin blinked.

"Yup," said Kitry, winking at Jin. "The 1990 Intent act bogged down the chimps good and plenty. Lots of times I can't even prove intent by current standards. But I still want a pass."

Marshall rose, flushed. "Well, what about Wallenstein's Theory of Existential Probability-Loop Meaning?" She turned her papers face-down.

"What about it?" said Kitry.

Marshall sat.

Shuster lifted his chin again. "Well, Jin, we can all be thankful that Dr. Newcomb was not at the 12th Annual Psychoempiricist Linguistics Concordance."

"But," said Jin faintly, "what about all those books? Didn't chimps write . . ."

"Poetry?" Shuster charged the word with complete revulsion. He very deliberately turned and drew a slim volume from the bookshelf: Pongo's "To A Branch Darkly." He held it between thumb and finger. "Is blank verse an expression of intelligence at all? Didn't the head of Arcane House say, 'My dog could write blank verse.'?"

"Oh, really?" said Jin. "You mean you read 'The Paws Of Kilimanjaro'?"

Shuster glared.

Marshall shook her head. "The current definition of language renders poetry invalid." She put the papers in a drawer. "A species has to produce a novel."

Sambal Goreng had written "The Ides of Spring" last year. The novel only sold 1,000 copies and got some pretty bad reviews. One critic called Sambal's imagery "obsequious."

"A best-selling novel," amended Marshall.

"Which Sambal has a better shot at this time," said Kitry. "And if this goes, all those clerical chimps and factory chimps are gonna have to be paid basic minimum wage. Tsk. So if you'll give us a pass, we'll get on with it."

"All right," said Shuster, punching out a disk.

Jin took the opportunity to flee.

Kitry was puzzled. Shuster never coughed up a pass without a fight. She was even more puzzled to hear his laughter as she scooted down the hall to Sambal's cubicle.

But there was a novel to write.

When they returned Sambal seemed incandescent. His usual reluctance to go back to the cubicle showed not at all. Kitry and the guard could barely keep up with him. Collette under his right arm, micro-mini computer in his leather harness, Sambal jumped up and down in front of the cubicle, signing, "Hurry! Literary fires are raging!"

"Dr. Newcomb?" Sallie, another grad student, poked in. "Little Tipp is having an identity crisis. I can't talk her out of it." Her voice started to quaver. "Can you come?"

"Right," she said.

By the time Kitry had convinced Little Tipp that "Being And Nothingness" was not really a model for the young orangutan's life, it was late. She dragged home to a delayed dinner.

"So you really think this is the one?" Basil hunched over some tea at the kitchen console.

"Yup," said Kitry, sticking her feet out for Robot to massage. "I haven't read anything so pretentious since Starshine's 'Who Dealt This Mess Anyway?' The critics will drool." She sniffed the air. "Dinner's burning, little brother."

"I know," said Basil seriously.

"I'll get it," beeped Robot.

Basil squinted into his tea.

"The editors at Magnum House are very excited," lied Kitry.

"Good," said Basil. "Wait until I tell the gang at Ron's Robotix Roundhouse."

No Flying Dutchman appeared during next morning's MagTube ride, so Kitry phoned Sambal's editor early enough to catch him.

"Absolutely not," said Mr. Graham. "I will not tolerate another display of primate temperament. And his first novel lost money for us, remember? So if the finished manuscript is not on my desk by 10 a.m. sharp May the 15th, your contract goes out the window. Good luck finding another publisher." He rang off.

Then Jin popped into her office, whimpering about his

thesis.

And a call for help flashed from Sambal's cubicle.

Kitry felt distinctly harassed. She was sure her hair stood on end. She shuttled like an electronic messenger from Shuster to Sambal, editor to grad student, staff to visitor.

She wasn't even aware of how many days passed when Sambal summoned her with a very peremptory message.

She stood in his cubicle, gasping with fatigue, feeling several dendrites burst into flames. "What?" she snapped.

Sambal hooted. "Deadline," he signed, and handed her a disc of "Golden Fruits."

She sat down on Collette, who lowed in protest.

"Hadn't you better run?" signed Sambal.

Kitry left Collette's fur ruffling in the breeze.

She sat in the Oklahoma-Kansas MagTube, clutching the disc. Were editors fuming already? And why the hell were they so archaic? Why the damned hell had they never installed modems? *Publishers*, she thought bitterly.

She hardly noticed the train stop.

"Flying Dutchman!" squealed a nearby five-year-old. It tugged its mother's sleeve, echoing the words again and again in piercing staccato. Mom beamed at Junior's cleverness.

Kitry gnawed her knuckle. She saw the contract sprout wings and take off. She saw Shuster cut a caper.

Much later, she crept into Magnum House and stopped outside Graham's door. She turned to Kimba the receptionist. "What's going on in there?" she signed.

"They're playing Rocket to Romance. And they sure don't want to be disturbed," signed Kimba.

"How long have they been at it?"

"Hours."

Hopefully, Kitry explained her mission. Kimba pursed her lips. "I'll give them the disc when they come out. And say you were here waiting since ten, but had to leave." She made a friendly face. "Good luck," she signed.

It worked. Kitry marched into Shuster's offices and asked him for a long leave of absence.

"All right," he said mildly, and punched it in.

She left his offices slowly. Funny, she thought. You'd think he would want to obstruct us.

She slid into Sambal's cubicle. He looked up from drawing a moustache and bad teeth on a picture of Shuster.

"What?"

"Get your stuff together," said Kitry. "Magnum is sending us on a promotional tour. Basil even managed to get himself fired from Ron's so he could join us."

Sambal hooted. As they struggled down the hall with Collette and luggage, Kitry thought she could hear Shuster hooting, too. Hmm.

It was quite a tour. One critic insulted Sambal at a book party and Kitry avoided bloodshed by diverting the chimp's aggression towards some furniture instead (Lady Devon, their host, said she would have preferred Sambal to shred the critic.). But "Golden Fruits" got mostly raves, was translated into all known languages, and hit it big in every other medium as well.

On return to the Institute, Kitry was happy and tan, Sambal happy and rich, and Collette happily fat. After depositing Sambal in his cubicle, Kitry marched into Shuster's offices.

She thrust some sales figures at him. "Here," she said. "Oh, don't bother to scream. This was going to happen sooner or later. Shame, isn't it? All those bosses having to pay minimum wage, you having to say 'good morning' to the chimps. Aww, you'll get used to it. There *is* a slight family resemblance."

Shuster smiled. Kitry flinched.

"I'm afraid," he said, taking the sales figures and shredding them, "that we were far too imprecise in our previous efforts to define language. While you were out gallivanting the worlds, we at the First Concordance of Unilateral Psycholinguism decided . . ."

"At the *what*?"

"Control yourself, Dr. Newcomb. As I was saying, we came to the conclusion that a best-selling novel could merely be an unfortunate reflection on coarse popular taste in literature. Therefore unacceptable. For a species other than man to be considered truly sentient, concrete proof of the ability to think in a rational, scientific manner must be shown. The species in question must produce a workable unified field theory which will stand up to . . ."

He never finished. He was suddenly flat on his back, covered with papers from the Concordance.

Sambal took the news more philosophically. He was,

after all, a wealthy chimp now. He put Collette in Kitry's lap. He offered her a grapefruit.

"I'm finished here," said Kitry, when she had calmed down a bit. "I've had it with this whole stupid field." She peeled the grapefruit and gazed at the pictures of all the authors Sambal had put up over the years.

She stood up suddenly. Collette slid off and meowed.

"What?" signed Sambal.

"Hell, why not?" she said. "We'll start a writer's colony." Sambal jumped up and clapped.

When Basil visited The Golden Fruits Retreat, things were humming along.

Dozens of happy primates worked on novels, on how-to books, on religious tracts. Kitry led him to Sambal, busily working on his trilogy.

Then she led him to the Retreat's special guest. The young, brilliant pygmy chimp, Zippy Hawking Einstein, was busy, too.

His work on a unified field theory was humming along at a rapid clip.

Sign of Hope

•

Adrienne Lauby

Placed and tucked and pillowed for the night, but Taditt
didn't want to sleep. Didn't want to? Or couldn't? What
difference did it make! Only that, lately, she lay awake many
nights with the sounds of sleepers filling the tent, until gray
light showed at the smoke hole and she suddenly plunged
into dreams. Often she slept through the morning.

Sometimes she didn't mind. And sometimes she did.
She trusted the buffalo wisdom of her body, which paced
her days and nights with a genetic knowledge honed by
centuries of migration: The weather changed. Acceptance
and flexibility were crucial.

But frequently a tribal prairie dog stood on its dirt
lookout in her mind, chirrking out a warning. "WISE, is it
now? You always KNOW, don't you? But you don't do your
share of the work. What would happen if everyone behaved
like you?"

Chatter, chatter. Warn and scold.

At least tonight she didn't have to work to understand
her wakefulness. Plenty of others were awake tonight and
not just in this tent. Today had marked a long-overdue
occasion by commemorating a blizzard which had killed and
changed so many twenty years ago. What could not be
completed at the time was now accomplished.

Before a give away and feast there was always a build-
up in excitement. It would be a few more days before the
tribe shed their raised emotions.

Taditt sighed, eyes opening and closing on darkness.

This morning her tall grown son had come to her
breakfast fire and, as though casually and not for the benefit
of the young children sitting nearby, asked, "How was it
again? Tell me about Aunt Nora. When did news of the
blizzard reach France?"

Over breakfast! Before anything else! The children crowding closer, her son's dark lean body and all that old long story!

Oh, to her it began like any ordinary day (Taditt closed her eyes and pictured it as she spoke). Nora woke up and jigged the toggle switch of her citizen's computer program. She sipped warm tea from an orange thermos bottle which lay on the pillow beside her as the daily headline categories slowly rolled onto her screen. Like all the generations of morning newspaper readers, she wanted to know what had happened as she slept. And, unlike them, she had access to first hand information, more than she could possibly absorb.

Nora was awake earlier than usual that day, a large-boned woman with enormous brown eyes who slept in a white flannel nightgown trimmed with lace. Sometime during the night her green flowered bedspread had hit the floor so, as she read, she wiggled to tuck the flannel around her toes.

Another push on the toggle with the back of her hand and a question appeared on the screen under the category of NATURAL DISASTERS.

AFTER WEEKS OF COLD WINDS FOLLOWED BY AN UNEXPECTED SEVERE SPRING BLIZZARD, ONE HUNDRED ARE DEAD IN THREE SMALL COMMUNITIES OF THE U.S.A. STATE OF SOUTH DAKOTA. THIS REPORT FILED AFTER ONE DAY OF RESCUE OPERATIONS. DEATH COUNT MAY RISE. SHOULD NORMAL EMERGENCY DISTRIBUTION BE INCREASED?
YES? NO? NEED MORE INFORMATION?

Nora liked to begin her citizen's duty with emergency issues and her computer program was set for it. "It wakes me up better than coffee," she often said. Today she hoped that someone else's problems would take her mind away from her own. She nudged the toggle to ask for more information and twenty or so categories appeared.

NORMAL DISTRIBUTION AMOUNTS
HISTORY OF AREA
ESTIMATED NEED BY LOCAL RESPONSIBILITY

MESSAGES FROM SURVIVORS
PRESENT CONDITIONS
POSSIBLE CAUSES OF EXTREME WEATHER
PROJECTED EFFECT ON WORLD ECONOMY OF IN-
CREASED
    ALLOTMENTS . . . ON LOCAL ECONOMY
WEATHER FORECAST FOR AREA
STATEMENTS BY POLITICAL GROUPS . . . BY CHARITY
    GROUPS

and so on (more information than she could possibly absorb), until the final category with its blank fill-in lines.

OTHER QUESTIONS?

Through the flounces of her green matched curtains Nora saw the light outside change from gray to gold. She dutifully called up MESSAGES FROM SURVIVORS and added RANDOM SELECTION as the screen presented notices written during the two-day storm: "Has anyone seen my mother? She drove south on P42 Tuesday to go to the dentist . . . Can someone bring more comfrey leaves to the hospital? . . ."

After the storm the messages began to address a wider world, and Nora deleted RANDOM so she could carefully read each one: "My husband was out with the horses and has not returned. Please send more heliocopters. Maybe he is alive and suffering. Please help us."

"Begin with the people," Nora's mother always said. "Start and end with living human beings."

Since that teaching at her mother's side, Nora had trained with many others, but her mother's words, more often than not, still determined her approach to voting.

Another twenty minutes and, her room brightened by sunlight, Nora was ready to vote. She'd finished the messages from survivors and their friends, the figures for normal distributions, estimates of need by the local Responsibility, and most of the articles under PRESENT CONDITIONS. Her hand wavered on the toggle near HISTORY OF AREA but, with a look at the time, she transferred the information to her personal reading file instead. Maybe she'd get to it. Her reading file was crammed full, enough for three years, but there was a new flu going around. Maybe she'd get sick and be able to do some reading.

She transferred a small donation toward a heliocopter rental from her bank account, called up the original question, and answered it, YES.

WHAT PERCENTAGE OF INCREASE?

Nora ignored the follow-up and cleared the screen. Her back ached. She'd done the best she could for now. She'd settle for the average increase suggested by YES voters. The baby would be awake any minute and her attendant came at nine.

She leaned against her pillows, trying to relax the muscles which had tightened while she worked. No sound from the baby's crib yet. Shelby had run a slight fever yesterday afternoon and Nora worried she had caught the flu virus which had half of Paris home in bed. Any sickness now and they might label her irresponsible for taking Shelby out in the cold to the rally. Nora didn't want any strange twists thrown in at this late date, not with her Committee of Experts and Concerned Strangers coming at noon and their report almost sure to influence the final vote. But the grape pickers had been sitting outside the most expensive restaurants in Paris not eating anything, drinking only water for over a month. Now after the huge weekend rally, wine sales were down and the growers were back at the bargaining table. She and Shelby had been part of that. And Shelby had slept through the night. Maybe Nora's luck would hold.

Then Nora couldn't lay still any longer. She reached toward the toggle, then waited impatiently for a new computer display.

SHOULD NORA F., SEVERELY DISABLED BY CERE-BRAL PALSY FROM BIRTH, RETAIN CUSTODY OF HER DAUGHTER, SHELBY?

"Oh, yes. Yes," Nora begged as if the world could hear. "Yes, for sure I should . . ." finding nothing new in the debate and information sections, she called for the final question.

CURRENT VOTE STATUS?
MAJORITY REQUESTS MASS POLLING.

In the middle of the night Taditt woke, aware of the

outside of her body, the angles of her bones at her elbows and shoulders, the rain she'd anticipated in the rising wind some hours before. The air felt warm. Maybe the rain would fall before turning to snow. She was surprised she'd slept. The young prairie dogs chased around her mind, racing back and forth among the many stories and people of the give away day. She had had so many opportunities to please herself and others, with her tired body caught between. Now her tongue lay hard and painful against a rough tooth. She pulled her arm from the heavy robe and stretched it above her head to soothe a few of her aching joints. Sleep, said the buffalo weight of her body.

Yes, sleep. Sleep well in the memories. Remember once again the kindness of your brother, not that terrible storm. Remember Willa Eagle's third daughter as she spoke before the give away, standing with five others to say her mother had lived through the storm, seen the suffering and not forgotten.

In the same way that the give away was made in the names of the dead and the large size and beauty of the gifts honored those who had gone too suddenly to honor themselves, Willa's daughter told the story as Willa would have done, not speaking of herself, but of another who had suffered more. This way, the daughter reflected her mother's great generosity and her listeners agreed, commenting audibly, "Yes, Willa always thought first of others. Willa was like that."

Taditt curled her arm against her chest.

Sleep. Think of the richly decorated white deerskin dress which drew all eyes as Willa's daughter spoke and all remembered.

She must have thought she'd need a new name. "Runner Like the Wind" was a joke to someone who could only lie without motion on a pallet in the Lakota Relief Center. The wailing she'd done that morning had turned her eyes hollow, taking every feeling from her body. But she still grieved.

It was hard to bury her family so soon. Although she understood why — with so many dead the ceremonies could not be held separately for each one — the fact of it stayed hard. She stared into the high oval ceiling far above, tracing the steel girders that crossed through its empty air. Blowers as loud as the blizzard winds filled the room with stale warmth. But despite their efforts, cold drafts stole past the wooden plank floor to drift through the building. Taditt (Runner Like the Wind) shivered.

— Her brother, with whom she'd shared a childhood, crushed under the tent when it collapsed in the section where he slept with his wife and their ten-year-old child. All three dead. She'd never replace his protective loyalty, forever miss their mutual obligations, and grieve his wife and child.

— Her mother and two aunts, the last of their family generation, who died later that morning from the cold and pain. Her mother. Her mother.

— Her own legs, useless after a tent pole cracked against her back.

— Her right arm, amputated yesterday when her blood continued to refuse its frostbitten flesh.

Through the racket of the blowers, a familiar laugh broke into her sad catalogue. A baby played on a brown wool blanket beside her, shaking his gourd toy in the air, laughing as the seeds rattled inside. Only this precious child remained, her son who came like a gift last spring after she left her husband's tent to return to her mother's family. Only this small human she'd named Sign of Hope was uninjured and strong.

"That's how it is," one of the medical team had said. "In every tragedy, there's always a few miracles."

Sign of Hope flung the gourd across the blanket and looked at Taditt with round black eyes which instantly and silently brimmed with tears. Taditt called for help, shouting to be heard over the blowers. She couldn't nurse with the pain drugs in her body. That, too, was hard. She twisted herself up a few inches, trying to see if someone was coming.

At least her legs didn't hurt. They felt heavy. They tied her hips to the floor and made it impossible to crawl to help her baby, but they were numb. It was her absent arm which throbbed and sent wrenching jabs toward her chest. Her almost-relative Willa Eagle appeared with a warmed bottle of goat's milk.

As Willa fed the baby, her lips pursed in a croon and Sign of Hope curled close to her body, kicking and grasping with satisfaction.

Taditt imagined her baby's year-old body next to her breasts and flinched, terrorized by the thought of those strong feet landing like fists among her bandages.

For years before the storm, Willa Eagle had shared work and visiting with Taditt's mother, and in the past few days she'd spent many hours caring for the grandchild of her friend. When they arrived here, Taditt's duties had been with her dead relations, first her mother and aunts, then her brother and sister-in-law. Now, with the burials and surgery over, Taditt's duty was to care for the youngest, weakest member of her family, her own baby. This time, duty and desire matched perfectly. If only her body . . . her body . . .

"Shall I take the baby while you rest?" Willa asked.

Sign of Hope lay in Willa's arms, asleep, milk dribbling from the corner of his tiny mouth. Taditt smiled. The pain drugs made her smile possible but this baby gave the reason.

Kindness such as Willa offered might grow. In spite of her body, Taditt must take her own part before Willa's kindness grew into a wall between a mother and her child. Somehow she must find a way.

"I would only ask you to change the diaper and bring a voice box with a screen," she answered. "I have not yet entered a song of praise for my absent relations."

Willa was kind. Willa was truthfully kind. The diapering was accomplished and the computer plugged nearby. Taditt awkwardly used her left arm to enter her code and clenched her teeth against awakening nerves as she waited for an empty screen. The computer blinked and made a request of her instead.

WILL YOU CONSIDER A QUESTION WHICH HAS ARISEN FOR A WOMAN OF YOUR AGE GROUP?

Maybe she would enter the tent of Howard Eagle and live with Willa's kind hands and willing heart. Willa said their tent had suffered no damage and her male relatives had all survived. There was also her father's brother-friend, the man who had camped with his family across the canyon this winter. Perhaps he would welcome her for the sake of her father and his grandchild. Many tents would be widened this summer. Many tents would disappear with the spring rain.

WOULD YOU PLEASE CONSIDER A QUESTION . . .

Taditt turned her thoughts outside herself. The computer held duties beyond the stabs in her body and heart, beyond even family and child. Her grandmother had taught her such duties always come first.

"We (the Lakota, our family) do not need shouts or punishment to know everything in the world is of importance; those we see and honor with our presence and those we cannot see, but honor no less."

Taditt had not always followed her grandmother's teaching. She would not always do so in the future. But today she accepted the computer's request, and in her memory, grandmother approved.

SHOULD NORA F., SEVERELY DISABLED BY CERE-BRAL PALSY FROM BIRTH, RETAIN CUSTODY OF HER DAUGHTER, SHELBY?

Taditt immediately asked to see and hear Nora with her baby. In the videotape which followed, she watched a young woman pilot an electric chair through a kitchen doorway. Nora's neck sagged as the chair halted, throwing her brown hair over her face in long straight strands. Slowly she raised her head and focused at the camera, finding it in the corner of her eyes. The computer translated into Lakota as Nora spoke.

"I want to take care of my baby," she said (and Taditt could not tell her slight slur from a language accent). "I only need a little extra help. No one else could love Shelby more than I do."

The camera focused on her hand as Nora fumbled with the chair controls and Taditt could watch no longer. She grabbed for the "pause" button and froze Nora's image in front of her. How could Nora raise a child when lifting her own head was a chore? Is this how it would be for herself, for Taditt? Was she seeing her own future? Seeing Stubborn Awkwardness, who would now replace Runner Like the Wind? How could she raise Sign of Hope without use of her legs and only one arm? How could she live without running, walking, without every freedom she had taken for granted last week?

Taditt thought she had spilled the last tear from the dammed reservoir behind her eyes. But she was wrong. A fresh spring gushed and covered her face with water. Tch. What would grandmother say about this? It was necessary to cry for her relations, but for herself Taditt must find solutions. She stopped the tears and steadied herself to begin the tape again.

She listened and watched as Nora rolled through her home using her voice to activate machines, carefully and slowly manipulating food and laundry.

"These straps hold me in the chair," Nora said, "Shelby rides in the baby pack on my stomach when we go outside. Before Shelby was born, I went to a month of special training about parenting and we found many tricks to help me."

Nora pointed to the large zipper which made it easy to open her yellow blouse to nurse. Another woman brought Shelby into the room and placed her in the baby pack. Taditt reversed the machine and leaned forward to watch as once again Nora held her baby. Nora braced herself to support Shelby's fragile neck and back while the baby pack supported her weight. Taditt, who had not tried sitting yet, much less carrying twenty pounds of moving child, was impressed. Nora didn't talk much more. When she finished her house tour, the camera lingered. Nora looked down and spoke to the baby. Shelby blinked once, blew a saliva bubble and smiled widely.

Taditt smiled too.

Impulsively she queried direct, "WOULD NORA F. TAKE A PERSONAL CALL FROM ANOTHER DISABLED MOTHER?"

A child stirred and someone half-rose to replace the robes. The rain was softer, the air colder. In the dark gray outside it was snowing and Taditt felt like a wise buffalo, slowly straying down a narrow valley toward the wind break of a canyon wall. Sometimes the shaggy head dropped to graze the tough grasses which were quickly disappearing under the lightly drifting snow.

For the first half of the ceremonial day the storyteller had drifted in just this way, visiting among the tents in the casual way of Taditt's son to tell stories of each family's relations during that terrible winter. The storyteller could draw new meaning from stories heard so often they flattened with the telling. She could connect the stories of different families and frequently remembered details others didn't know or had forgotten.

But after the large gift distribution, to which every family had contributed, the storyteller rose and spoke to all of them. Again, Taditt heard her story told.

In this same winter in Ecuador, there was a woman called Johnson (the storyteller began). And Johnson never voted on disasters.

"Why bother," she said, most often speaking out loud but only when she was alone. "There's plenty of people who like that kind of thing. They get to check the figures and make sure no one's padding budgets or dipping free at public wells. It makes them feel important."

Johnson, in fact, rarely voted at all and her life had changed very little when the five-hour work day became universal to allow for mass participation in government. Long before the hook-up of the International Citizen's Computer System, she'd earned the equivalent of a citizen's credit by research in a sub-sub-group of PLANT GENETICS — AMARANTH WHEAT, 3,000 FOOT STRAINS. She also exchanged theories with a peer group under MIGRAINES. She'd done this work by her own choice and would go on doing it no matter how other fools decided to run the world.

Johnson had come the night before to the traveler's hostel in Colonche, a short woman wearing a bright red shirt and a expensive jacket torn across one shoulder. Her various bags filled most of the entrance room and she riffled several before finding her computer card and hostel ID. No one asked but she explained she had come from Guayaqull in a car full of Ecuadorian relatives and had her bags confused in the process. Not HER relatives! She liked Ecuadorians more than most, but not enough to take on any as family. She had more family already than she wanted, thank you very much; been born with more than necessary, and they expanded every time she returned home. Naturally, after that ride she'd come to the hostel tired, and now was afraid she'd lost some piece of equipment in the dark. Colonche was supposed to be her rest stop, a three-day holiday by the ocean before heading back to the humid interior . . . IF, that is, she hadn't been misinformed about the accommodations . . . IF she managed to get back to Guayaqull in time to catch the expedition group . . . .

No one in the Colonche hostel was surprised when, by mid-morning of the next day, Johnson discovered a hole chewed in her tent by some rodent. Or maybe a dog.

"It doesn't matter if it was the mayor's kinkajou," the

191

morning manager told her, his voice heavy with sadness for her troubles, his eyes light with humor. "There's no place in town to fix it or get another."

Where Johnson was going, there were no hostels. She needed the tent. But she hardly wanted to rush back to Guayaqull on the off-chance she could get it fixed there. She ate a big fish lunch to calm her stomach, then approached the guest computer with a scribbled list in her hand. She punched in her code number, language and cultural preference (English twentieth century. "When people still talked with some degree of precision"), and skimmed the headlines.

A blizzard in South Dakota had rampaged a Native American Traditional Area. Lakota. She'd studied that linguistic group the summer she'd dropped out of college. The death count was way past a hundred, and freezing cold was screwing up the rescue operations. Typical. What a mess . . . But what did people expect, trying to live in the fourteenth century?

Johnson never voted on disasters and she didn't have time to play around with old memories. She hoped she could find someone to bring her a new tent from the capital. She queried for the regional taxi system. Maybe she could still figure out some way to get her vacation in.

The screen flickered and presented her with a green and orange banded message.

Shit. Another majority request. Ignore at your own risk. Shit. Lately, they came up with these urgent issues every week. Pain in the butt! If the majority cares so much, why don't they just decide? People always want to drag everyone into their enthusiasms. Human nature. This computer voting gives them a perfect opportunity.

Johnson would have ignored the message but she needed the computer to help with her tent. The two-day down-time penalty would end her vacation for sure. She sighed and punched in agreement.

Okay, what is it?

SHOULD NORA F., SEVERELY DISABLED BY CEREBRAL PALSY FROM BIRTH, RETAIN CUSTODY OF HER DAUGHTER, SHELBY?

Naturally! One of those human tragedy things.

Johnson was so irritated she considered voting to put

the kid in a foster home out of spite. But Johnson didn't really hate people. She had even tried once to have a home and friends. But something about living around people always got her involved in their problems. This Nora thing was a perfect example. She couldn't quite write off this girl after she'd been forced to get involved, not even on her vacation. She queried for the family details.

KIN
BLOOD FAMILY (BASIC INFORMATION)
NORA'S BLOOD FAMILY CONSISTS OF AN ELDERLY MOTHER WHO CAN OFFER NO PHYSICAL SUPPORT. SHE MAINTAINS DAILY TELEPHONE CONTACT. QUALITY OF MUTUAL EMOTIONAL SUPPORT RATED FUNCTIONAL TO GOOD. GO ON?

Yes. (Damn it!)

NORA REPORTS EXTENDED FAMILY WITHIN THE DISABLED COMMUNITY. DAILY PHONE CONTACT WITH JEAN P. AND FLASH C. WEEKLY OR BIMONTHLY GROUP CONTACT. RANDOM SURVEY SHOWS NORA IS WELL KNOWN WITH HIGH POTENTIAL FOR EMOTIONAL SUP- PORT AND PROBLEM SOLVING WITHIN HER COMMUNITY. POTENTIAL FOR PHYSICAL SUPPORT — VERY LOW.
MARGUERITE V. HAS BEEN NORA'S ATTENDANT FOR THREE YEARS. THEIR RELATIONSHIP IS RATED GOOD TO EXCELLENT. NORA HAS TWO OTHER ATTENDANTS WHO HAVE WORKED FOR HER LESS THAN SIX MONTHS. GO ON?

Yes. (But this is it. Make it short.)

NORA HAS EMERGENCY ARRANGEMENTS AND PERSONAL CONTACT WITH TWO NEIGHBORS. SHE MAINTAINS COMPUTER AND/OR LETTER WRITING RELATIONSHIPS WITH APPROXIMATELY TEN INDIVIDUALS, VARIOUS AGES AND GENDERS, VARIOUS ABILITIES AND DISABILITIES. RANDOM SURVEY REPORTS THE FRIENDSHIPS ARE CONSIDERED MUTUALLY BENEFICIAL. GO ON?

No. Skip to health.

HEALTH OF MOTHER AND CHILD.

NORA HAS REGAINED LEVEL OF FUNCTIONING SHE
HELD PREVIOUS TO PREGNANCY AND BIRTH. ABLE TO
LIVE INDEPENDENTLY WITH FORTY HOURS OF ATTEN-
DANT CARE PER WEEK. WITHIN LIMITS OF HER DISABIL-
ITY, HER HEALTH IS EXCELLENT. SHELBY IS SIX MONTHS
OLD, ABLE-BODIED, NO PHYSICAL PROBLEMS.

So? What else do you want? The kid is doing fine and
there's people to keep an eye on things. Give the woman
her baby. Motherhood and apple pie and all that.

Johnson put the original question back on her screen
and stabbed the vote button.

YES

ANY FURTHER CONSIDERATIONS?

She squinted at the keyboard and typed rapidly with
two fingers. Return in three years with Committee of Experts
and Concerned Strangers for health check. Double food,
housing, and transportation options for both mother and
child. Twenty-five percent additional attendant hours.

ANY FURTHER COMMENTS?

Stop bothering me with this obvious junk. Use your
common sense, People!

VOTE ENTERED.

The circle of people had packed closer as the storyteller
spoke. The friendship between Taditt and Nora was itself
practically a legend and they were eager for new details. But
now, when the storyteller turned to leave, even Taditt was
disappointed. Millions had voted on Nora's case. Why choose
to speak of this person in front of the assembled tribe?

The storyteller appeared to notice their dissatisfaction.
She glanced at them over her shoulder.

"Oh." She raised one eyebrow. "Does my story bore
you?"

As they looked at the ground with shame for allowing
such impolite feelings to show, the storyteller allowed a rare
laugh to escape.

"Well, so might you be," she said. "The computer was bored that winter too."

She turned again to face them and everyone realized the ending had been carefully faked to insure their interest in what was to come. They smiled broadly. The storyteller had many fine tricks.

At that time there were three medium capacity computers in charge of operating the Citizen's Network. From Montreal, Soweto, and Beijing, they handled routine matters, such as Nora's custody fight, in a small area of their circuits.

When 90 percent of the world's citizens had voted, they announced the decision: one-half of 1 percent in Nora and Shelby's favor. When the friendship between Nora and Taditt grew into the formal Lakota relationship of sister-friend, they noted the event in their ongoing tabulation of socio/psychological and cultural effects of the Citizen's Network.

But, as I said, they were bored with all that. What they enjoyed most during the few years which surrounded our winter blizzard was an esoteric guessing game which had much in common with the twentieth–century U.S. practice of polling. In this particular six-month period they sought a voter who would always reflect the majority view. The typical voter, perfectly typical.

Statistically, such a voter was inevitable, yet the Montreal computer took an extra millisecond before pointing out the significance of the Nora vote.

"She's done it again."

"Johnson?" Beijing asked.

"Not only voted yes, but came up with the exact increase in housing, transportation, and attendant care."

Soweto entered the conversation for the first time: "It's because she hardly ever votes. Nothing to speak of. An occasional effect."

"You'd like to ignore her because she's arrogant." (Beijing)

"Self-absorbed." (Montreal)

"Selfish!" (Soweto)

"But fair-minded." (Beijing)

"Come on," Soweto said firmly. "You can't say this is a true representation of humans. Selfishness with random streaks of fair play? That's nineteenth–century British colonialism, twentieth–century U.S. imperialism . . ."

Can a computer shrug?
Montreal did.

Although many lay quiet or crept about the edges in consideration for those who were already stoking fires and beginning the food, the tent was alive now with open-eyed children and moving adults. When snow fell, the tents were always more crowded.

Taditt had slept again. But she didn't feel rested. Should she get up? Change her clothing? Which tasks would she work with today? The adolescent who helped her this week would come soon to ask these questions. Inside Taditt a buffalo shook its head to tumble the snow from its matted curls and leaned closer to an overhanging bank. A prairie dog rotated its body, curling deep into the grass lining of the den where it planned to sleep out the storm.

womanmansion
to my sister
mourning her mother
•
hattie gossett

(for brenda h.)

is it really true that your mother will spend forever and
    ever and ever as a servant on her knees revolving
    around the throne of someone named god/master
    like the preacher said at the funeral

revolving on her knees and shouting hallelujah halle-
    lujah hallelujah glory be to the name of this god/
    master person

was the preacher correct when he said that death is
    the only and the ultimate freedom cuz it alone allows
    us to go up through the skies to this dude god/
    master

cuz the preacher made it clear that this g/m person
    is a dude

and he made him sound like a white dude at that
              although i have heard that the g/m
              dude can be black too

i really hate to think that after working and slaving
    to meet the demands of various masters on earth
    all her life like it said in the obituary that your
    mother is going to have to spend eternity as a
    servant on her knees revolving around anybodys
    throne
              riding an assemblyline merrygoround
              forever and ever would make anybody
              tired& bored&dizzy&sick&crazy

isnt heaven supposed to be a happy place

if there has to be a god can she be a committee of women
dedicated to wiping out earthly oppression

a committee of the struggling women of all races classes
ages and sexual preferences united in one mind/
body

and so if your mother indeed will experience an afterlife
couldnt it take place in womanmansion

couldnt it be that right after your mother was deposited
in the earth the womanmansion transport committee sent a special private solarpowered jet for her

and the jet sped her through the horizon gently setting
down at womanmansion airfield where a waiting
steamfueled limousine whisked her to the front door
of womanmansion itself and the committee of
allwomen in one mind/body was out on the front
porch with the drummers and dancers and poets
to greet her and lead her to her own private suite
in the welcome wing of the mansion where the way
has been prepared for her to lay up and rest herself

while the music of bessie smith mahalia jackson ida
cox clara ward big maybelle dinah washington and
billie holiday and their choirs and orchestras flows
through the speakers in her suite in the heavenly
home your mother will get her nerves together have
a manicure a pedicure a shampoo and oil treatment
get her fro shaped up take a steambath a whirlpool
bath a sauna or all 3 do some limbering up exercises
get massaged in fragrant warm oils whenever she
feels like it

plan out her menu by the week and have her tasty
healthful lovingly prepared meals served promptly
at the appointed hour

get her wardrobe together

lay up in her bed of angeldown mattresses and pillows
covered in finely spun silk and cotton
                    sheets changed everyday

and talk on her phone as long as she feels like to whoever she wants to without worrying about the bill or worrying about somebody interrupting her conversation and asking her where their socks are or if theres anymore greens in the icebox

visit her friends

have company come in

sit on the porch sippin mint ice tea or limeade watchin the evenin sun go down

get clean and go out at night without worrying about money or being mugged

work out her deep thoughts

go for long walks on the beach or in the forest

swim in the ocean climb trees and mountains

and when she feels rested and ready

she will participate in pleasant structured meetings with small groups of women
> *after theyve finished their collective chores*

in their meetings they will talk about many matters

including how to make their supernatural wisdom and powers available to us their sisters daughters mothers grandmothers granddaughters still laboring on earth for this man

cant you just see your mother sitting down with the righteous native american women the wise african asian and latina women the indomitable afroamerican and caribbean women the cleareyed white women

the women who are the farm workers the pink collar workers the unskilled factory workers the service workers the whores the wives and mothers

cant you just see her putting her head together with theirs and them collectively fixing up for us monthly care packages of fresh vegetables books pamphlets movies videotapes dried medicinal herbs magazines

and newspapers warm blankets organic birth control
devices sample legislation fresh fruit juices archi-
tectural plans fresh air ideas on economy and health
baby clothes military and political plans clear water
soothing sleep restorative mental and spiritual energy
nonnuke fuels nocholesterol fried fish and cornbread
with *femme noire 2000* champagne on the side

if and when they want to they will be with men

men wont be in power of course and they will live
somewhere else and take care of they ownselves

your mother will be in the position of dealing with men
secure in the knowledge that she got her own
womanmansion

needless to say her sexlife will be truly ecstatic cuz it
will be completely on her own terms

reproduction wont be a problem since all female babies
who die and all aborted female fetuses will automatically come to womanmansion

plus women who really really want to have babies will
make use of various and wonderful methods of
impregnation not all of which will involve men

and of course the womanmansion childcare center will
be the lastword in loving infant and early childhood
care and training

and since they are in heaven your mother and her
sisters wont have to worry about weather or laundry
or budget cuts nor concern themselves with ex-
ploitative personal relationships retirement plans
rent or ma bell neither will they study rape nor war
nor any kind of emotional or economic ripoff and
of course they wont have any problems around age
or race or physical/mental condition sexual preference or class

if your mother in her earthly form worked hard loved
her family and her people suffered the physical and
mental repercussions of oppression and still kept
on struggling and encouraging you to struggle and

still kept on struggling right on down to the wire

if she went through all this

if she went through all this

doesnt she deserve something more in eternity than that pootbutt preachers paltry pronouncement of forever going nowhere in circles on her knees in front of somebodys throne

Contributors' Notes

Adrienne Lauby was raised in a large Nebraska farm family and is currently writing a novel about lesbian punks. Another of her stories can be found in the disabled women's anthology *With Wings*. She's white, feminist, lesbian, and forty years old. She writes that "Sign of Hope" "benefited from the book *Waterlily*, written by ethnologist-linguist Ella Cara Deloria in 1940 and published last year by the University of Nebraska Press. I have also been inspired by the insight of teacher, performer, and concerned citizen Jan Levine, and the struggle of Tiffany Callo on behalf of disabled mothers. All mistakes, of course, are only my own."

Barbara Krasnoff "'Signs of Life' was inspired by my experience as a sign language and interpreting student at the New York Society for the Deaf. It was there I developed great respect and love for a language that dances as it communicates — and learned about both the satisfaction and the stress that accompany the job of interpreting. Although I did not, finally, enter the profession, I made many good friends who are interpreters, and it is to them that this story is dedicated.

"Incidentally, there is an official Code of Ethics which is followed by members of the Registry of Interpreters for the Deaf, and which includes the total confidentiality of all interpreted conversations. I hasten to add that it is not as strictly enforced as in this story.

"I am thirty-five years old, was born and bred in Brooklyn, and earn my living as alternately a writer or editor for computer magazines (depending on what mood I'm in). I am the author of one nonfiction book called *Robots: Reel to Real*, which was published by Arco Press in 1982 and is now out of print, and numerous articles about data-base management systems, modems, lap-tops, and similar unpoetic topics."

Caro Clarke "I am a white, middle-class Canadian living in London, England. As 'J. P. Hollerith,' I have had poetry published in two anthologies. My two passions, aside from her whom I adore, are history and speculative fiction. I am a radical feminist separatist dyke."

Charlotte Watson Sherman is a Pacific Northwest native, although she often feels the flow of the South in her veins. A husband and two daughters often listen to her stories, and her poetry/prose has appeared or will appear in *IKON, Backbone, Obsidian II, Painted Bride Quarterly, Portland Review, (f.) Lip, Morena, New Rain, Gathering Ground: New Writing and Art by Northwest Women of Color*, and others. She is the author of a children's book, *NIA and the Golden Stool* (Winston-Derek), and a chapbook, *Womb/Song*.

hattie gossett is a member of the wild wimmins clan operating out of northern harlem as a writer/performance artist/wall street dreadlock office temp. "womanmansion" is excerpted from her first book *presenting . . . sister noblues/firebrand/1988*.

poetry essays recipes performance works written by hattie are published in major anthologies periodicals journals. her poem "king kong" was performed in the off-broadway poetry/drama starring vinie burrows titled *her talking drum.* other works have been performed by urban bush women (dance-theater ensemble) casselberry-dupree (reggae band) evelyn blakey (jazz vocalist/bandleader) robbie mccauley (actress).

in the course of her travels hattie performs & presents workshops at festivals shelters theaters schools jails bars conferences community centers museums group homes. she has appeared as feature artist with edwina lee tyler & a piece of the world (percussion performance ensemble).

Judith Katz was born in Worcester, Mass., in 1951. Her plays have been produced by the Washington Area Feminist Theatre, the Omaha Magic Theatre, Chrysalis Theatre Eclectic, and At the Foot of the Mountain. She was also part of the team that wrote *Toklas, MN*, a lesbian soap opera. Her fiction appears in *The Coming Out Stories; Sinister Wisdom; Fight*

Back! Feminist Resistance to Male Violence; Hurricane Alice; and *Evergreen Chronicles.* She is currently at work on a new novel. "The Amazing Disappearing Girl" is an excerpt from her first.

Kiel Stuart is a member of the Science Fiction Writers of America (whose *Forum* she edited from 1985 to 1988), the Authors Guild, and the Writers Alliance, of which she is the executive editor. Her stories have appeared in many journals and anthologies, including *Tales of the Witch World 1; Magic in Ithkar 3;* and the *Best of Horror Show* anthology. Among her other recent publications are "Muscle Envy," in *Muscular Development,* and "Pro Wrestling — Heroes and Villains" and "Work Out with Weights," both booklets from the National Research Bureau.

Stuart tries "pushing the envelope," challenging herself physically with bodybuilding and powerlifting. She is currently working on a novel, *Jack the Dreamkiller,* based on some of her work in the muscle magazines, and is developing an anthology (*Future Sweat*) of such fiction, with some well-known contributors.

She is also an artist who incorporates her bodybuilding visions into her work ("Bodyscapes"), with exhibits on Long Island and elsewhere. In addition, she enjoys making custom jewelry and painted shirts.

L. Timmel Duchamp lives in Seattle, equipped with a closet capacious enough to hold most of her manuscripts. She first began writing fiction while holed up in a library carrel preparing for the oral portion of her doctoral exams in European history. When on its fourth submission the manuscript of her first novel met with physical violence, she realized her books were probably destined for private (rather than public) circulation. To date she's written ten novels (nine of them sf, none of them published), as well as a handful of essays published variously for political and academic consumption. "O's Story," her first fiction publication, is a spin-off from the nonsequential cluster of books known as *The Frogmore Saga,* which so far includes *The General's Daughter* and *The Asymptotic Woman.*

Laurell K. Hamilton "'A Token for Celandine' is my second short story sale. Marion Zimmer Bradley purchased my story 'Stealing Souls' for a new anthology tentatively entitled *The Sense of Wonder*. My first book is making the rounds of publishers. It is set in the same world as 'A Token for Celandine' and 'Stealing Souls' but uses different characters and countries. It is the first book in a series. A first draft of the second is already complete. A third, unrelated book is nearly ready for an editor's eyes.

"I am twenty-six and happily married. Our fifth wedding anniversary is in August 1989. My hobbies include reading, scuba diving, jogging, and lifting heavy objects to no apparent purpose. I also grow African violets, collect dragon figurines and a few select teddy bears. We have a yellow-naped Amazon parrot with a vocabulary of several hundred words. My familiar is a cockatiel that just loves to have her head scratched. We have a canary named Snert, after Hagar the Horrible's dog, and last but not least a very pushy lovebird."

Lorraine Schein is a New York poet and sometimes cartoonist. She attended the Clarion SF workshop long ago but has only started writing science fiction again in the last few years. Her poetry has appeared in *Heresies*, *The New York Quarterly*, *Exquisite Corpse*, *BLUE LIGHT RED LIGHT*, *Star*Line*, and *Ice River* magazines, among others, and her own chapbook, *Dead Frogs*. New work will be in an upcoming special science fiction issue of *Semiotext(e)*.

She likes to write in mutant genres, and all of her science fiction is based on her real life experience. "The Chaos Diaries" is a musing on the feminist implications of physics' Chaos theory; she still hears the first line of it as a voice in her head sometimes, and wonders what that means.

Mary Ellen Mathews "I'm a freelance computer consultant and occasional manuscript reader for Baen Books. I have taken various writing classes; the most notable one was Shawna McCarthy's workshop at The New School. This is my first sale."

Nona M. Caspers "My fiction and poetry have been published in literary journals such as *Hurricane Alice*; *Plainswoman*; *Evergreen Chronicles*; *Negative Capability*; and *Fall Out*.

Two stories recently appeared in the anthologies *Stiller's Pond* (New Rivers Press) and *Testimonies* (Alyson Publications). I am currently working on the final draft of a serious novel about a young lesbian feminist who is abducted by a fundamentalist Christian woman."

R. M. Meluch "I have a B.A. in theatre, with an acting/ directing emphasis, from the University of North Carolina at Greensboro. I also have an M.A. in ancient history, emphasis in Greece and the Near East, from the University of Pennsylvania. I travel a lot, and have worked at an archaeological dig at Tel Aphek (a.k.a. *Pagai*, "the Springs," in Alexander's day), Israel.

"My science fiction novels are *Sovereign; Wind Dancers; Wind Child; Jerusalem Fire; War Birds;* and *Chicago Red,* all published by New American Library.

"Currently I am working on a novel centering on the Battle of Britain, so I've been making a nuisance of myself with RAF and Luftwaffe veterans.

"Am a born again environmentalist.

"For a science fiction writer it is very embarrassing to be allergic to cats. Nevertheless, there is a vociferous Siamese cat that has designated itself my familiar and waits in ambush outside my front door, which is in Westlake, Ohio."

Rosaria Champagne was born and raised in Chicago. She holds degrees from Wittenberg University and the University of Pennsylvania. Presently, she teaches in the Center for Women's Studies at the Ohio State University, where she is completing her Ph.D. in the department of English.

Shirley Hartwell, lesbian, 54, was born into the white working class in Baltimore, where she still lives with her lover and no cats. She has this to say about her novel-in-progress: "Our history, especially our history before patriarchy (called prehistoric), has been stolen, distorted, suppressed, and burned. It is dangerous for us to know that, in Itu's words, 'human nature didn't always exist, that there is another way to live.' I started this novel in the faith that we *do* know, that such knowledge can never be totally destroyed, that it is with us somehow: handed down in small and obscure ways, stored in our DNA, resting in our universal unconscious. So I started to write a historical novel. As I talked about it, people began to refer to it as fantasy or science fiction. Fine by me. I know that in fantasy lies the truth. I started by writing what it was like to live through the patriarchal takeover. By the time I had finished the first section, a major portion of the novel, the characters had made it clear that they would refuse to participate in a novel about their defeat. They want to win. They will not allow a takeover."